AF580849

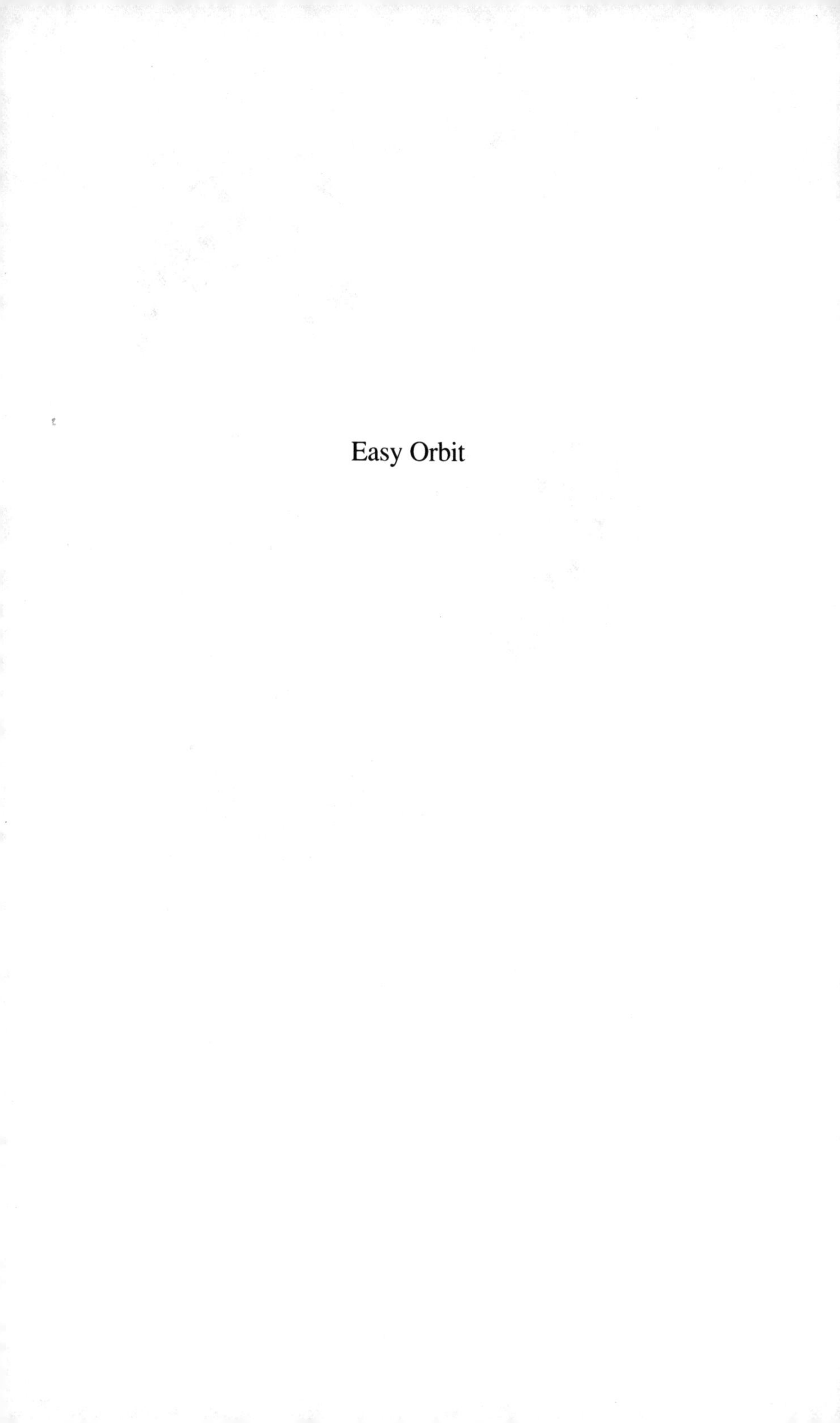

Easy Orbit

Tilted Planet Tales Number Three

Easy Orbit

Edited by James McEnteer

Illustrated by Kathleen Thoma

Tilted Planet Press
Austin, Texas

Tilted Planet Press
P.O. Box 8646
Austin, Texas 78713

Tilted Planet Press is an enterprise committed to peaceful revolution. True and lasting change comes not through violence but through a change of mind and a renewal of spirit.

First we must see through the empty materialism of our age. Next we must realize that we built this culture, that we are still building it, and that we can build according to a new vision. Then we must begin to build new institutions for a new age.

Tilted Planet Press labors in that cause. We aim to present good literature, to act as an outlet for new ideas occurring to new writers, and to advance toward a new world.

The text of this book was set in Times Roman on a Macintosh computer at the office of Tilted Planet Press. The type was output on a Linotronic 100 at the office Resource Graphics in Austin. It was printed on non-acid Glatfelter paper by Thomson Shore of Michigan, in a press run of 2000 copies.

Library of Congress Cataloging in Publication Data

Easy orbit.

(Tilted Planet tales ; no. 3)
1. Short stories, American--Texas--Austin.
2. American fiction--20th century. I. McEnteer,
James, 1945- II. Series.
PS559.A9E27 1986 813'.01'08976431 86-14474
ISBN 0-912973-06-4 (alk. paper)
ISBN 0-912973-07-2 (pbk. : alk. paper)

Contents

Introduction

The stories in this collection represent the voices of our contemporaries and neighbors, here and now. You could say Texas fiction is larger than the state in which it is written, because writers have psychic mineral rights that go down deep. You might also make a case for fiction being a more dependable resource than petroleum, always in high production whatever the fair market value.

Written by Austin area residents, often set in Central Texas, the fiction here does not focus on purely regional issues, but instead addresses the larger concerns of the human mind and heart. Not surprisingly, in a world of divorce and dislocation, most of these tales center on relationships—of women to men, children to parents, inidviduals to their evolving circumstances.

None of the stories is set in historical or future time, though several do contain fantastic elements. Confined to the present moment, the tales manage to remind us that the past—our own and that of the human species—impinges on the present. Our modern problems are variations on the ancient dilemma of what it means to be alive.

The tales here give us a wide range of subjects, styles, and points of view. That diversity of outlook is probably the most satisfying and informative feature of this collection. Perhaps, as the surface of our society appears ever more homogeneous—franchised and televised, interstated and malled—each of us develops increasingly individualized ways of dealing with It All. Anthropologists are discovering new linguistic dialects and micro subcultures, especially in urban areas, evolving within but out of sight of, the larger common culture. These stories reach beyond the scope of politics, beneath the spotlight of mass media, closer to where we really live.

The task of editing was made both easier and more difficult by the hundreds of manuscripts which arrived in answer to our call. Given our luxury of choice, it was easier to find good material, but harder to exclude finally some well-written work because of space constraints. We thank all those who submitted manuscripts. It was a pleasure to learn how much writing is going on in Austin, and how much of it is good. Several stories here are the first published by their authors. Although quality of work was our only criterion for inclusion, we are particularly pleased to introduce the new authors to you. Because none of these sixteen stories has appeared before, the reader has the opportunity to share our pleasure in a unique homegrown product good enough to export anywhere.

James McEnteer

Authors

John Campion was born in Dallas, Texas to James Campion and Mary Kucera Campion. He has five brothers and sisters. His translation of *El Sueño* (Thorp Springs Press), by Sor Juana Ines de la Cruz, was the first in English. He was one of the founding members of The Open Theatre—a non-profit arts organization. Campion was one of the editors of *PANGAEA*—an anthology of the International Texas Poetry Series published by The Open Theatre In 1985. *Sippapu the Kiva, an Inverted Bat, or The Medicine Man Speaks,* was just published by Goat Boy Press in a special edition.

Diane Castleberry, a native of Philadelphia, has lived more than half of her twenty-six years in Austin, and sets her fiction in central Texas. She began writing poetry in junior high school and studied literature in high school and college. While at the University of Texas, she co-founded *Wellspring,* literary journal of the UT English honors program.

About writing, she says, "Fiction is a way to share. Writing fiction is also a wonderful way to detach from day-to-day life and look close up at the dynamics of relationships at all levels. Mostly, I find time to write in cycles. When I'm stuck, I put my stuff away and go back to reading, reading, reading."

She is employed with the Austin Rape Crisis Center's Child Assault Prevention Project, where she educates elementary school children in strategies for preventing abuse. A mother of two preschool children, she lives with them and her husband in Austin. She contributed a story to the second volume of *Tilted Planet Tales.*

Susan Rogers Cooper, a fifth generation Texan, was raised in the Dallas area, attended East Texas State University, migrated to Houston in the early 70's and finally made it "home" to Austin three years ago. She began writing at age twelve, when she found a copy of *Catcher in the Rye* and discovered the written word could reach beyond *Nancy Drew—The Clue of the Leaning Chimney.*

A people-oriented person, Ms. Cooper has been involved in volunteer work for many years. In Houston, she spent six years as a telephone crisis intervention counselor and a trainer of volunteers for "Crisis Hotline Inc." In Austin, she helps run the volunteer-training program at the Center for Battered Women. She works full time as an administrative technician for the City of Austin. She lives in North Austin with her husband of fourteen years and their eight year-old-daughter.

Nan Cuba is a freelance writer living in San Antonio. She received a B.A. in education from the University of Texas in 1970 and taught school for ten years. She has published investigative articles in *San Antonio Monthly, San Antonio Magazine, Third Coast, Universal Family, Science '86, D Magazine,* and *Life.* For the past two years, she has been researching the story of serial killer Henry Lee Lucas. Her book on Lucas, *I Didn't Kill Nobody But Mom,* will be published by Corona Press. Her story, "A Bridging" appeared in the August, 1986 *Crosscurrents*, and another story, "Caricature of a Fulfilled Woman," appeared in the anthology *Voices of America.* She participated in the 1986 Bread Loaf Conference.

Cuba hosts a television program, "The Art of Writing," on which she interviews writers, poets, agents, publishers and editors from across Texas. She calls the show a "writer's mini-conference on the craft and the industry," and reports that audience response has been extremely favorable. She is married to an attorney and they have two children.

Tamara Stanfield Fish was born and lived for 27 years in Jonesville, Michigan, a rural agricultural village near the Ohio-Indiana line. Though she left Hillsdale County in 1980, she returns to her small-town roots again and again in her writing, for her perception of life is intimately tied to that experience of place. She finds the unique qualities of small-town life universal and these provide the impulse for her fiction.

She has a B.A. in English from Hillsdale College and an M.A. from Michigan State University. She taught high school for five years in North Adams, Michigan, worked in the Michigan Attorney General's office and taught composition for three years at Weber State College in Ogden, Utah. She came to Austin in August, 1985, to read and write fiction. "If I Should Die" is the first story she completed in Austin.

James McEnteer has published stories and poems in the United States and Canada. A former newspaper reporter, he currently teaches in the University of Texas journalism department, where he is working on a Ph.D.

Born in Mississippi, he grew up in Ohio and Pennsylvania, attended college in Connecticut and earned a master's degree in creative writing at the University of British Columbia. Not averse to the odd job, he has picked fruit (apples in Washington, blueberries in Maine), appeared as a contestant on a television game show and once managed a discotheque and bowling alley in Monrovia, Liberia. He contributed stories to the first two volumes of *Tilted Planet Tales*.

Jenny Lou Peña was born in Kerrville, Texas, in 1945 and grew up on the campus of the Schreiner Institute. She graduated from Tivy High School and from the University of Michigan, Ann Arbor, with a B.Mus. in wind instruments and a Michigan teaching certificate. She returned to Texas to earn a Texas teaching certificate.

She has held a number of jobs, teaching music privately and in public schools, working for the IRS, and as clerk and buyer for retail stores in Austin and San Antonio. She teaches clarinet and piano privately and performs as a soloist with the Waterloo Winds and other chamber ensembles. She reviews classical concerts for the Austin *Chronicle*, is forming a computer-formatting printing business with a friend and paints in acrylics in her spare time. She and her husband, Jose Guadalupe Peña, have a son, Alexander, three. "Lies" is her first published fiction.

Steven Phenix was born July 3, 1963 in Austin. His great-grandfather came to Texas in a covered wagon with his wife, "Big Mama," great-granddaughter of George Bernard Shaw. Phenix wrote "101 Ways to Drive People Crazy," in second grade and "Randy Holmes, Boy Detective," in fourth. In high school, he wrote subversive tracts for a teen-terrorist group that released 50 white mice in the school as a protest against the oppressive environment. Later, he chained shut the chamber door of the school board and slipped his fiction through the mail slot, making literary use of his captive audience.

On the six-year English degree plan at the University of Texas, he waits tables at a restaurant three nights a week. The rest of the time, he writes and rewrites his stories on a word processor at the *Westlake Picayune.* In lieu of payment for computer time, they make him take out trash. He comments, "If my fiction never takes off, I have my experience in waste disposal to fall back on and someday I hope to move up to nuclear waste." "Quality Time" is his first published story.

Ray Reece, born in Colorado during World War II, has been a perennial and worried Westerner ever since. As a high school boy in Fort Worth, he worried about his pompadour, which eluded the control even of Royal Crown Pomade. At Texas Christian University, where he took a B.A. in English, he worried about racial segregation. At the University of Chicago, where he took an M.A. in English, he worried about the existence of God. As a journalist in New York City, he worried about the Vietnam War in particular and the seemingly rapacious character of U.S. capitalism in general. At the University of California at Santa Barbara, where he taught comparative literature, he worried about the death of the antiwar movement.

Back in Texas, seeking to make moves in Austin, he worried about not being in Manhattan, where his Sensitive Intellectual Friends still lived. Then he worried about the energy crisis and wrote a book called *The Sun Betrayed: A Report on the Corporate Seizure of U.S. Solar Energy Development.* Whereupon, finding himself typed as an Energy Writer, he worried about life after solar power and began digging into his bulging file of Love Story Germs. Now he is worried about adult illiteracy, minimalism, overpopulation, the browning of the biosphere, childlessness, and going bald.

Michael Reynolds was born November 1, 1945 in Shawnee, Oklahoma. His formal education, through high school, was in the Catholic system. He attended the University of Oklahoma, Central State University and Oklahoma State University. He has traveled extensively throughout the United States, Canada, and Mexico, finding refuges in Florida, Quebec, California, Oaxaca, and Texas. Divorced, he has a daughter and two sons. He has lived in Austin since 1981.

His writing has appeared in regional and national publications in this country and in Japan, France, and Canada. In 1981, Full Count Press published his first volume of poetry, *Desperate Acts.* His work in this volume is the first chapter from "Burning The Deer," part one of *Under The Dome of Scorpius*. He is now at work on his second novel, *American Opportunity*.

Isabella Russell-Ides arrived in Austin in 1981 on the back seat of a motorcycle with two hundred bucks in her back pocket and her man on the front seat with his foot on the pedal. They came to see "Nashville Road," a play they co-authored, produced at Center Stage (now The Ritz) on Sixth Street. The play won the Austin Circle of Theatres award for best musical. Austin seemed to be saying yes to them, so they said yes to Austin and stayed.

Their next play, "Star Friends," turned into their wedding ceremony. Isabella loves the way art and life rub shoulders with each other. She says, "I always like to tell the truth, but what tickles me is telling it slant, so that the truth tells on itself and surprises me." Her first book of poems, *Getting Dangerously Close to Myself*, will be published by Slough Press as soon as Isabella works up the courage to let go of the manuscript.

Claudio Segré was born in Palermo, Italy, and grew up in Berkeley, California. He holds graduate degrees from Stanford University and from the University of California at Berkeley. He was formerly a reporter with United Press International in Los Angeles and with the *Wall Street Journal* in San Francisco. Since 1970, he has lived and worked in Austin, where he teaches modern European history at the University of Texas.

His articles and reviews have appeared in newspapers such as the *Journal* and the Jerusalem *Post*, and in numerous scholarly journals in the United States and Italy. His books include *Fourth Shore: the Italian Colonization of Libya* (Chicago, 1974) and a forthcoming biography, *Italo Balbo: A Fascist Life*, a study of the Italian fascist politician and aviator. He is the recipient of Fulbright and National Endowment for the Humanities fellowships. He and his wife, Elizabeth, are the parents of three children.

Russell Smith is a native of Eastland, Texas (population 3,747) but has, to date, never written of small-town sexual awakening, familial degeneracy, high school athletics, enigmatic elderly imbecile/sages, crusty farm widows living alone in spiritual communion with nature, trailer parks, incest, evangelical christianity, tragically-fated inter-ethnic love affairs, or the primal struggle of Southwestern agricultural man against the pitiless elements.

Smith, 30, worked as a newspaper journalist for six years after graduating from the University of Texas and is now a speechwriter with the Texas Department on Aging. He has lived in Austin for 11 years.

Pat Ellis Taylor was born in College Station, Texas in 1941. She began writing journals early as a way to converse without necessarily having anyone to talk to, since a military father kept her on the move during childhood. At eighteen, she settled in El Paso, where she eventually graduated with a master of arts degree from the University of Texas at El Paso in creative writing and folklore. She grew to love the border country and its people. From her explorations in the West Texas mountain areas came her first book, *Border Healing Woman: The Story of Jewel Babb,* which won a Southwest Book Award in 1981.

She has also won a National Endowment for the Arts writer's fellowship and the Austin Book Award for her first story collection, *Afoot in a Field of Men.* A third book, *The Godchaser,* is scheduled for publication this year. Currently she lives and works in Austin as a poet and free-lancing spirit, with headquarters at Paperback Plus Bookstore, and performs her stories and poems frequently in bookstores, libraries and bars around the state. She is married to Chuck Taylor, who is also a poet, and between them they have five children, who have all grown to be performers also—musicians, songwriters and poets. Both she and her husband are contributors to *Tilted Planet Poems.*

Andrea Winkler has lived most of her life in Texas. She travels frequently in Central Texas, where she likes to "collect" small towns. She grew up in Corpus Christi, where it was too hot and humid to do much save write, read, or swim—all of which she did in abundance. When she was thirteen, her family moved to Austin. After high school, she taught creative writing at Camp Mystic, near Kerrville. Currently, she is working on a master's degree in social anthropology.

She finds it "interesting to see what different people find necessary and meaningful. This seems to lead into fiction as well as fact; anthropology has made me many stories, a novelette, and an imaginary society richer." She has a passion for French and Russian operas, choral masses and requiems, and medieval motets. Her family is owned by two cats, an unruly Doberman and an Afghan hound. "We enjoy making up words and names (an anthropologist friend wanted to study our ‘language’) and all of us, including the animals, have at least eight nicknames apiece.”

Brian Yansky is a connoisseur of state universities, having spent time at the Universities of New Mexico, Iowa, Minnesota, and Texas. He has held a variety of jobs, including golf course caretaker on Cape Cod, farm laborer in Virginia, waiter in New Orleans, library worker in Houston, bartender, waiter, and lawn-maintenance person in Austin... in pursuit of minimum economic survival and maximum writing time. Lots of stories and two novels later, he thinks he's getting better.

Though his politics are to the left, he is right-handed, and is proud of having taught his dog to shake, speak, fetch, and lay. He tries to write every day, finds it difficult to begin new work and notices that when work is finished and sits on the shelf for a few months, re-reading it is like seeing someone on the street you know you know, but can't remember from where. Surprises keep him writing, the realization that the subconscious has been leading him in a certain direction all along, something said just right, or a character wiser than he is. He has lived in Austin six years.

Illustrator

Kathleen Thoma grew up in Washington, D.C., where she began to draw and paint at age three. Her mother, also an artist, encouraged these early efforts. Always a voracious reader, she began early on to illustrate the stories in her children's books. She took private art lessons until college, where she studied fine art. She has a B.S. in fine arts from Northern Virginia Community College and a B.F.A. in studio art from the University of Texas.

As a student, she worked as an intern at Sagebrush Studio, under Tom Curry. She began to free-lance while in school and has continued as a free lance while holding various jobs with local publications as advertising art director and graphic designer. Her illustrations have appeared in *Third Coast, New Texas* and *Destinations* , among other publications. She has worked for the City of Austin and recently completed a series of illustrations of endangered botanical species for the State of Texas. She plans to illustrate more books, especially for children, where she can combine her artistic skills with her imagination.

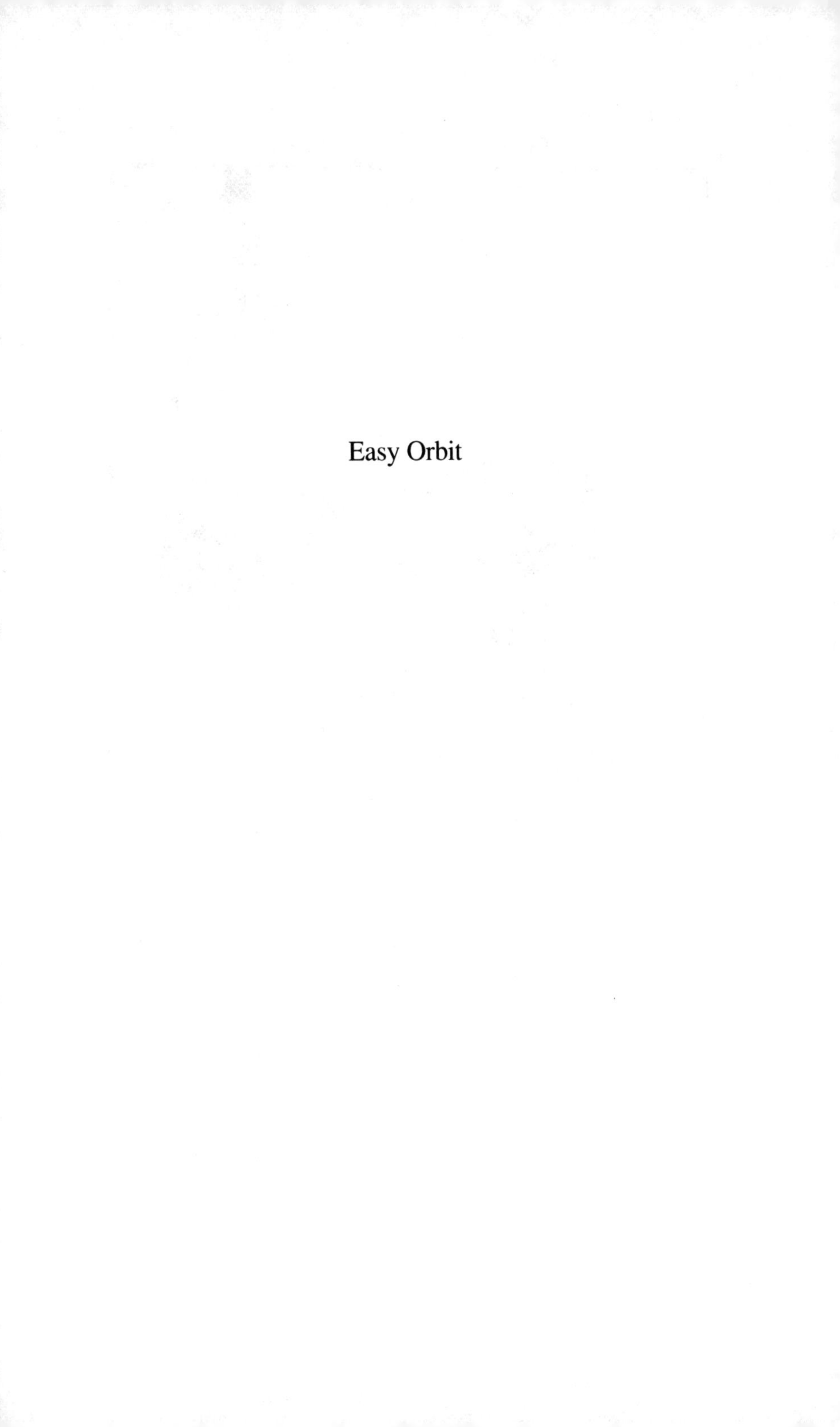

Easy Orbit

Kathleen Thoma

LIES

Jenny Lou Peña

When Sarah asked me how I liked her recipe for malted pancakes, I told her the truth. I'm not sure if our friendship can withstand so hard a test. "Why on earth did you tell her?" groaned Rebecca, who witnessed it all. I've thought about that a lot since, in the mornings as I brush my hair, at night as I dice carrots for supper. I'm not really sure at all. Perhaps the responsibility of being believed is too great.

I remember all the conscious lies I've ever told. Four.

When I was a very young girl, my grandfather was left in charge of me while the older womenfolk were out. He said he'd scramble us up some eggs. I said I didn't want him to because he'd get shells in them. He bet a quarter he wouldn't. He didn't either. They were great. But I claimed mine had shells and I got the quarter. I didn't do it for the money. I just hated to be wrong.

Once, before going to bed, I dripped water on my toothbrush and claimed I'd brushed my teeth. Guilt and thinking I could feel my teeth rotting away kept me awake until I got up and brushed them.

When I first learned to print my name, I was so proud I printed it everywhere. I even scratched it through the shiny blue paint of my Uncle Theron's brand new pickup truck. He asked me if I had done it and I said "No" because I wished I hadn't. He shook his head and said he wondered "who had done it then...someone surely musta".

I was thirty years old when I told my fourth lie. I had just been divorced and had moved to a gigantic apartment complex on the outskirts of San Antonio. I lived alone in a three-room apartment with a balcony, a pool I was too self-conscious to use, and a little yellow parakeet named "Birdie". I was so uncomfortable alone in a strange city that I had to steel myself to buy groceries on the way home. There was a convenience store within walking distance, one of the reasons I had chosen the apartment, but I never got up the nerve to use it. I worked long, hard hours as an assistant buyer in a large retail store in the heart of the city. The pay covered rent, gasoline, and minimum groceries. I had no extra cash, but it didn't matter much. There was no time or energy for entertainment and I would never have had the nerve to go anywhere anyway.

I had left all my dear friends behind and had not yet made new ones. I was very isolated except for regular phone calls from my friend, Sherry. She was afraid that, in my lonely state, I would fall easy prey to some man who did not value the intricacies of my mind or heart. She had pondered long over the perfect going-away gift, finally settling on a kit for a macramé plant hanger. She had compiled it herself and watched with shining eyes while I unwrapped and examined the twine and pins. "To keep you out of trouble" she had exclaimed "and because I know how you like to work with your hands. Look, you just..." and she had sat lovingly twisting and braiding and pinning and chattering. Then, it had looked like fun, but later alone, I had sat hunched over it braiding and unbraiding until my fingers were raw and my neck ached. Finally, I had put it away, unfinished.

Later, I had dreaded her phone calls because she would always say "How's the macramé coming?" and I would squirm and twist and say I hadn't done anything on it. One time I was just too ashamed to say that anymore. It was a Tuesday night in midsummer. It must have been the end of June because we were working terrible hours preparing for inventory. I remember pausing halfway up the stairs to my apartment, leaning against the cool, wrought-iron rail, and breathing deeply of the sweet summer night. I relaxed my tired eyes on the glowing blue water of the deserted pool. It had to be very late for the pool to be empty. The shrilling of my phone pulled me up the stairs. I caught it on the third ring.

"Hello. Sherry? Hi! How's your little family? Oh, yeah. I'm fine, tired though. Just got home from work and have to be back tomorrow at eight and...I'm sorry, what?...the macramé? Oh, uh, yeah, uh. It turned out fine. Uh...it looks just great." The lie slipped out so quickly. I clamped my mouth shut to catch it, but it was too late. "Huh? This weekend? Friday night? Oh, sure. I work Saturday but we can visit Sunday. The kids can sleep on the floor. Okay. See you then."

I stood a long moment and stared into the darkness, then flipped on the light and drug a chair to the closet. I dug through the junk on the top shelf, pulled down a big brown bag and dumped its hodgepodge of pins and twine across the maroon carpet. Three strands were plaited—the rest, a tangled octopus.

I turned on all the lights, settled crosslegged on the carpet and began the untangling. Birdie whirred to my shoulder and dug in his little toes, calling "Wheet! Wheet! Smack. Pretty bird!" He hopped to my hand, and viciously attacked the worms of twine. Impatiently, I flung him away.

Wednesday morning I walked stiffly into my office (cramped and red- eyed from a night of macramé) and dialed the phone. "Hello? Is this Tony's Craft Shop? I have a macrame project started. It has to be finished by Friday. Is there any one there who..." Line by line I crossed them off. Finally, with only two shops left, a woman with a whiny voice agreed to take a look.

When my lunch hour arrived, I grabbed the big brown bag and rushed down the escalator, ignoring the DO NOT WALK sign. The directions had sounded so clear on the phone but in the street I made several wrong turns, retracing my steps each time. Finally, I found the shop with 2316 CHARLIE'S MACRAME AND YARN in chipped red letters over the door. The window was littered with fading signs taped to the glass at odd angles...SPECIAL SALE...20% OFF...NEEDLES OF ALL SIZES...WOOL YARNS... The edges were curling, and little drifts of dust had collected on them. The tape was browned and peeling. I entered.

The woman stood motionless as a manikin, staring through me and beyond. Neither the ringing bells, as the door opened, nor the hollow sound of my footsteps, caused her to blink. I turned and peered curiously through the plate glass pane, but saw nothing except smudges and the street beyond. I shifted my gaze from the window and stared, instead, at a black tar triangle where a heel or chair leg had ripped off a corner of linoleum tile. I saw the woman's feet, perched high on narrow black heels, open- toed, with thin, graceful ankle straps. My gaze traveled up reedlike legs encased delicately in sheer black stockings, but stopped where her bony bird knees disappeared beneath a heavy gray skirt. I fidgeted and dared a quick peek at her face, but she still stared. Dust tickled my nose and I sneezed. The woman's calm grey eyes focused on my face and her pinched voice asked "May I help you?"

We spread my failure out on a dusty glass counter. She clucked and murmured, fingering the twine. "This is the rough kind...so hard on my hands...I don't know."

"Oh, please...please." I heard myself beg.

"Well, I'll try" she finally whined "but I'm not promising anything. Call Friday and see."

"How much will it cost?" I asked, looking away so she could not read my poverty.

"Oh, $25 I guess". She sighed.

Because I didn't have twenty-five dollars, I had to spend lunchtime Thursday again sweating my way through the maze of city streets. I turned down an avenue so narrow and winding that the searing rays of the noonday sun couldn't find their way in. For a moment, the shade seemed a welcome relief, but the breeze could not get in either. The heat and the stench were soon overpowering. The avenue was lined with bodies leaning against the wall; dirty men with bold eyes, old women (hands groping outward, palm up for coins). I had no change to give, so I averted my eyes guiltily to the sidewalk just in time to avoid stumbling over the outstretched legs of a wino, sprawled across the walk, gurgling melodies from loose unshaven lips.

I was so busy not looking at the people I missed the number 354 and the sign 2ND HAND BARGAINS BOUGHT AND SOLD. Before all of those eyes I turned, retraced my steps, and entered the shop.

The neat little man who strutted forward looked like he belonged anywhere except on this street, in this shop. From under my arm I unfolded a red wool blanket and from my purse I drew a gold ring wrapped in kleenex.

"You want to sell." His voice was crisp.

I nodded. He glanced briefly at the ring, then weighed it. The blanket, he opened completely, examining it for holes or stains. He handled them carelessly, as if they had never belonged to anyone, as though the ring had never been worn on a hand caressed by a lover, as though no breathing body had snuggled cozily beneath the blanket.

"$27" he barked. "I'll give you $27."

I nodded numbly. He pulled a thick pad from a drawer and boldly printed BLANKET RING $27. I filled in my address and phone number and signed it in triplicate. I wondered if that was in case I had stolen them. The register rang and I was back on the street, dodging stares.

Friday morning the woman at Charlie's Macrame answered the phone on the fifth ring.

"Nope, sorry. I haven't finished. If business is slow, I might get through." As the day dragged on, I snapped at everyone. I called her at three, at four, at four thirty, at five. Finally, at five-thirty, she said "Yes. I'll be through in a half hour. We will be closing up. Don't be late."

The vice president was approaching, paperwork in hand. I ducked behind a rack of hanging robes and took the back elevator to the street. The evening was beginning to cool, but dust and humidity hung like a cloud.

The door to Charlie's Shop was locked and the lights were out. I pounded loudly on the door with the flat of my hand. There was no answer. Tears stung my eyes and nose. As I turned, the door opened and the woman peered out.

"You make quite a racket." she said sourly, and thrust a bundle into my arms.

I paid her the $25 repeating "Thank you...thank you...thank you..." as she shut the door.

It seemed to take forever to get home in the Friday rush hour, but, once in my apartment, I moved rapidly. Standing on tiptoe on the kitchen chair, I screwed a large hanging-hook into the plaster ceiling. Tiny white powdered flakes floated to my hair and scattered like snow on the maroon carpet. I hung the beautiful, intricate macrame with its shiny, yellow beads in the corner between the long, blue couch and the picture window. Slipping my best Swedish ivy into it, I arranged the strands carefully around the sides. The vacuum swiftly sucked up the evidence. As I brushed the last of the ceiling dust from my hair, the doorbell rang. "Wheet!" Birdie called and there was a whirr of wings.

"Into the house quick, before the bird gets out!" Sherry yelled.

They all poured in. Gene hugged me and headed for the refrigerator. Matthew was a good two inches taller than I remembered and squirmed out of my embrace. The twins, on the other hand, were only too ready to give me big, gooey, peppermint hugs and kisses, then took off chasing Birdie, who winged his way from room to room chirping loudly. I turned to hug Sherry, but she wasn't even looking at me. My gaze followed hers to the corner of the room and the intricate design of braids and beads, twists and frizzes that hung there. She took it in her hands and turned and tugged.

"It's beautiful" she gasped. "The tension in the braid is just right." I stood very still. Her voice continued, happy, excited, "You're ready for a harder project."

K. Thoma

Quality Time

Steven Phenix

Good lord, my head hurts. I must have drunk a whole twelve-pack last night. After the game on Friday nights, everybody meets at a virgin cul-de-sac in the hills. We call them Circle Parties: meeting at the fringes of civilization to drink, fight, and hopefully fornicate in the bushes. Last night it was just a road in the wilderness. By the middle of next week, our tree covered cul-de-sac will be topped with luxury homes. And by the weekend they will be filled with young upwardly mobile professionals. And in every garage, a Mercedes. In every kitchen, a smiling bride with the nickname Dottie or Pooch. In every living room, a VCR; in every backyard, a pool, and in every bathroom, a bitter young man sits on the side of the tub, jerking himself and dreaming of a better world. And by the next Friday night, all the angry self-abusers will be forced a little further into the woods.

Last night at the demarcation line between bush and bulldozer, we had one hell of a time. Lenny, my best friend, threw up on Margaret's new Gucci shoes. Jack Rudd and four other football team captains kicked this one kid till his ribs broke. And a chubby, yummy, strawberry blond named Trish ignored me the whole night. I'm just too shy.

Oh god, my throat is dry. I stumble to the bathroom and stub my foot on the laundry hamper. The room spins like a ride in the amusement park. I must still be drunk. The cold, sweet water from the faucet washes out the dead buzzards in my mouth. Never again, I swear I'll never get that drunk again.

The telephone rings and the back of my head breaks off and falls into the bathtub. I pick up the receiver knowing it will be someone mad at me for something I was supposed to do, but didn't.

"Where the hell are you?" It's Dad and as usual, he's mad. "You were supposed to meet me for brunch and you're an hour and a half late."

"Oh shit."

"What?"

"I mean, I'm sorry, Dad. My alarm didn't go off. I'm on the way."

"Did you pick up the brake pads for the truck? Or did you forget?"

"Oh no, I went to the parts store last night," I lie. I did forget we were going to fix the truck today.

"Okay, see you in fifteen minutes."

"Dad, I've got to take a shower. It will take me at least forty-five."

"Forty-five minutes for a shower? It only takes me eight minutes. That's all it should take. I'm not going to wait. I'll go ahead and order breakfast. What would you like?"

Breakfast, yuck. My still-drunk stomach trembles at the threat. "I'm on a diet, Dad. How about just a big glass of orange juice."

"A diet, Jesus Christ. See you in forty-five minutes."

I take some aspirin, throw on some overalls and a dirty purple shirt, kiss Mom goodbye, throw up the aspirin outside the parts store, get the pads but forget the brake fluid, and fly down to the restaurant in forty-eight minutes.

"You're late," Dad says.

"Sorry, didn't have any clean towels."

"Your mother not doing the laundry, eh?"

"That's not it at all. Let's not bring her into this, okay?"

Dad grunts and returns to his migas. The scrambled eggs covered in hot sauce and tortillas vibrate on the plate while he forks. His throat makes a greasy gulop sound as he swallows. Suddenly it's high tide and I excuse myself to go throw up.

Then I float back to my lifeboat of orange juice and spend some time with my father. Since the divorce Dad has been real busy with his new job and his new girl friend with the firm abdominal muscles. So Dad has to pack a week's worth of love and support into a forty-five minute lunch. Quality time, he calls it. I think the term was invented by the same people who invented concentrated orange juice.

Lately I've been getting in trouble in school. My grades are dropping and the principal has threatened to set aside an honorary desk for me in the detention hall. And last week I was kicked off the cross country team for fighting. So the powers that be—Mom, the divorce lawyer, and the guidance counselor—feel that I need a stronger paternal presence. Which is odd considering the fact that before the divorce my father and I would watch television together and we would strain muscles trying to fill the sixty-second commercial breaks with meaningful conversation. Fatherly advice amounted to: "Boy she's got great tits." So we will spend this Saturday fixing my 1968 GMC pickup truck. And since I bought the thing last summer, rebuilding the truck is the only father-son tradition we have, short of watching television.

Dad eats breakfast while I study the surroundings. The Number One Bar is done in black and red like a banquet hall for a satanic group of Shriners. Black leather booths, black chairs, black tables, and black quarter panels. Red carpet and red wallpaper interrupted by a few Western paintings. The waitresses wear red cocktail dresses with black pompons at the hem. The place seems to be dominated by fathers brunching with their sons. I guess if I were a father who is worried about his son's manhood, I'd take him to the Number One Bar.

And like all the other fathers leering over the waitresses, my father has that Recently Divorced Look. To celebrate his newfound freedom his shirts are unbuttoned one button below the virile male level and one above Chicano pimp. He sucks in his paunch so he's not really fat. He combs over his salt-and-pepper hair so he's not really bald. He suns under lamps till his skin is football brown, so he's not really unhealthy. All in all, he looks not really happy.

"How are the girls treating you?" he asks.

"Like a love-slave, Dad. I have to beat them back with a club." He laughs at our father-son bawdiness.

"But you don't really have a girlfriend yet."

"No, I just play the field."

"Then you've gone out on an actual date?"

"Not in so many words, no. But sort of. I sort of went out a couple of times with girls and all."

"Don't worry about it, Skip. You're probably still in the cooties stage. It'll happen, just relax."

"That's not it. It's just that well, women slow you down. They weaken your legs. I've got a few things I want to accomplish first, then I'll worry about women."

"You got those genes from your mother. But try to have a little fun on the way to your first million, okay?"

I want to ask him if I should have fun like he did, behind Mom's back. But out of respect for quality time I keep my mouth shut. Then, as Dad pays the tab, he flirts with Viola Gene and her big country boobs. As usual, she loves the lines he's stolen from "Love Boat."

"Oh, you cute thang, you," she pats his hand. Dad grins and kicks me under the table to show me that's the way it's done.

Out of the dark, manly confines of the Number One Bar and into the blinding day we take Dad's car in search of brake fluid. Furious that I forgot, my father rages from stoplight to stoplight like a bantam rooster in a wooden crate, flapping red against the sides.

At the parts store, Dad puts on his good ol' boy accent and tells dirty jokes to the Gimme Caps behind the counter. "... and then his wife says, 'My God, Leroy is dead.' Hyuk, hyuk. I've noticed in parts stores and in tackle shops my father's sun-lamped neck turns West Texas red.

Then we pick up my truck and drive out to my father's big empty house. Divorce settlements are usually nasty. But with cool aplomb, my parents' marriage was dissolved like a business partnership. The settlement: he got the house, she got me.

Besides my father's furnishings, his electronic gadgets, and his girlfriend's overnight bag, the house is empty like a wedding vow. I hate going there. It feels like Christmas morning and I didn't get the bicycle I was promised. We drive into the circle driveway and I pull the tools from the back of my truck. Colonel Fanning (retired) half salutes us from behind the fortifications of his sculpted bushes. My dad waves, grins, and mouths the word "asshole."

Colonel Fanning (retired) sees landscaping in terms of global power. He believes if one insurrectionist blade of crabgrass is allowed to grow, they will soon be landing in San Francisco. So, from his bunker of a front porch, he marshals whole battalions of wetback laborers against the insidious forces eating away at America's roots and shrubs.

"How are the mealy worms this year, Colonel?" my father yells across the lawn.

"We can see the light at the end of the tunnel," he hollers back.

Dad positions the rolling jack under the rear suspension. Then he gets on one side and I on the other, and together, we remove the lugnuts. "Son of a whore," Dad issues the first epithet of the day when one of the lugnuts sticks. After drowning it with Liquid Wrench and banging with a hammer, he finally squeaks the sucker loose. We are ready to begin a long afternoon of skinned knuckles and stripped nuts.

"You know, when I was a kid," Dad says from the other side of the truck, "we had an old Buick we called Shenita. Know why? Shenita new brakes, Shenita new tires. Get it? Shenita new muffler."

"Have you ever thought about a career in professional comedy," I pop off while I pull at the cotter pin with a pair of rat-nose pliers.

"Son, you could make a living as a professional wise-ass." He called me son. That means he's getting testy and I need to watch my mouth.

"Son of a bitch," Dad hollers. "Son of a bitch, I broke the son-of-a-bitchin' cotter pin." I hear him throwing tools around, looking for another pin. From experience I know how to remain as inconspicuous as possible till he burns himself out. When I was a kid and I heard Dad come home and throw his keys in the brass bowl on the bookshelf, I went and hid in my closet. If no brass gong announced his arrival, then it was safe to continue playing.

Dad finds a spare pin and starts to settle down when his portable phone starts to chirp like a cricket. "Get that, will you," he snaps.

"Hello?"

"Jimmy, honey, I was just laying out here topless by the pool, under this warm, hot sun and I just called to say I was thinking of you." It is Sandra, my father's former secretary and current lover. I didn't say a word.

"Jimmy?"

"No, this is Skip, his son."

"Jesus Christ," her voice lost its girlish dance. "I mean, is your father there?"

"Hang on." I walk around the truck and look at my father. I stand there holding the phone for a few dramatic seconds, then say, "Jimmy, honey, telephone for you."

"Jesus Christ," he mumbles. He walks the phone into the house and yells at Sandra for calling him now. I continue working. If this were Dad's Porsche instead of my truck, I would strip a bolt or drop metal filings down the carburetor. I am pissed off with a capital P. I hate Sandra, that aerobics slut. And I hate my father and his obsession for flat-bellied women. And while I'm at it, none of the men that court my mother are good enough.

As if on cue, up walks Mr. Bledsoe, the biggest jerk in the neighborhood. When I used to sneak out of the house at night, Bledsoe would mention to my father in passing, "Oh I saw your boy out roaming the streets last night. You need to keep tighter reins on that child." And my father would thank him for his advice.

Mr. Bledsoe walks with his hips slung forward and his ass pinched like his shit is valuable and he's afraid to share. He waves at Colonel Fanning (retired). The Colonel smiles but I can see him mouth the word "asshole" as Mr. Bledsoe crosses the street towards me.

"Working on the truck I see."

"Yep."

"What did you say?" Bledsoe has the biggest black pores on his nose. They look like moon craters and they wink at me when he flares his nostrils.

"I said, 'yep.'"

"Ah, but you meant to say, 'yes sir.' Didn't you?"

"Yes sir." I hate Mr. Bledsoe. He has hair on his ears that curls up like wings.

"You know, you could probably see what you were doing better if you'd cut your hair."

"Yes sir," I say. Boy I want to tell him off. But I remain servile, till tonight. Then I'll drive over his mailbox with my truck.

"How's your mother, boy?"

"Just fine."

"Just fine, what?"

"Fine, *sir*."

"I was very sorry to hear about the divorce. Both your parents were good friends of mine. Do you know what they should do? They should go to a counselor and..."

I interrupt him by smashing my hammer against the frozen brake pad. And I keep hammering till he storms off to tell his wife what a horrid and disrespectful child I am.

My father returns in a darker mood. Normally I stumble all over myself trying to placate King Jim, the Tyrant, when he swells with red rage. This usually just makes him angrier. Thirty minutes after his anger is spent, he starts exuding boyish charm and expects me to forgive him. But today I'm ready to fight back. I'm ready to stand up to him.

"Look at this pad. The friction polished it to a shine," I say. I want him to draw his gun first so I can claim it was self-defense. He doesn't even look up from his work; he just grunts.

So I put in a big wad of my favorite chewing tobacco in my mouth and lean over the truck above my father. In sixth grade, my friends and I began chewing tobacco. We also shot craps with our lunch money. How we middle-class kids picked up the bad habits of urban and rural

Texas, I'll never know. Now I chew because I enjoy the reaction spitting in public provokes.

I chew till the leaves form a supple ball in my left cheek. Then I lean over Dad and spit a big brown glop that drops on his socket wrench. King Jim's head jerks up and his eyes bulge out.

"What do you chew that shit for. Dammit, that's disgusting. Spit it out. Now." I take the tobacco out with my fingers. "I didn't know pretty boys chewed tobacco," he says. So I throw the wad down and it bounces off his work boots.

He jumps off the ground and comes at me in a crouch. The cords of his neck stick out red and inflamed. "Boy, have you lost your fucking mind?" he says through clenched teeth.

"I guess this means quality time is over," I pop off.

"You bet it's over, Mister. And I've got a few things to settle with you. I'm tired of your pouting and brooding. You walk around all the time like somebody ran over your dog. We got a divorce. So what. It happens. Your mother and I couldn't work it out. You may not understand it now, but wait till you have a family of your own. Then you'll understand the pressures involved." His face relaxes a little. He takes a deep breath. "And another thing, your mother says you come home stinking drunk every weekend. That's not going to happen anymore. Do you understand me?" I just glare at him. I don't say a word, afraid I might cry.

"And your mother said you got kicked off the cross country team for fighting. What was that about?"

"This kid said you were a jerk-off, adulterizing, son of a bitch." Dad raises his fist to backhand me. I step back and pick up a wrench. I am bigger than he is but he has fury on his side.

"What are you, a man now," he taunts. His voice trembles with rage but he's not shouting. HIs voice is low, almost a whisper, and it scares me more than the shouting. "Come on," he says, "I brought you into this world and I can damn sure take you out." He reaches for me, but then stops in mid-lunge. "Shit, here comes Bledsoe. Cool it."

"Am I interrupting you boys?" Bledsoe asks.

"No, no Henry. I was just showing Skip a wrestling move I used in college. Right Skip?" I nod my head. I'm shaking all over and my knees feel funny.

"Good, that's wonderful," says Mr. Bledsoe. "That's what the boy needs at this point in his life, a strong paternal presence."

That does it. Angry tears start to sneak down my face. I grind my jaws so I won't sob. My father notices. He directs Mr. Bledsoe over to the curb to inspect a fire ant bed. I crawl under the truck and bang my hammer against the suspension so nobody can hear me cry.

After a bit, I regain control and try to breathe without gasping. Dad and Mr. Bledsoe return to the truck. I can see Bledsoe's blue jumpsuit and white tennis shoes from under the truck.

"I see you and Skip are working on the pickup truck," he says. "Maybe when you are through here you can fix the mower and finish the lawn." I can hear my father give a polite, social laugh.

"It sure needs work," Bledsoe says. "See that new coat of ivory paint I put on my house. I got it on sale down at Everett Hardware. You ought to go down and pick up a few gallons yourself, you know."

"Thanks, Henry, I'll keep that in mind," Dad says, his voice cool and modulated. I can see his feet take a few steps backwards, away from Bledsoe.

"Say, I saw your girlfriend leaving the house real early the other morning." Bledsoe steps closer to my dad. "What's her name?"

"Sandra."

"Sandra, right. Boy she is a looker. She's a lot younger than your wife, isn't she. How is Grace? Is she holding up well?"

"She's just fine." Dad taps his foot like he is keeping time to a marching band.

"I'll tell you what, if you and her would just go to one of them marriage counselors, I'm sure she would forget about all about this divorce nonsense. If not, I hope you got a real sharp lawyer. Don't let her pull anything over on you, no sir."

"Thanks for the advice, but the divorce is already finalized." Dad is still calm. I would have said, "Mind your own business, you hairy-eared freak." Then knock him upside his head.

"But I tell you, that Sandra is one hot cookie. She's an aerobics teacher, right? Mm-mmm she's a looker. That's what you need, Skip." He kicks my feet hanging out from under the truck. "You need a pretty girl like your father has. I never saw you bring home any girls when you were living here. But I bet you've met some real humdingers at your new school, huh?" He kicks me again. I want to take my hammer and smash his toes. He practically called me a faggot in front of my father.

"How are things going at the agency, Jim?"

"Business is up, but I've seen it better." I can detect a little tension in Dad's voice now.

"Well, if you would stop advertising in those conservative business magazines and place your ads with the local paper, I'm sure things would pick up. They've got a bigger circulation."

Then I see Dad's feet step real close to Bledsoe's. "Goddamit, Bledsoe, don't you tell me how to run my business." Then I hear a blow. I hear fist against face. And Mr. Bledsoe is on the ground with me. I must look as surprised as he does. I can still see the white imprint of a fist on the side of his jaw. My dad pounces on him and they both roll around the driveway.

I crawl out from under the truck to get a better view. It looks silly, two grown men wrestling on the ground. Colonel Fanning's wetbacks run over and yell encouragement in Spanish. Colonel Fanning (retired) threatens them for leaving their posts. My father and Mr. Bledsoe grunt and cuss while they scuffle. Neither one lands a solid punch.

It's all very funny, but I'm angry. I can't believe my father let him insult me and then tell him how to run his home and family. Dad let Bledsoe drool all over Sandra and he didn't do a thing. But he decked Bledsoe for criticizing the agency. What a hypocrite. For a moment, I entertain the thought of calling the cops and telling them about the two madmen fighting on the front lawn. What a kick that would be to see my father and Bledsoe hauled off to jail. Dad in handcuffs.

Dad has Bledsoe in a terrific headlock. Bledsoe reaches up and pulls Dad's hair. Dad howls but I notice his wide-mouth bass of a grimace flatten into a grin. He is enjoying himself. In fact Dad has always believed in "growth through conflict." Bledsoe continues to pull Dad's hair. With his free hand, Dad cuffs Bledsoe's hair-covered ears till he goes limp with surrender. Dad beams and bloats with victory. I can tell he has grown tremendously with this conflict. Suddenly I begin to laugh. I don't know why, but I'm laughing in my gut like never before.

Dad picks up Bledsoe and shoves him towards home. Bledsoe runs off to tell his wife what a horrid family we have. He'll probably tell his lawyer too. Dad smiles at me and laughs. The wetbacks laugh too, but they're not sure why. Colonel Fanning (retired) kisses both sides of Dad's face and hugs him like some French guy giving a medal.

Dad comes to me and puts his arm around my shoulder. His cheek is scuffed from the pavement. He smells like oil and sweat. I am embarrassed by his touch and the look in his eye. I expect him to say, "Here son, have a Lifesaver." Instead he laughs. "Come on," he says, "let's go have a beer."

"Jeez your face is a mess," I say and wipe the dirt away from his wound. He winces at my touch, but he still smiles. "Bledsoe damn near pulled out what little hair you have left."

"C'mon wise-ass, I'm buying the Shiner Bock." Then not bothering to wash the grease off, we head downtown for a drink. We drive right past the Number One Bar and, instead, we belly up to a fern bar where my friends hang out. Here the angry self-abusers drink manhood without fear of an ID check. Dad feels uncomfortable.

"Nobody will know, Dad. Just act like you belong," I tell him.

Inside Pandora's Box

Diane Castleberry

OCTOBER

Celina stood, a gimme cap pulled low over her black curls. Her eyes grew darker, flashing in irritation. She hated outings with his family, and this afternoon was no different. Sensing her mood, Danny shifted his attention to her.

He reached into the ice chest and picked up a pear, wet from the melting ice. He walked over to where she stood. She turned her back. He wiped the pear off on his t-shirt, stopping beside her, shoulder touching hers. He gave her the pear without comment. She took a bite and turned to look up at him.

"Come on, it's Kara's birthday," he coaxed.

She shrugged.

"Lina," his shoulder dropped. "She's my sister, just be a little civilized."

She glared at him from under the hat's brim. "I've been a lot civilized, damn it. And it's not just her. It's all these people together." She gestured with the pear.

Danny chuckled, "As if there were a hundred people here..." he slipped his arm through hers. "Come sit down. After we eat, we can leave."

"Where will we go?" She rested her chin on his arm.

Danny backed up to sit on the picnic table and Celina leaned on him. He wrapped his arms around her. "Well, we can always go home," he began.

Kathleen Thoma

"Danny." Kara was coming around the corner of the shelter that shaded the table. "Come play for us before supper." She tugged lightly on his arm. Her eyes smiled up at him, as blue as his own.

Danny looked at Celina, questioning. Her face was deceptively blank, inches from him, and he wanted to smack her. He turned his gaze back to his sister. "Go get my guitar, there near the hammock."

Kara went quickly. Danny turned Celina in his arms. "Whatever it is with you, you're making this real hard for me." His voice dropped.

She pulled away from him and walked toward the hammock that Kara bent under to get the guitar. Without a word, she lay down in it, swinging gently in the sparse shade of a mesquite tree. She closed her eyes, pushing the cap low over her face.

It wasn't long before she heard the dissonant sounds of Danny tuning his twelve-string. She forced herself to unclench her fists; dangling a leg from the hammock, she rocked there wondering what he would play. There were voices passing her; his older sister Judith and her friend brought lawn chairs nearer to enjoy the entertainment. She opened her eyes to watch as his audience collected slowly. His father stretched out in the grass with Kara. He went from tuning into a song without introduction. The quiet minor key of the ballad was a complement to the surroundings and became part of the cool breezes. His voice wove a story built from an old poem; he searched libraries for ancient ballads and prose poems and resurrected them. The care that had gone into the choice of each note gave the story an engaging intimacy.

Celina looked away from the group toward the overarching granite formations that crowned the park. At that moment, they would've been more pleasing to her if they'd been a lot closer to Austin. She felt isolated. The offer to leave would probably not come through. The family was going to spend the night, and after the dinner the two-hour drive back to town wasn't going to look as good as a night under the stars. She sighed, trying to let some of the tension go.

"Lina." Danny's voice. She lifted her head. "Come over here," he patted the bench space beside him. "Judith wants to hear her song."

She paused, a frown creasing her brow.

"I can sing it with you." Kara offered.

Danny shook his head without taking his eyes from Celina's "No, it's arranged for an alto."

Celina got up and went to sit beside him. He began to play again. The duet was peaceful and slow, written for Judith's stillborn daughter. Judith rarely requested to hear it, though Celina and Danny sang it together occasionally when he performed. Their voices were in the same range, blended together, meshing subtle harmonies. Celina always enjoyed the singing, but she was not a performer; lights and crowds were too invading.

Danny continued playing smoothly into another song, avoiding silence. Celina followed, singing the low harmony to an old John Denver song. The song had everyone humming or singing along, and people moved to get their plates for supper as he finished it up.

Danny put his guitar away, making room for those who wanted to sit at the table. Celina wasn't particularly hungry and she waited, leaning against the shelter. She watched Kara follow Danny to the hammock where he rested the guitar case in the grass. There were people near and she couldn't hear what they were saying. She watched Kara get too close, and Danny's face change as he moved her away. It was a ritual she'd observed many times. She wondered that Kara never figured it out and gave up. Kara wanted a lot more than Danny gave her. Celina turned it over in her mind— what did Kara need from him? Danny met her gaze, walking back to the table, Kara in his wake. He reached and Celina took his hand. He lifted his hat off her head and kissed her, soft and fleet.

Danny found two empty lawnchairs for them and they ate dinner. Judith and her friend Marissa came to sit with them. Marissa asked questions about Danny's career that Judith answered with only occasional nods from Danny. His family almost always referred to him in the third person as if he weren't there, even discussing his needs and ambitions. After several minutes, Celina felt her nerves stretch tight. She never understood how Danny lived with it.

She put her fork on her plate and excused herself. The trash sack was behind the shelter and she tossed her plate in, most of the food uneaten.

She stretched her arms out, arching her back. Danny put his hands at her waist. She jumped a little.

"Sorry," he laughed, letting her go. "It's almost cake time, you want to walk to the car with me and get the gift?"

"Sure." She shrugged her shoulder indifferently. Danny took her hand, weaving his fingers between hers. He was always warmer and his hand warmed hers. She wondered what he had gotten for Kara. Choosing gifts was something he did well.

They'd driven out in her brown Toyota wagon. It treated them only slightly better than his old MGB on the road, and held considerably more gear. Danny's duffel bag shared the back seat with the tent. He dug through it for a moment, pulling out two small packages. "Here."

He handed her a small flat box. "That's for you," he added in response to her furrowed brow.

She opened the box quickly, letting the top drop to the pavement. Nestled in cotton was a bracelet. She took it out, examining it in the fading sunlight. The pattern on the surface was a delicate vine. She fit it on her narrow brown wrist. The bracelet complemented the silver and gold braid of her wedding band. Danny caught her arm to see how it fit and looked.

"I like it." He let her arm drop.

"Thank you." She kissed his shoulder.

He tossed the box onto the floorboard of her car, retrieving the top from the ground. "Come on." He started back toward the campsite, she fell into step beside him.

The cake was on the table when they got there, holding twenty-four candles. After a boisterous chorus of happy birthday, Kara blew them out. Watching Kara open her gifts, Celina was struck by how much it felt like a kid's party. She got a beer out of the ice chest.

Kara had saved Danny's gift for last. By the time she opened it most everyone had lost interest and gone to pull lawnchairs closer to the fire. The earrings were pretty gold filigree hoops. Kara put them on. "I love them," she smiled at her brother, turning her head. "What do you think?" Danny took her chin in his hand, pulling her hair over her shoulder, sandy blonde curls. He nodded approval.

Celina turned away. The cold beer tasted good. She moved to stand nearer the fire. Judith's friend Marissa began explaining something to her, with a gentle slur that didn't come from too much beer. Celina sat crosslegged on the ground, glad to focus her attention on the woman she barely knew. Behind her, she was aware that Danny and Judith cleared the trash while Kara took her gifts to the car.

The air cooled as the sun dipped to the horizon. Fireflies signalled each other at the edge of the creek. Celina listened to conversation wander from topic to topic. "Hey." A tug on her hair made her look back. Her husband leaned over her. Another tug and he slipped the kelly green hair ribbon off, letting a mane loose. His face reflected in the firelight, upside down, ghostly angles.

"Danny, don't." She pulled his hand away. She leaned back, inviting him to sit. He shook his head, instead pulling her to her feet.

He took her hand, tight, close to him. "Come." They stepped away into dusk.

"Where are you going?" Kara, on the path back to the campsite spoke to Danny.

"Nowhere."

Those kind of answers were always bait. Celina frowned, unseen in the approaching dark. Kara stopped in their path.

"You didn't set up your tent; are you leaving?"

"Not right this second." Danny didn't want to talk.

"Aren't you going to stay tonight?"

Danny and Celina looked at one another. She could feel his hand tightening on hers. "Well... what do you want to do?"

He knew she wanted to leave. She clenched her teeth. She was tired of always being the dissenter, the spoiler. She didn't know how to respond. A sigh escaped. She shrugged a shoulder. "I kind of thought we were going home. Later," she ventured, finally.

Kara moved closer. "Oh, y'all stay." There was a whine to her voice that Celina knew well and didn't trust.

"We're just going for a walk. We'll be back." Danny evaded, taking a step.

"Where to?"

"Alone." He dismissed her, pulling Celina behind him. They walked in silence for a hundred yards. Celina thought the odds were good that Kara would follow. Realizing that she'd held her breath, she almost laughed. Danny looked at her. "What?"

"Nothing; I do not like her."

"So you giggle?"

"Nerves." She leaned closer as she walked. "Bitch," under her breath, involuntarily.

"Lay off."

"Danny, admit it, she drives you crazy too. She whines. She hangs on you." Hearing her words, she flashed on Kara's face. "She's hot for you. That's it, isn't it?" She laughed.

"Shut up."

"Not much of a joke, huh?" He'd let go of her hand, slowing his pace a little.

She looked back at him, his face in shadow. She pursued it, "What is going on with you?"

"Nothing. It was a long time ago." He wasn't really talking to her, looking back over his shoulder. "I didn't mean it."

"What are you talking about?"

"Kara; she just won't let go. She doesn't understand about now. You."

"She's your sister." There was a shadow of distaste in her voice. She recalled her own discomfort when Kara got too close to him. The possessiveness. The hostility. "Lover?"

"I didn't mean it."

She stopped, a chill across her shoulders. He watched her warily. As often as he lied to her, this wasn't it. Too many things fell into place. He got a pack of cigarettes out of his pocket. His gestures lighting up were painfully familiar. He looked out of place here among trees. He needed smoky bars, dim stage lights. He watched the ground now, like he did when they visited his mother's grave. Midnight journeys. The pain of his mother's death, his music, Kara. He refused to share. The crush inside her was almost physical. He stood apart, and there was no place for her.

"I hate you." It came out between clenched teeth. Suddenly furious, she swung and slammed her fist into his jaw, sending him backwards several steps.

"Christ." A second swing missed and he grabbed her wrist, twisting.

She took a breath of surprised pain, as the bracelet cut into her skin. He let her go as her knees went to the ground. Her knuckles hurt from hitting him; she rubbed her stinging wrist. "Son of a bitch," she bit her lip.

"What is the matter with you?" He jerked her head back, both hands tight in her hair, his voice low and harsh.

"You." Her neck ached with the pull.

His face was so close she could feel his breath. "You understand." The demand, hot in her face, was followed by more harsh words. She didn't hear; his grip was too painful and she didn't want to know. He was too close, his voice too loud.

"Stop; stop it. Stop it," grinding out of her throat. He pushed her away and she scrambled to her feet. They stared at each other, shadows.

Celina walked. Then, panicked and ran. Past the idle playground and into the bathrooms. She swung open the stainless steel door to a stall, aware that no one followed. She locked it behind her. She sat down, then she stood again, turning around in the tiny space. She cried out, banging against the metallic walls. Sound vibrated in the hot, humid air. Retreating, she sat on the toilet seat. Pulling her feet up, she hugged her knees. For a long time her mind was gloriously blank.

"Celina?"

Her face fell to her hands.

"Are you in here?"

"No."

A laugh. Uneasy. Judith. "Come on. What's going on?" There was a gentle knock.

"Nothing."

"Lina."

Celina got up, unlocking the door.

Judith pushed it open. Unceremoniously, she took Celina's arm and pulled her out.

"You guys have got to quit fighting like this." She gazed for a long moment at Celina's face. Celina didn't meet her eyes, remembering a time Judith had nursed bruises and scrapes. This was more, felt worse, yet, in the mirror that stretched the length of the room even her face was blank. Judith's voice went on. Celina let herself be led to the bench opposite the showers. Judith's hands soothed. She deftly wove Celina's thick hair into a french braid that fell heavy, traitorous. Celina didn't listen, let the monologue drift around her. Eventually she let herself be talked out of the bathroom.

The night was cold and very dark; Celina shivered. Danny was outside, leaning on the wall. Celina looked at him and, for just a second, she could see through him, as if he were standing behind himself, gaunt, waiting. Her fear reflected in his eyes. She pulled back into herself and he was just standing there, waiting for her.

NOVEMBER

There was a light on in the back of the apartment when Danny opened the door. Celina closed her book. She listened while he came in through the kitchen and stopped near the table. Habits: in the morning she would find his guitar by the table where he'd set it to sift through the mail. He leaned in the bedroom doorway. The light from her reading lamp reached far enough so she could see him clearly.

"How'd it go?"

"Good." He sounded pleased with himself. "Nice crowd, and towards the end I played some of my stuff." He sat on the edge of the bed. He unlaced his boots and kicked them off. He checked his watch. "You're up late." He wanted to touch her—she was close—but he didn't. "Couldn't sleep?"

She shook her head. "What time is it?"

"After three." He watched her stretch out her back. "You should've come out tonight; it would've been more fun." He tossed her book on to the floor. The low light reflected his eyes.

"I would've gotten drunk. Might've felt good."

He shook his head. "I would've made you work."

She laughed. He loved her laugh; he relaxed back on the bed. One afternoon on a beach, he had tried explaining that to her—her laugh. It had sounded trite and romantic at the time. She tucked her feet under him, to warm them, he guessed. He wondered how often she touched him just to get warm. Her touch, gentle and strong, was always cool against him.

Celina sighed, snuggling back into the pillows. The silence was deep; the basement room had no access to the outside. Much later, Danny rolled to stand up, and she'd been half asleep. "What are you doing?"

"Going to bed." He dropped his shirt close to his desk and rummaged through some things there for a moment. He sorted cassettes, one into the cassette deck, one to the shelf, one into his box. He pulled the small wooden box out from its home under his desk and returned to it the cassette of his mom singing nursery rhymes. He tapped a beat on the side of the box. The varnish had long since worn away, leaving the wood exposed.

He had found the box in his grandmother's attic, old then. It had held his personal things for more than eighteen years. He lifted out a high school picture of Celina: pigtails and cutoffs. He looked at her now, her hair wild and dark, all over the pillows. She didn't know about his collection of photographs of her, or the crimson ribbon he'd saved from a date. It suddenly seemed a long time ago. His journal was there, near the bottom, unused. He dug to the corner and found the ring his mother had given him, tossing it back on top. He closed the box, a phrase in his mind. He looked at his wife again. She was just barely asleep.

He went out to the living room. Taking his guitar out of its case, he sat on the floor in the dark. He played a simple melody and then worked it. Celina got up and stood near the bedroom door, listening. Occasionally the instrument became part of the man. His first mistress, truest love. She couldn't see him and didn't need to. His music was more than revealing. She walked over, silent. Danny stopped playing when she touched his hand. "You said you were comin' to bed."

"I lied." He pushed his guitar up on to the couch and pulled Celina on top of him. "I'm sorry."

"Sorry," she echoed. His mouth was against her face, then he kissed her. Her skin, soft with rose musk and something faintly hers, was greater invitation than the press of her mouth and hands. He pulled her down on the carpet, remembering the first time they had made love, eight years ago in his father's house, on the sly, on the carpet of Danny's old bedroom, two floors above where they were now. He tasted her familiar taste. She laughed, low.

She was wet with his sweat when she sat up. Her brown skin glistened in the faint light from the bedroom lamp. She leaned very close to his face. "I love you."

Her voice sounded bottomless. He heard the gentleness, but felt the intensity of her staring and he opened his eyes. Her hair curled away into darkness around him. He had found those words in countless lyrics, and he smiled slowly. Reaching out, he put his hand in her hair. "So what does that mean? 'I love you?'"

She shoved against his shoulder, affectionate, frustrated.

"That's a weird thing to say."

He moved from her reach and stood.

"Please talk to me." Her voice chased him.

Without looking at her, he walked into the bedroom. She got to her feet and followed. In their bed, propped by pillows and blankets, Danny hummed softly, willing her to sleep. It had been a long time since he'd wanted so much to cry and he fell asleep uneasy.

Celina's eyes came open, her body waking, hair burning along her spine. She glanced around the room, found nothing, not even an ominous shadow. She shook it off, burrowed close to Danny. He moved in his sleep, accomodating her.

DECEMBER

Danny was sprawled on the floor, propped against the couch with his guitar in his arms. His fingers picked a complex melody that drifted into the kitchen. When she'd first met the Martin twelve-string, she hadn't known she would have constant accompaniment. It had its good points, but not today. His music wove into her, too much a part of their life; she couldn't just not listen. With a quiet sigh, she wished him out of the house, knowing that he was the one staying.

She'd packed a carton, filled with enough kitchen stuff to get her started and not leave the kitchen empty. She picked up the strapping tape and carefully sealed the carton. A shove with her foot moved it closer to the door. Still listening, she sat in a chair at the table, gritting her teeth. Deliberately she thought back, itemizing, sorting, sure she hadn't forgotten anything. She ran her hand through her tangled hair, standing, feeling unsure. "Danny?"

The melody stopped, mid-phrase. She heard him getting to his feet. She took a step and leaned against the doorjamb. His face was a mixture of resignation and confusion. She couldn't read his eyes at all. Glancing around the room, he didn't meet her gaze. "Done?"

She nodded. She checked her pocket for the keys. "Yeah, I'm going."

He walked toward her. "Need a hand?"

"You could help with this box."

"Sure."

He searched the kitchen for a moment, and she wondered if it was so different. Of course, with all her things gone, it would have to be. He lifted the box and she opened the door. He maneuvered up the concrete stairs with ease. She watched him for a moment before letting the door shut softly on her back.

The sun was flat-Texas-brilliant, radiating off the pavement. She narrowed her eyes against the flood of light, climbing the stairs to street level. Danny fit the box into the back seat of the little Toyota.

"Thank you." She smiled.

A corner of his mouth lifted. "It'd feel silly to shake hands."

"I know."

"I don't like this. I want you to come back."

She nodded, looking past him, over his shoulder.

"Will you?"

A shrug, "I don't know yet." She didn't want to go into it again.

"Celina," he used her full name, made her look at him; his voice held a familiar note. Stay with me. I need you. Things that came easily in his lyrics. Things that didn't get said. He took a breath.

Instinctively, she put up her hand before he moved. She touched his collar, his shoulder. "I'll call you tomorrow, okay?"

He nodded, the muscles in his jaw tightening a little. She stood on her toes to kiss him.

"Bye."

He didn't answer.

He held the car door for her while she slid behind the wheel. The huge house over their basement apartment was empty, she noted with relief. It would've been too hard to say anything in view of his family. She started the engine and he closed the door. As she backed the car out of the driveway, she had a fleeting sensation of escape. Danny leaned against a tree, watching.

Her relief vanished into despair. In the five years they'd lived together, she had left him three times, although he didn't count the two times before they got married. Two weeks ago, after the yelling and hitting had died in a standoff, she had filed for a legal separation. He'd been maneuvered into surprised silence and she'd moved out, a few boxes at a time. The cottage was set in the shelter of trees near the back of a friend's property; they would let her stay there as long as she needed, rent free. Dead liveoak leaves crunched under her tires as she parked in front of the house. The doors had no locks, which seemed odd to her. She hadn't told Danny where she was staying.

In this smaller kitchen, she unpacked the carton she'd sealed half an hour ago. She set out some hamburger to thaw. The phone rang. She went quickly through the small house to her bedroom.

"Hullo?" She stretched out on the bed.

"Hi, it's Kara." The voice felt like icy fingers on Celina's back.

"Hi."

"Danny says you want a divorce," Kara started slowly. "I didn't know..." Celina hated even the pace of her words. "I'm sure you don't want to talk to me, but I feel like..."

There was a long pause and finally Celina asked "How did you get my number?"

"Danny."

Disbelief kept Celina silent. Kara never spoke to her unless it was unavoidable. She felt a prickle of danger.

"Was it me, Lina?"

"What?"

"Why you left him this time."

"You were right; I don't want to talk to you about this," Celina spoke carefully. "There's no..."

Kara interrupted, "Don't come back to him. We don't want you."

Her anger folded in on itself for a moment and didn't let her breathe. Celina hung up. How dare that bitch have such a soft voice? But the anger, the madness, didn't stop the crush of fear. She could still see Danny's face, still feel the anguish. She went back to the kitchen. She got a cup out of the cabinet and put it under the tap. She stared at the clear amber as it filled, without seeing. Then there was cold water on her hands, and she didn't want it. She emptied it out and looked around the kitchen again. Slippery, the cup fell from her fingers and shattered on the wooden floor. "Aw, Jesus." A sob came up, and she kicked into the splinters of glass. What she really wanted to do was strangle Kara. Her thoughts tumbled in confusion for a minute.

She sat down at the table and stared at the floor. Because her mind was busy, she didn't hear the creaky noises that the house made in the breezes. The sun slanted light in and she watched it reflect prettily off the glass shards. Her love for Danny twisted sharply around inside. She sat motionless. For years she'd thought, felt maybe, that the quirks in their relationship had something to do with her. And she'd worked so damned hard. The memories ached. Coils of red-hot barbed wire.

Frustrated, she slammed her fist onto the table top. It hurt. Made her know she was still alive. She rubbed her hand, still stinging. It was too painful to deal with Kara's soft, gold threads of incestuous possession. Her fresh horror left her hollow with the sense that perhaps even her own anger and passion was somehow twined through Kara. She stood and turned, glass crunching beneath her Nikes. Her car keys were on the counter by the door. She picked them up.

On the way back, she argued with herself. Through eight years, her love barely touched whatever scar Kara left on Danny. Celina couldn't be part of it any more, but she needed something. When she pulled the car to a stop in the drive, she felt some of her momentum slip away. Other cars were there. The house seemed to impose. But then, even more yelling and screaming would make her feel better, less alone. Judith's car was at the curb. Celina wondered if she knew her little brother and sister made love all those years ago; read more than rivalry into Danny's explosive reaction to Kara. She went up the front walk and rang the bell.

Jeremy Logan answered the door. "Lina. Danny said you finished moving out today."

She nodded and took a breath, trying a smile. She would always be awkward with his father. "I need to talk to Judith." She stepped in.

"Well, she's upstairs somewhere." He gestured to the stairs, already looking past her.

"Thanks." She went up. The carpet upstairs was deep and silencing. The hall was long and she glanced at each door. Kara's bedroom door was slightly ajar, and Celina stared. After a second, the door swung away. Kara looked back at her, surprised. The delicate cheekbones lightly sprinkled with freckles were deceiving.

No words came.

Kara backed up, edging the door closed. The latch clicked shut.

"Kara," Celina lifted a hand to hit the door, but stopped. She touched the wall, rough beneath her fingers. Her lips pressed together, she walked past, trailing her fingers on the opposite wall. She knocked on Judith's door.

"Lina, hullo." Judith's smile was a welcome, and it hurt a little. Judith touched her shoulder. "Danny came up after I got home from work. He said you packed up. Today was it. I'm glad you're here. I thought we wouldn't get a chance to talk."

Celina came into the room and sat on the floor by a window. The view reassured.

"Lina, what are you going to do?" Judith asked aloud, and the question haunted. Celina looked up at her, silent. She shrugged.

"I can't; there's nothing. . . . I don't know." She stopped.

Judith sat on her bed and a wooden box behind her caught Celina's gaze. "Danny's box."

"Yeah, he brought it up this afternoon; I haven't had a chance to look inside yet." Judith touched the worn edge of the box. The wooden box had a hinged lid. Danny hid things there. Celina had never looked, but out of it had come his journal full of poetry and lyrics, a cassette of his mother singing, an old ribbon from Celina's hair. He had shared with her and she'd never pushed that trust. She couldn't think of any reason for that box to be so out of place. Judith reached out and pushed hair away from Celina's eyes. "Are you okay?"

Celina dug her fingers into the plush blueness of the carpet. "There is so much of Kara with him," she started. Judith's blank, listening eyes made her stop. She didn't even know the words, or the truth. "Judith, don't you know? Tell me. . ." Judith shook her head, looking past her. Then she looked back again. Celina forced the words. "He loves her, differently than you, or me." Judith's eyes closed; her face in the light was pale, creamy, golden. For a second, Celina wondered why Judith had no freckles. And unexpectedly, she needed to know why Danny had given his box away.

She stepped up and lifted the lid of the box, feeling oddly sneaky. Judith looked in with her. Junk. And Celina recognized the attachment to every item. She saw herself—pictures—a bright-red satin ribbon, and notes in her own hand. She lifted a crumpled piece of paper. Just a note to tell him what time to meet her. She'd written it at least six years ago, and signed it 'yours, Celina M.' She let it fall back into the box. He kept all of these things. "I need to ask him."

Judith touched her arm. "What does he say?"

Judith had been there and comforted and not understood. Celina shook her head. There wasn't anything coherent. "I'm gonna go downstairs for a minute."

"Talk to him?"

"Yeah," Celina pulled away, her fingers lingering on the corner of the box.

Judith walked down with her and through the kitchen, while Celina went down the inside stairs to the apartment. She opened the door, wondering if she should knock now. The guitar was where she'd seen it last, resting on the couch. "Dan?" She patted the case lightly as she passed and went through to the bedroom. "Dan?" The bathroom door wasn't quite shut. She tapped gently, looking down. The door moved slightly under her hand. There was blood in the neat square grouting of white tiles. She pushed the door open.

Danny was lying on the floor, on his side, his arms tucked under his head like a small child. A puddle of blood surrounded him, staining his white t-shirt, his jeans. Something inside of her froze and, for a moment, she looked away. Then, in a shadow of her mind, she moved. "Dan? Danny?" Her voice was surprisingly loud. His six-foot-three frame dwarfed the room. His arm was warm and she grasped his shoulder, shaking gently. "Goddamn it!" She leaned close to his face. Gold freckles stood out on a stark white skin. She felt no breath on her cheek. He didn't move at all. She heard her voice counting slowly; her chest was tight, her own breathing scarcely there; she got scared. The tile hurt her knees. She tugged and pulled his arms out from under his head; he had done a good vicious job.

"Judith!" She yelled, her voice reverberating against the walls. "Help me! Danny!" Her voice fell. She shifted his shoulders flat to the floor, tilting his chin back. She took a deep breath, covering his mouth with hers; she gave the breath to him.

"Lina." Judith was at the door. Celina looked up, imploring, and saw Judith's face go blank with shock.

"Go back and call EMS." Celina's voice was even, in startling contrast to her panicky face. Judith took in the scene; for a moment her eyes darted, sorted. With one backwards step, she fled.

Celina leaned over and rested her hand on Danny's neck. Her nerves were so jangled that she didn't know what she felt. She closed her eyes, but could find no trace of a pulse. Fear took her breath, her thoughts indistinct, "Don't do this...;" her words were a rhythmic whisper. She positioned her hand on his chest and waited for the flutter of a pulse. A faint gift. She took a deep breath, and watched his chest rise and fall with her efforts to resuscitate. She counted aloud, worked without thought.

Heavy, fast feet on the stairs distracted her and the noise of voices and bodies rose. "Okay, now listen," a low voice near her. "Take a deep breath; we're gonna switch." He counted with her, quiet and sure, then she could lean away.

Space became a premium and Celina moved backwards, stepping into the tiny space of the shower stall where sounds echoed a little. As she watched, staring at the efficient ministrations of the paramedics, she sank to the floor, her knees coming up under her chin. She was so tired that it hurt, inside and out. "He killed himself," an incredulous whisper sliced from across the room and, for just a second Kara, stood in the doorway. Celina wiped at her face, hiding; sobs made her choke and bend her head. She gave in and lay down, curled in that tiny space, the tiles cold against her cheek. She just listened. Voices, now familiar, were loud and sure. Forcing and then receding with the clatter of a gurney.

"Hey." The same low voice near. "Come on, talk to me." She was forced to turn over. "Sit up for me." He didn't give her a whole lot of choice. His hands were strong, pulling her out. His eyes were sharp, assessing. "I can't leave without checking you. How do you feel?"

Her surprise was a blank stare, then a puzzled frown. In the distance the ambulance screamed away. There were two of them.

"He might be all right. The cops are on their way. Is there anyone that you would like to have with you? I can call somebody for you. Are you okay?"

Celina frowned, knowing that nothing was that plain, that easy. She wondered why these guys wore white. Over his shoulder she could see Judith standing in the doorway. The man's eyes were still on her, dark and concerned. It was getting hard to breathe; her mouth and nose tingled a little, numbing. She put her hand against her face and tried a deep breath. His eyes narrowed. There was blood drying on her hand; things were closing in on her. She shook her head as if to clear it.

"I think I'm gonna be sick." She whispered. He leaned further to look into her face. She paled, thick bangs concealed her eyes. She started to cry, shoulders shaking, her stomach cramped. He hoisted her, moving to the sink. She threw up, sick; feeling herself shake in this strange man's arms made it worse. Someone wrapped a blanket around her, pulling it tight. He was speaking to her and his voice soothed, but she didn't know what he said. Her stomach was empty, tight. Glancing up, she drew back from her reflection. Cracks in the mirror radiated out, distorting everything. She rinsed her mouth out with cold water.

It seemed as though people wanted to get into the bathroom. Celina wanted to get out. Away from the mess. For the first time, she saw glass in the blood, remnants of a shattered bourbon bottle. The smells threatened her. The room shrank. She shrugged away from the EMS technician and left. She passed Judith in the hall—not a glance, not a touch in that narrow walkway. There was a cop on the stairs who did not look as she went past to the kitchen.

She had a sense of people moving near, around the room, around her. In her kitchen. She shook that stray thought out of her head. "I need to go." She spoke to no one in particular. Danny's father turned and met her gaze. There was surprise, mixed with recognition.

They looked at each other for a long time, silent though the room was filled with noise. "Are you sure that's a good idea?" His voice was very deep, hard to hear. Kara had gone in the ambulance to the hospital. Celina felt it across her shoulders and didn't say it.

She nodded, panic still in her face. "You tell them." She backed up, letting the blanket drop away. He watched her turn and walk through her living room. There was newspaper spread across the coffee table and she folded it neatly, absently. He thought she was going to cry. For a moment, she didn't move at all. Then she picked up his guitar case, weighing it in her arms. He watched her leave, soundless, by the outside door.

Celina set the guitar in the passenger seat of her car and climbed behind the wheel. She pulled away from that large house for the second time in a day, past an ambulance and police cars in the dusk.

It was dark when she got to the cottage. Inside, she went back and rested the guitar case on a corner of the bed. She didn't turn on any lights, instead going through to the bathroom, wanting to be cleaned. In the bathroom, she turned on the water. The sound of the shower was an ordinary comfort. She stripped off her clothes, leaving them in a stiff, crumpled heap on the floor.

Reluctantly, she stepped under the water, turning it as hot as she could stand it. She scrubbed at the brown streaks on her arms that had been Danny's blood. The air grew steamy. Her mind reeled a little. Crisis. The harshness of all the violence Danny had trusted her with in those years, suddenly turning in on himself. She knew that they would call her later, wanting to know things she couldn't give, didn't have. She washed herself thoroughly, the fresh rose scent of soap was calming, normal.

When she turned off the water, the quiet felt sudden. She wrapped a towel around her dripping body, leaving puddles behind her down the hall to the bedroom. She sat on the edge of her bed and turned on the cassette deck. Danny's voice, a half-laugh, came into the room. She knew the melodies, even the intricacies of his voice, as if they were her own. She recognized the introductory strains and background noises; she'd been cleaning up after dinner when he recorded it. The suddenly too-familiar lyrics didn't hold together for her anymore. Leaning back against the headboard, she pulled her knees under her chin, closing her eyes against the dark night, fists tight. For long moments she searched her mind, body; no escape. Nowhere to go. Without knowing, Danny held her. She could not leave him.

She heard her own voice, crying. Her skin was damp and cold; water dripped from her hair onto her shoulders. She reached out, unfolding, and turned off the tape. Across the bed, she pulled his guitar case to her and opened it. Her fingers gently touched the strings. No sound came; laced through strings at the first fret was a wrinkled and dirty kelly green ribbon.

"Happy Birthday, Dear Rachael"

Susan Rogers Cooper

MONDAY

("My left tit's sagging!")
"Shit!"
"What you say, honey?"
"Nothing. Just talking to myself!"
("Shit!")

Rachael lifts her left breast. She examines her naked body in the full length mirror. The left breast definitely sags.

("Dear God, please make both tits alike.")

She giggles as she pantomimes both breasts falling to the floor. She leans closer to the mirror. Counting her wrinkles. Counting gray hairs. She winces as she pulls out a gray hair.

("At the rate I'm going, I'll be white headed or bald in a month!")

She turns around, looking over her shoulder at her body in the mirror. Studying her hips, her thighs.

("Peach jello!")
"Rachael, are you ever coming out of there?"
"In a minute!"
("Go play with yourself!")

She pulls on her robe and opens the door.

"It's all yours!"
("I hope you drown in the shower!")

Making breakfast. Cold cereal for Jason. Hot cereal for Justine. Coffee and juice for Jeff and herself. Getting dressed. Finding clean

Kathleen Thoma

blue jeans for Jason. Pinning a tear in Justine's hem. A runner in two pairs of pantyhose, one brand new. Leaving the house. Find the cat. Put him out. Turn out lights. Turn up the air conditioning to 85º. Justine with Rachael in the Vega, Middle School bound. Jason with Jeff in the company car for the high school. Kisses good-bye. Waves. A new week.

("I'll be forty in six days. If I live.")

At work. Tight smile.

"Mr. Johnson, If you don't look for work, you don't get paid. That's how it works. Simple."

"How can I look for work when there ain't no jobs? Answer me that, woman!"

("You scare me. You terrify me. You're so big and so black and so angry. I marched for you at Selma! In spirit.")

"Mr. Johnson, you've got to look. I can't tell you how. Go any place; apply for anything. Just come in here with names of companies and persons contacted on that sheet of paper and you'll get your money. No names, no money."

He reaches across her. She flinches back in her chair. He picks up her telephone book, rifles through to the Yellow Pages. Grabs the paper and a pen and starts writing down names of companies. Slams the book down and sticks the paper in her face.

"This do?"

"Ah...for now. Next week, come in prepared. I must warn you, though, the computer does pick out claims at random...."

"Fuck the computer."

"Certainly, Mr. Johnson. Good-bye."

("Fuck you, Mr. Johnson, and the horse you rode in on!")

A finger wiggling at her seen through a glass partition. Mr. Roderick. A summons.

"Yes, sir?"

"Rachael, were you having trouble out there?"

"No, sir."

"It looked like it to me."

"No, sir, no trouble."

"I have to look out for my girls. Can't have some big buck bothering my girls, now can I?"

"No trouble, Mr. Roderick."

("You prick.")

"Wouldn't you be happier working in job placement? We have a lot of secretarial openings and a lot of applicants. I'm sure you could handle that well."

"I'm quite happy where I am, Mr. Roderick."

("You pig sucker!")

He looks at his watch. At his papers. He is really too busy to be wasting time on this.

"Very well. If there's any more trouble, though..."

"There was no trouble this time, Mr. Roderick."

The look. The heartache of insubordination.

"That will be all, Rachael."

"I'd like to decapitate him and tell God he died."

"You're overreacting."

Coffee break. Jerry sitting across from her. Wearing a blue striped shirt with white collar, grey jacket with patches on the elbows. Very sexy.

"So, you have a birthday coming up soon, huh?"

("God, don't let him say how old! Don't let anybody say that word!")

"Gonna be forty, huh?"

"Life begins, and all that crap."

"Well, I must say, you look damn good...."

("You're very charitable at twenty-eight....")

"Thank you."

"What's wrong?"

"Rodprick."

"He's always wrong. What's new that's wrong?"

"Nothing."

("I'm going to be forty in a week and I want your body. No big deal.")

He reaches over, takes her hand. Holds it next to his.

"Can you tell which hand belongs to the twenty-eight year old?"

She pulls her hand away.

"Amusing."

"Shit, Rache; talk to me."

She sighs. She squirms. She makes a rat-a-tat-tat with her nails on the table.

("I lust after your young, firm body.")

"I'm afraid I've got the 'I'm-going-to-be-old-in-a-week blues'!"

"You'll never get old, babe. You're the youngest woman I've ever known."

("Does he mean I'm childish?")

Smile. "Thank you."

"Did you hear what Manuel said Rodprick said to Loraine?"

"No..."

"Well..."

Tight smile. Noncommittal. Frozen. Automatic.

"Have this filled out before you come back in two weeks. After that you can mail your claims in and your checks will be mailed to you."

"Yeah, okay."

("Cretin.")

Paper in left hand. Stamp in right hand. Right hand to left hand. Depress. Repeat. Get up. Walk to Jerry's IN basket. Smile. Smile returned. Walk back to desk. Smile.

("I got a Master's in English Lit for this?")

"I'm sorry, Ms. Jenkins, you have to have the full name and address of your last employer on here."

"They went out of business. There's no one at the old address."

"Do you know the new address?"

"Somewhere in South America."

("Shit!")

Tight smile. The day wears on.

Dinner over. Kids in their rooms. Rachael and Jeff in the living room.

"I figure if we can put $20,000 in an IRA this year, with that, what we've got in C.D, my retirement and profitsharing and your state benefits, honey, we're gonna be shitting in high cotton...."

("When we're dead, you prick! I'm not old! Goddamn you! I'm not old!")

"Walt told me there's a condo near his up on Marble Lake for sale. Thought it would be a good investment for our retirement. Want to go look Saturday?"

("I want you to die so I can have fun on your insurance money!")

"This Saturday? I don't know, honey, we'll have to see."

The phone rings. She gets up. "I'll get it."

It stops ringing. From upstairs, a disgruntled voice:

"Mother. It's for you. It's Grandma."

("I can't handle this.")

"Thanks, Jason."

"Hello, Mom?"

"Rachael, what's wrong with Jason?"

("You probably disturbed him while he was masturbating.")

"Nothing that a few years won't cure, Mom."

"Well, I certainly don't remember you or your brother's being that surly when you were teenagers."

("Shit, Adam didn't come out of his room for four years. That's not surly?")

"Times have changed, Mom."

"Haven't they? Your father and I were just talking about that. We can hardly believe our little girl is going to be forty in a week! My goodness, Rachael, you make me feel old!"

Discreet giggle.

"I can hardly believe it myself, Mom."

("Because it isn't true. It's a bad dream. I'm going to wake up in my dorm room and have to get ready for a date.")

"This was going to be a surprise, but you know I could never keep a secret from you, Rachael...."

("Try.")

"Adam and Jenny and their kids and Michael and that woman..."

("Her name's Amanda. Amanda. Nice name. Try it.")

"...are all coming in this weekend for your birthday. We're going to have a big blowup Sunday just for you, darling...."

("Just send cash....")

"...so tell Jeff and the kids. We'll probably all come over to your house Saturday. Jeff can barbecue. You know how he loves to show off his new gas grill! And then Sunday, we'll be at the old homestead. It should be just loads of fun! What do you think?"

"Wonderful. But you shouldn't go to any trouble on my account."

("Or I'll hear about it for the next forty years.")

"Trouble? How often does my little girl turn forty?"

("Not too damn often, thank God!")

"That's very nice of you, Mom. I'm sure we'll all enjoy it."

("If I slit my wrists Saturday night, I should be dead before the party begins.")

"Besides, a party is just what Jeff needs. He doesn't look well. Have you been feeding him right?"

("I put his bowl down on the floor, what he does with it...")

"Mom, he's a grown man...."

"Don't tell me about grown men! I've been married to one for almost fifty years!"

"Jeff's been playing tennis a lot lately; all that exercise..."

"Is he taking his vitamins?"

"I buy them, whether or not he takes them..."

"He's your responsibility, darling...."

"No, Mother, he's not. Jason is my responsibility. Justine is my responsibility. The cat is my responsibility! Jeff is a grown man and he's responsible for his own actions! End of discussion."

"You don't have to bite my head off!"

Sigh. "I'm sorry, Mother. I guess I'm not in a very good mood."

"Well, I should say you're not!"

"I'm sorry."

"All I can say is I hope you straighten up that attitude before Sunday."

Sigh. "Yes, Mother."

"Do you want me to give any message to your father?"

"Please send him my love."

"He gets your love and I get your attitude?"

"If he had called, he would have gotten my 'attitude'."

"And I would have gotten your love?"

She smiles. "You always have my love, Mom."

A sigh on the phone. "Well, I can tell you I'm not really looking forward to this weekend. What with Michael bringing that woman home..."

"She's very nice, Mom. Just give her a chance."

"Nice? Her ex-husband has the custody of her children. What kind of woman can she be?"

("Tired.")

"Give her a chance."

"Well, I have to go draw your father's bathwater, dear. I'll talk to you later."

"Good night, Mom."

"Good night, darling."

TUESDAY

She leaves the shower, towel-drying with her back to the mirror. No need to look. She remembers.

The morning is the same. The mornings are always the same. The sameness makes her crazy. The sameness makes her want to scream. The sameness is her sanity. Her routine. The difference is making her crazy. The difference is she will be forty in five days .

Coffee break with Jerry.

"You have no idea what it's like to be a woman turning forty."

"That's true."

"You can't even imagine."

"That's true."

"I hate men. They have it so goddam easy. We get old; they get distinguished."

"What's this 'they' shit?"

"I don't think of you as a man."

("Like hell, I don't.")

He laughs. "Thanks a lot. But I'll try to take it as a compliment. I guess."

"Believe me, it is."

"Is Jeff helping you with this? I mean, he's already turned forty, hasn't he? Can't he give you some insight?"

She makes a noise. A snort? A sigh?

"Are you going to be like this all week? It's going to drive me crazy."

"Thanks for the support."

"I don't mean to be unsupportive, I just don't know what to do."

("Take your clothes off.")

"Just listen, I guess. You certainly can't make this boo-boo go away."

"What?"

"Sorry. Mom-talk."

He reaches over and lightly touches her hand.

("I'm going to cream in my pants")

"Rache, you're the most vital woman I've ever known. Chronological years really mean nothing..."

("At twenty-eight...")

"...it's how old you are inside."

She smiles. He leans back.

"Have you been to the Fellini festival yet?"

Sigh. "No. You know how Jeff is about foreign films."

He laughs. "Yeah, that's right. He'd rather stay home to read."

She leans her head in her hands. She's thoughtful. She's plotting. "What would you say if I told you I'm thinking of getting a divorce?"

He's stunned. "You're kidding! Hey, Rache, you and Jeff are a team! You're perfect for each other." He's thoughtful. "Could it be just part of the 'I'm-going-to-be-old-in-a-week blues'?"

"Five days does not a week make."

"Huh?"

"Nothing."

Looks at watch. Time to go. She hopes he'll walk in front of her so she can watch his ass. He stands aside to let her pass. She sighs.

("There's something wrong with my mind. I'm going crazy. I'm losing reality. I'm a sick woman. I need help.")

"Next line, please."

("Do I really want Jerry? He's a friend! Is it impossible for me to be friends with a man? Am I a sexist? Is it just Sunday? Is that all it is? All it is! Jesus, that's enough!")

"No sir, I'm sorry, your claim has expired. You can file for an extension if you're still looking for work..."

("He's beautiful. A beautiful person. Fuck it, a beautiful bod! A bod? Far fucking out! Shit!")

"You must have the full name and address of your last employer. There's a phone book on the table over there."

"I'll lose my place in line."

Sweet smile. "That's true."

("I wish they'd all die. No, I wish they'd all find jobs, that's what I wish. Then maybe I could get a job. That's what I need. Another job. I'd miss Jerry. I don't want to leave Jerry. I'm afraid. Of everything. Oh, God, I'm so afraid.!")

Paper in left hand. Stamp in right. Depress. Repeat.

("Do I still love Jeff? Did I ever love Jeff?")

Smile. She remembers.

The phone rings.

"Ms. Albright."

"Mrs. Albright? This is Rainier High School. Mrs. Schultz speaking. Your son Jason has been sent to the office. This is the third time this month he's been caught fighting. I'm afraid we need to have a conference with you and your husband."

"Is he all right? Has he been hurt?"

"A torn shirt and a busted lip. Other than that, physically, he's fine. I'm afraid, though, the problem is beyond the physical."

"He's been fighting? I don't understand. I didn't know about this!"

"We've sent notes home to you, Mrs. Albright."

Silence. Notes never received. Notes crumbled in trashcans. Notes torn up and scattered in the wind. Notes flushed down toilets.

"Hey, lady, I've been waiting in this line for a goddam hour."

Tight smile. Cover phone with hand. "I'll be right with you."

"Mrs..."

"Schultz."

"Mrs. Schultz. I'm afraid I never received the notes. I didn't know a thing about this."

"Perhaps your husband had some inkling..."

"If he did he would have mentioned it."

Discreet laugh. "Well, Mrs. Albright, men tend to think their sons aren't 'macho' unless they get into a couple of fights."

Indignation. "My husband is not like that! We discuss these things. If he had known about it, I would know about it!"

A sigh from the other end of the phone.

("She thinks I'm a rotten parent. She's right! I am! I am!")

"We'll need to see you and your husband in the office as soon as possible, Mrs. Albright. There may be the necessity for a suspension."

("Oh, God, I'm gonna kill him!")

"Will tomorrow morning be soon enough?"

"How's nine?"

"That'll be fine. Thank you for calling."

("Now go ruin someone else's life, you bitch! I don't need this! I can't handle this. What's wrong with him? Why is he doing this to me?")

Tight smile. "Sorry to keep you waiting."

Dinner is waiting. A cold dinner Justine is waiting. A hot Justine. Why is everyone but her in the den? Why is she being excluded?

Jeff stalks. Rachael sits perched on the edge of a chair. Jason sulks, slouched low in his chair.

"Tell me what the fights have been about. Do you know? Can you articulate that much?"

A noise. Sounds like a pig grunting. Their first born. Such a good baby.

"Jeff, calm down." To Jason. "We would appreciate some comment from you, Jason. Some explanation."

The grunt sounds almost like a word. Possibly, "I dunno." Could have been "Um bahgawa."

"Jason!" Jeff is losing his patience.

Big, brown eyes look up from their position low in the chair. Cocker spaniel eyes.

("I want to hold him. I want to cradle his head in my arms.")

She rises from her chair. Sits on the ottoman in front of Jason's chair. Takes his hand. He tries to pull away. She holds on.

"What's going on, honey?"

Cocker spaniel eyes fill. Honey. Mommy's little man.

"I dunno."

Jeff sits on the ottoman with Rachael. He places his hand over their two hands. Rachael's eyes fill. It used to be so good. Wasn't it?

"I dunno. Some guy says something. I get mad. I dunno."

"Sticks and stones..."

"Ah, shit, Dad..."

"Watch your language in front of your mother, young man!"

Rachael sighs. "Jesus Christ, Jeff!"

Jeff shrugs. "What the fuck."

Rachael feels the hand in hers. So big. When did this hand get so big? The feeling of the small hand in hers for safety, for love, the small hand reaching out for her help, holding a moist chocolate-chip cookie or Cookie Monster by his big bug eye. The small hand was big now. The big hand struck out in anger. The big hand was so angry. She can feel the anger through the skin. The anger is hot. The skin is smooth.

"We want to help, honey. We want to talk to you...no, that's not right."

She searches.

("Help me, Dr. Spock!")

"We want you to talk to us. Communicate with us. Maybe you're not mad at those boys who say things, maybe you're made at us. At yourself?"

She looks to Jeff. He shrugs. He is saying, "You're on your own. You started this shit."

Jason pulls his hand away. He gets up. He grabs the top of the chair, the knuckles of his big hands white in his death grip on the back of it.

"Can I go to my room?"

The Cocker spaniel eyes are dull.

("Is he on drugs?")

"Yes."

WEDNESDAY

A short, pudgy man. Large smile. Hand outstretched.

("His teeth are capped.")

"I'm Doug Marshall, principal of Rainier. I'm sure sorry we had to meet under these circumstances."

Waves them to chairs. Rachael perches, Jeff sits erect, Jason slouches.

("Sit up, Jason. Try!")

Big smile. "Well, boy, what do you think needs to be done?"

Silence. Jeff nudges Jason.

"Huh?"

Mr. Marshall stands up, rests a plump ass on the side of the desk. Smile replaced by worried, professional frown. Shakes his head sadly.

"Jason, Jason, Jason."

Jason slouches further into his seat.

("Why are you so angry? What did I do? Did I potty train you too early?")

"This has got to stop, young man."

Silence.

("I don't like you, Mr. Marshall. You are not a nice man. You don't really care.")

"Mr. and Mrs. Albright." He walks back to his chair. Plops his plumpness down into its depths. "I'm afraid we're going to have to put Jason on a ten-day suspension if this happens again." Points a finger at Jason. "Do you understand, young man?"

"Yeah."

Mr. Marshall's head comes up. His eyes look down on Jason. "I beg your pardon?"

Grudgingly. "Yes, sir."

They are dismissed. Big smile from Mr. Marshall. Pat on the back for Jason. He did good. What did he do? Nothing.

They say good-bye at the door of the school. Rachael thinks about kissing her son good-bye. Not at school. Not macho. They leave.

Jeff walks her to her car.

"What do you think?"

("I think I'd like to rip out his caps and blow cold air on his stubs.")

"I don't think it was very effective, do you?"

Jeff shrugs. "No. Not really."

They look at each other. Strangers look at each other the way they look at each other. Strangers smile and say, "Have a nice day."

He opens her car door for her. He smiles. He says, "Have a nice day."

She smiles. "You too."

THURSDAY

Granola bars and milk for the kids. Coffee and juice for the adults. Hectic morning. As all mornings.

At work. Note on her desk. See Mr. Roderick.

"Yes, sir?"

"Close the door, please, Rachael?"

She closes the door.

("I'm getting fired. I know it. I've done something terrible. Oh, shit, what did I do?")

He smiles.

("He's enjoying this. He's always hated me.")

Drums fingers on his desk top. "Rachael, you've been with us now how long?"

He looks at her file in front of him.

("Oh, shit! It's a test!")

Smiles. "About two years."

He nods.

("One for me!")

"Are you happy here?"

Tight smile. "Definitely."

("Here it comes!")

He stands. He goes to his window overlooking the peons, hands in pockets, the general surveying his troops.

"Margaret Newman is retiring at the end of the year. Were you aware of that?"

"Ah...yes, I believe she has mentioned it to me."

A smile. “Her position as Section III Supervisor will be open at that time.”

Rachael nods.

“Would you be interested?”

(“Is there any money in it?”)

“I wouldn't be opposed to discussing it.”

A disappointed look.

(“He expected me to kiss his fucking ring, I suppose.”)

He returns to his desk. Fingers drumming on desk top. A frown. “Monetarily, it isn't much of a promotion, but it would put you in line for a managerial position at some later date.”

(“If anybody ever dies!”)

“A move like this could safely guarantee you a future with the state for life.”

(“That makes me all warm and fuzzy.”)

“It certainly sounds like a splendid opportunity, Mr. Roderick.”

(“I should be writing sonnets, lecturing on the merits of Shakespeare versus Bacon...”)

He stands, holds out his hand. Rachael takes it. They shake. “Let me know what you think. You have until Monday. Talk it over with your husband.”

(“See if Daddy says it's okay.”)

“Thank you.”

Dismissed.

“Guarantee me a spot with the state for life. Seems to have an ominous ring to it, don't you think?”

Lunch with Jerry. Tacos on a park bench. Birds singing, a light breeze.

(“And thou beside me...”)

“Rache, grab it! Really! With you as Section III Supervisor, we could get away with murder!”

(“God, he's so young!”)

“I've been thinking....”

“Hum?”

(“I want out! Of all of it! I don't want to be Section III Supervisor!”)

“The money sucks.”

“It sucks a little less than the money you make now.”

"The raise would probably put me in a higher tax bracket and I'd bring home less than I do now."

He shakes his head. "You know, your attitude could stand a little improvement."

("Fuck my attitude! Fuck you!...In a dark room, with a rosy light, a little Bach fugue on the stereo...")

"Sorry, I'm in a pessimistic state of mind at the moment."

Sigh. "Damn it, Rachael, people turn forty every day. Probably several times a day! You're getting a little carried away with this. This promotion could mean a great deal for you; it would put you in line for a managerial position...."

"Right. Right. Okay. Forget it. Let's don't talk about it. Okay?"

He shrugs. "Okay."

They leave the park.

("What could I possibly find attractive about this mundane little man?....His ass. He's got a great ass!")

("I'm losing my mind. I know it. I can feel it. It's all slipping away from me.")

Phone. "Ms. Albright. No, that number is..."

("I've got to hold on. To what? Shit, I don't know. My marriage? Why? Do I really need it? Do I want it? Could I make it on my own? Oh, shit, that's scary! Whoa!")

Phone. "Ms. Albright...You'll have to bring that in. Yes. The downtown office. Or a branch office. What section of the city do you live in?"

("Seventeen years of marriage down the tubes. Is that what I'm saying? Really? Do you want that?...No...Really?...No. I don't want that....Then what do you want?...A chance! All I want is a fucking chance!.... A chance at what?...I don't know....Youth! That's what you want. A chance to get your youth back. You're like some fucking middle aged man who leaves his wife to fuck twenty-two year olds!...No, I'm not! This is serious!...What is?...It's my life, damn it! The rest of my life!...")

Phone. "Ms. Albright...One moment, I'll ring that line...."

("If I took that promotion, I wouldn't have to sub for the receptionist. There is that...If you took that promotion, you would be guaranteed a spot with the state for life....There's a couple of thousand murderers and rapists who are also guaranteed a spot with the state for life. One prison's as bad as the other....My God, you're so fucking melodramatic! You make me sick! You're a self-centered, egotistical fool....Sticks and stones...Did you think of your children? Huh? Did you ever once stop to consider how they might feel? Not to mention your husband. You remember him, don't you? The man who loves you? The man who plans on spending the rest of his allotted time with you? Huh? Surely in all your fumbling around to find your true identity, you ninny, you haven't forgotten him?...To hell with it!")

FRIDAY

("Everybody I know is growing. I'm stagnating. My life is a cesspool. I hate my life. I hate Jeff! I hate me!")

"Rachael, have you seen the 101A forms? They're not in the file."

She reaches under her desk and pulls out a box. "Never got them filed. Sorry."

("Forgive me. I'm sorry. How can you expect me to file your goddam forms when my life is falling apart? In less than three days I'm over the hill. Rock bottom. The end of the line. Menopause and breast cancer. Varicose veins and sagging tits. Liver spots. Conversations revolving solely around who's died recently...")

"Yes, sir?"

Scans papers. They're filled out correctly. Miracle. Must be an old hand at this. Stamp. Process. Smile.

"See you in two weeks."

He smiles. It's a nice smile. An unemployed smile, but a nice smile.

("He was probably a salesman....God, you're getting cynical.")

The pressure is building. The terrors are weaving through her soul.

("This is my last day on the job as a young woman. Monday, it's all over but the shouting. God, I wish I could shout! I wish I could scream!")

"Ready for break?"

She looks up. Jerry is standing there. He looks good. He always looks good.

"As I'll ever be."

"Are you going to miss me when I'm old and gray?"

He laughs. "You are going to live through this, Rache. I swear! Turning forty hasn't killed anybody yet."

("Where'd you get your statistics?")

"There's always a first time."

He smiles. "You busy after work tonight?"

("This is it!")

"No..."

"I'd like to take you out for a drink to celebrate your birthday. Would that be okay with you?"

Smile. "I'd like that."

("He'll never make the first move. Not Jerry.")

"Jerry...(keep it light)...you wanna have an affair?"

"Black tie?"

"I'm serious."

("I can't believe I'm doing this!")

"Hell of a way to fuck up a friendship."

("I'm dead. My body doesn't know it, but I'm dead.")

She stands up. Escape.

He grabs her hand. "Rache, I'd rather fuck it up by making love to you than fuck it up by hurting you."

She laughs too shrilly. "Hey, Jere, it was a joke."

He laughs too soon. "Hell, I knew that."

"Besides, you're too old, I'm saving myself for a seventeen year old."

She escapes.

("I've really ripped it! He's got something on me now. It'll never be the same. He'll look at me and wince, thinking of his escape. God, I hate him!")

The pressure continues to build. There is no escape. The alternative to aging is death.

("I'm so fucked-up it's scary! My mind is mud. My senses have gone haywire. Pretty soon I'll start hearing with my nose and seeing with my ears! They're going to take me away. Padded-cell time. Drooling in my Cream of Wheat!")

"Miss?"

("I think I'll go lie down. In a fetal position. Back to basics.")

"Lady?"

("If I could just find out why...why I'm growing old. Because it isn't supposed to happen. How can it happen to me? I'm still young. In my head, in my heart! To be young and to be trapped in an old body. It's terrifying.")

"Hey, lady!"

("Does everybody feel like this? Fuck everybody! It's me! These are my feelings! This is how I feel! This is what will kill me. This is my life—my death.")

"Lady!"

"Wha..."

A line in front of her desk. The masses of unemployed.

"Wha..."

"Hey, you okay?"

"I..."

"Lady?"

She gets up. She is bewildered. Who are these people? Why don't they get jobs? These are the ten percent. This is Reaganomics. This is shit! She must say something to these people. Something that will make them go away. Something to set things straight.

"I can't help you."

"What you say, lady?"

"Don't you know? I can't help you."

Farther back in the line, a voice cries out, "What is this shit?"

"You have to help yourselves. That's all we have anymore. Our own vessels. We are alone on the sea of life. Each in our own vessel..."

"Lady, are you all right?"

"I'm going to be with the state for life. I've been sentenced. Have you been sentenced?"

"Ah...look...".

"Section III Supervisor. After that, the electric chair. No...I think they give injections now...."

The people in line look around. For escape, No one likes to watch nervous breakdowns. They're so untidy. So embarrassing.

A hand on her arm.

"Rachael, what's going on here?"

"Hi, Rodprick."

A snicker from the line. If you have to watch someone's breakdown, the least they can do is make it fun.

"Go to the lunch room now, Rachael. I'll deal with these people."

"Sign 'em up, Rodprick."

She grabs her purse. She heads for the front door. She can see Jerry. He is busy with papers. He is ignoring the situation. No guilt by association for him. No, sir!

She walks out.

("I wonder if they'll give me a reference?")

The Vega's engine starts, stalls, finally catches. She roars off, tires squealing on the pavement. She drives. The miles fly by. She is somewhere she has never been before. Or she is somewhere she has been too often. She doesn't see the scenery. There is none to see. She doesn't see the road. It's going by too fast. She doesn't hear the sirens roaring behind her. The roaring in her head drowns it out.

They go together for miles, Rachael and the screaming sirens. Her foot automatically reacts to a stop sign. The screaming sirens block her path.

A man approaches her car. He is in uniform. His hand rests heavily on his weapon. The one at his side, not the one in his pants.

("I think I'm in trouble.")

She begins to laugh. The man in the uniform with weapons both front and side looks at her strangely.

Her laughter is uncontrollable now. Her side hurts from laughing.

("He's going to shoot me so I won't have to grow old!")

"I'm sorry...officer...I..." she sputters through her laughter. "Just...a...minute...let me...catch...my breath..."

"Let me see your driver's license, ma'am."

("And see my true identity and age...you young whippersnapper!")

The laughter bubbles up and spills out again. He's a highway patrolman. State Police. A job with the state for life. A civil servant.

("Well, he certainly isn't being very civil!")

She giggles. She guffaws. She bellows. She weeps. His hand is on the door.

"Would you get out of the car, please?"

("Oh, God, I'm gonna have to walk a straight line!")

He motions to his partner who gets out of the car, bringing with him an unfamiliar object.

"Let me see your driver's license, please."

"It's...in the car."

She reaches in. She gets her purse. It spills out all over the road. She bends down to pick it up, grabbing for compact, breath mints, billfold, old bills, birth-control pills.

The officer spies the pills. He grabs them. "What's this?"

She begins to giggle. She begins to laugh. ("He thinks I'm high on birth control pills!")

"They're...birth control...pills..."

"Oh." He's embarrassed. He's very young.

He takes her license. He gets the object his partner has brought and holds out a breathing tube towards her.

"Breathe into this please."

She does. He waits. He reads the findings. He looks at his partner.

"I'm going to have to search your purse and your car, ma'am."

"Oh."

They search her car. They find nothing. They come back.

"What'ja take, ma'am?"

"Beg pardon?"

"What're ya on?"

"Drugs?"

"Yes, ma'am."

She giggles. "I'm not on drugs."

"Yes, ma'am."

"Really. I'm having a nervous breakdown."

The two officers look at each other. One scratches the weapon in his pants.

"Ma'am?"

"I'm going bonkers. Nutto. Bananas. Looney tunes."

"You realize you were going considerably over the speed limit?"

"Was I?"

"Yes, ma'am. About twenty miles over the speed limit."

She smiles. There is pride in her smile. Woman and machine. "Really?"

"I'm gonna have to write you a citation, ma'am."

"A ticket?"

"Yes, ma'am."

She nods. He writes her a citation. He admonishes her to drive more slowly.

She gets back in the car, watching the now-silent sirens roar down the road. She sits. All she can do is sit. Her muscles have atrophied. She is dying. Her mind is blank as she sits and waits for death.

One hour later, death has not come. She is tired of waiting. She starts the Vega, turns it around and heads back to town.

She is in the garage, digging through the rubble of ten years.

("Somebody needs to clean this mess.")

She finds the tent. The Coleman lantern. The butane stove. The old Army cots. She hauls them out, throwing them into the hatchback of the Vega. The cots hang out. She ties the hatchback down with an old rope.

People are talking to her. Justine is asking her what she is doing. She can't answer. A decision has been made. An inarticulate decision. The words of explanation won't come.

Jeff is there.

"Rachael, what are you doing?"

"Where's Jason?"

"In his room. What are you doing?"

"Get Jason."

Confusion. "Justine, go get your brother."

She turns to her husband. "I'm taking Jason camping."

"You're what?"

"Don't try to stop me."

"Honey, I'm not going to try to stop you! What are you talking about?"

"I quit my job today."

"Ah...if that's what you think best..."

Anger. "Obviously I must have thought it best since I did it! Don't you think?"

("You asshole!")

"Rachael, come in the house and let's talk."

"No. Get Jason some clothes. I'll buy food on the way. We're leaving now."

"Just you and Jason, huh?"

"Yes."

"Did you happen to forget you have a daughter? I won't bother to mention myself, God forbid."

"You can take care of Justine. She's thirteen years old. It's not like you have to change diapers or anything."

"Don't you think she might be hurt by this."

She turns. She is angry. "I need to do this. You could make it easier. You could make tonight special for Justine. You are her father."

He is angry. "What in the hell am I supposed to do with a thirteen-year-old girl? I don't know that to do with her!"

"Because you don't know her! You don't know Jason either. And you don't know me!"

Jason comes out of the house.

"Get a jacket."

He looks at her, turns, goes in and comes out with a light jacket.

"We're going camping. Get in the car."

She walks to Justine and puts her arms around her. "We'll be back tomorrow. I love you."

"Mom..."

Rachael gets in the car where Jason waits. She pulls out of the driveway, heading for the hills.

SATURDAY

Rachael pulls herself out of the tent. One corner is sagging inward.

("Great job, Rachael. You're a real trailer and tracker, woman!")

She starts a fire, puts on coffee. She kicks the tent.

"Wake up, Jason. The birds are singing, God's in his heaven, all's right with the world."

"Huh?"

She makes breakfast. They are silent. The horrors of the night before make them humble. Pitching a tent in the dark, finding out too late you have no flashlight.

They eat. They are silent. They clean up. They are silent. Rachael gets out the fishing poles.

"Come on. Let's go catch something."

"I don't wanna."

"Get your ass in gear!"

He is startled. This is his mother. He gets up and follows her to the lake. Marble Lake, the north side, not a condo in sight.

They cast their lines into the water.

"I had a mini-breakdown yesterday."

"Wha..."

"Nervous breakdown. Ever heard of 'em?"

"Yeah..."

"I got my very own yesterday."

"Um..."

"I decided...I hate my life...I didn't know what to do about it."

He looks at her. He is scared.

"I'll be forty tomorrow...it's weird what those zero birthdays can do to you...a circle, no beginning...no end..."

He looks at the ground. Trailing his fingers in the dry dirt. He looks up. Eyes make contact. The dullness is beginning to fade.

"Mom..."

"Your father's a good man...better than most..." She sighs. The water in front of them is clear and smooth as glass. It reflects. It reflects mother and son.

"It's a confusing world for a man...specially a man your father's age...being raised a man..."

She stops. She looks at her son.

("Does he hear me? Does he care?")

Jason speaks. "I don't understand what being a man is all about, I guess...the guys...they think about getting laid all the time...sometimes...I think maybe I'm...queer...a fag...I...I'm kinda...scared, I guess..."

She puts her arm around his shoulder. "The rituals of manhood. Pretty damn weird, huh?"

They sit. Poles dangling in the water. Touching. Arm on shoulder.

"I always wanted to do something with my life...that's why I went to college...I didn't mean to go for an MRS degree..." She sighs. A slight sob in the sigh. "I can't let this go on, Jason. I need your father 'cause I love him...I love him. I need you and Justine...I love you both so damn much! But I want to find Rachael Kincaid, that skinny kid who wanted to write sonnets...I want you to find out what it's like being a human being before you get all screwed up trying to find out what being a man is all about."

They are silent. Both somewhere else. Both very much together.

"Do you understand any of this?"

"Yeah, I think." He is quiet. Contemplative. "It's like...the fighting...I feel like..."

Rachael waits. He looks into her eyes.

"Am I a fag?"

She shrugs. "I don't know. Chances are you probably aren't...I hope I've taught you to respect women...I've meant to do that, anyway...Maybe that's part of your confusion...Sex is very confusing...it seems to get all mixed up with trickery."

"Yeah, I see that..The guys...there's this one girl...I've known her since first grade...she was a friend. They all say...she...does it. Ya know? They're all the time tryin to...figure out ways to...get her someplace. Alone. Ya know? I like her. I always have...we used to play together. Jimmy and Danny...they tried to get me...to, you know, go with them...one night..I didn't want to...It didn't seem right...."

She hugs him close to her. "Honey, you have to do what's right for you. You're the only one who knows what's right for you...just like I'm finally learning. I want you to know that now...I want Justine to know that now."

She laughs. "You know something...I actually thought I was liberated! Playing at going to work...dressing up in my high heels and panty hose, just like a real person!...And do you know what I got for my efforts?"

"What?"

"A chance at a spot with the state for life!"

"Are you thinking about quitting your job?"

"I already have, honey. I walked out yesterday in a huff...think that Monday, I'm going to the University and signing up for the Ph.D. program. My dream was to teach University level and that's what I'm going to try to do."

They smile at each other. Lives are beginning.

They unpack the Vega. Justine runs to meet them. "Mom! Gawd, you'll never believe it...."

Rachael hugs her child. "What, baby?"

"Daddy took me out on a date!"

"What?"

"We dressed up and he bought be a corsage and took me to dinner and to a play! Not a movie! A real play! It was neat!"

"That's...great..." Jeff comes out of the house.

"Help you brother unpack."

Alone with Jeff. "A date? Jesus, Jeff, she's thirteen, and your daughter!"

"We enjoyed it."

"How incredibly sexist."

"Shit! You take off and leave me holding the bag and when I try to do something about it, you start bitching!"

"I didn't realize spending the night alone with your daughter equated to 'holding the bag'."

"Don't get righteous with me! You took your son camping! Not your daughter. Boys go camping..."

"That's ridiculous."

"Is it? And by the way, I suppose you forgot your entire fucking family was coming over here today."

"Ah...yeah..."

"I called and cancelled."

"What did you say?"

"I said you'd flipped your lid."

"Thanks."

"Actually, I said you'd taken Jason camping and I had to go and I hung up quick. They probably think we're getting a divorce."

Silence.

He looks at her. "Are we getting a divorce?"

She looks at him. "Do you want a divorce?"

He looks at her. "I asked you first."

They both start to laugh. He walks up to her, placing both hands on her face. "In case I haven't told you lately, baby, I still love you. More than ever."

She pulls away. "Maybe that's not enough, Jeff."

"What do you want?"

"Freedom."

"That means divorce, doesn't it?"

"No. I want freedom...with you...through you...I don't know."

"You mean you want to fuck around?"

She laughs. "God, if you only knew."

"Knew what?"

She shakes her head. "I want to grow. I want to go back to school."

"You've always had the freedom to do that, Rachael. I've never stopped you. You have."

"That's not true."

"Yes, it is. Remember when Justine started first grade, I suggested you go back for your Ph.D."

She laughs. A bitter laugh. "Sure. You suggested it. But you weren't willing to put anything into it."

"Hell, I was going to pay your way!"

"Thanks, Daddy."

"Cut the shit, Rachael."

"How was I supposed to go back to school with two kids and the house to take care of? You weren't willing to help then, and I doubt if you're willing to help now..."

"That's not true!"

"It is true! If I tell you what needs to be done around the house, you'll do it, sure...but I'm still responsible. I'm tired of being responsible for everything except my own life! My own happiness! I want you to know it's time to do the laundry...I want you to know Justine needs new tights for gym, or Jason has to go to the orthodontist. I want you to know where the serving bowls go and how to clean a commode. Having to stand over you and explain everything is the same as doing it myself. Harder! I don't want to be totally responsible."

"Neither do I!"

"Why can't we both do it? Why can't we both have the knowledge of what needs to be done?"

He sits. He shrugs.

She sighs. "You're not willing to even list-"

"I am! Goddamn, Rachael, gimme a break! This has all come up so suddenly..."

"Forty came up suddenly, too."

"Is that what this is about?"

"At least you can't blame it on my hormones this time."

They look at each other.

"We can work this out, Rachael. It's going to take time and effort and a few fights...but we can work it out. What we have is worth whatever it takes."

She stands up. She walks to the window. "When you turned forty...didn't you have the slightest case of middle age crazies?"

"No!...Like what?"

"You know...attraction to twenty-two year old girls."

He laughs. "Good God no." There is a pause. He laughs again. "There was a thirty-five year old, though...":

"Who?"

"A woman at the office."

"What happened?"

"She got pregnant."

She whirls around. "My God, Jeff!"

He shakes his head. "No, not me. Before I could think it through enough to even approach her, she announced she was pregnant."

"Was she married?"

"No. Rumor had it the father was one of the Acapulco divers from her summer vacation."

("Not smart, but probably fun.")

"You're kidding."

"Course, long about the same time, Todd Wilson from Inside Sales took an immediate transfer to Alaska."

"And he was married..."

"With two kids and one on the way. I decided it was prophetic and took up tennis instead."

"That's why you started playing tennis!"

("I think I'll try handball. More aggressive.")

SUNDAY

Breakfast in bed for Mom and Dad. Burnt pancakes with too much butter, fresh squeezed orange juice with seeds floating on the top, raw bacon, and a rose. The kids on their own and the Sunday paper spread out on the kingsize bed.

Twelve noon. Dressed and ready to go. Pile in the car. Over the river and through the woods to Grandmother's condo...

Hugs and kisses. Brothers long time not seen. Children to coddle and coo over. Mothers to pacify. Roast beef and mashed potatoes. A birthday cake laden with candles.

Rachael looks at the candles.

("Trust Mom not to forget a single one.")

They begin to sing. Off-key voices, young and old. Mother's biting soprano filling the air. "Happy birthday, dear Rachael..."

("Shit, I can handle this.")

Kathleen Thoma

Burning The Deer

Michael Reynolds

I am here to bring you back to the dead, down years and across great distances from where I am watching. As I watch, I am remembering. There is no reason in remembering; it is a matter for ghosts. You are the excuse for the writing, for I can't go alone, without understanding, through memory's fall. Together, we see. If we turn our eyes away, the world goes berserk, instantly unbinding the assuring deception we have erected just there, on the edge of our vision where Ruin waits for Fury to subside, where Coyote waits to sing over the carbon that was once our bones. We are temporary circumstances here, carrying a curse of clearly-etched evil, a posit ancient and firm that—of a sudden—comes apart, leaving a cold, final ash upon the fingers left the living, a residue transmitting deep, inarticulate sadness like that glimpsed in the profound well of a dumb animal's eye. Behind that sadness, below its core, we see a cycle turning: humanity, chewing at itself greedily, pitifully and inexorably, mammoth in its horror, fucking itself over and over again to keep this miserable, straining *tableau morti* propelled phantasmally into cold, black rain. In this hammering rain is the Present, which I want to become memory. And, as I write, it will become memory because I say Memory rules my fingers and the words they seek, the flesh they sound, the voices they picture, if only I let it go. It is a puzzle how this works. It is the belief that it does work which conjures through time and distance, here to there—a highway.

Gazing down that highway, driving between the thighs of America, the convergence on the horizon always further, the destination residing in memory's imagining, unattainable at even the greatest speed—the illusion, the mirage of America's cunt, impossibly out of reach.

Now. I am there. And there is Gavin Barnes behind the wheel of his Cadillac, turning off that highway, leaving the concrete trajectory of his silver convertible, slipping through the monochromatic luminosity just before dawn, melting in its light, shining through its shadows; America's damaged seed swimming in Texas' native son, Gavin slows the compulsive night's journey by taking the road which leads to the one destination that can do him no further harm, where the failures, grief and mendacities are familiar, where pathological siblings and ancestors of his blood no longer frighten, to the asylum of long-dead and short-living family, to home.

The narrow asphalt and concrete road to his ranch was cracked, pocked and ragged from neglect as it rose from the highway and through the limestone gateway, plinths on either side mounted by wrought iron double-Bs—BB. The Caddy rattled over the pipes of the cattle guard and began a gradual descent alongside the first hill. When the road rose again, Gavin eased up on the accelerator, letting the car coast as it dipped into a black draw, damp and cool with cottonwoods that stood below the road, just above the creek. He could smell them, a peculiar animal odor he always associated more with flesh than plant. A mockingbird ran through some lonely changes just as Gavin switched off the headlights while the car silently rolled down the gentle curve and across the bridge at the bottom of the draw. When the Cadillac had nearly reached inertia, he accelerated with a tap of his foot and the car took off, up another curve, cutting back against the hill and away from the creek. The road went up to the left, then swung to the right, ascending another rise and, as Gavin pushed the convertible upwards, looking straight into an expanse of fading stars, the deer plunged directly from the sky, dropping down across Gavin's shoulder and into the back seat. He could smell the animal before he felt its hind legs kick past his ear.

He swerved the big car once to the right, chewing up the ragged edge of the road near a drop which would have ended back down on the bridge he had just crossed, then whipped the wheel left, slamming the Caddy into an outcropping of limestone.

Gavin could smell blood, felt it running down his neck as he lifted himself up to stand in the seat, bracing himself with one hand on the windshield. He looked back and saw the deer, its head twisted up, neck snapped and jammed into the corner between the armrest and seat cushion, its slight body slumped as if it were resting, two thin forelegs tipped with white where small broken bones protruded, framing its narrow head like a splintered crown. Its rear legs were splayed up behind the driver's side, the delicate hooves pointing to the lightening sky. Gavin reached out and touched one of them, holding it in his hand, ready for the animal to jerk in his grip. It was warm. But the deer didn't move as he bent forward, looking out through the night's whiskey and cocaine into the perfect dark eye of the dead animal. It glistened with knowing; in it, accusations flooded, tongues curled through voices without language and spoke in Gavin as the eye grew in his mouth, and before it choked him, he threw back his head, squeezing steel in one hand, muscle and fur in the other, and howled the terrible message to the stars.

There was silence. Then the mockingbird replied, adding to its song Gavin had heard down by the creek. He let go the deer's leg and pulled himself up to sit on the windshield, facing the rear seat. "Goddamn it all," he heard himself say. He could feel the night falling away, The heat of August was such that the hills could never cool quite long enough to shake the previous day's blaze and the temperature began climbing with the first hint of light. Gavin got up and turned around, sliding down with his hands to the wheel. He turned the ignition key and backed the Caddy off the rocks with a screech of tearing steel and a tinkle of broken glass. He braked and began rifling through the scattered pile of cassettes on the seat behind him... Albioni's *Adagio.* He pushed the cassette into the slot in the dash and baroque strings began building stately archways above the Cadillac as Gavin drove on up the hill.

He leaned over, pushed off the top to a styrofoam cooler and pulled out a can of Tecate beer, snapping it open while guiding the car with his elbows, and took a long swig before making a sharp right off the road to a caliche track that rose steeply through blue juniper, knotted oak and long, black strikes of buffalo grass etched sharply against a moon-white earth that seemed suspended in the air. He could feel the tires arhythmically battering over the ruts, his ass attuned to the broken earth while his head drifted out on the illuminating finger of the single headlight, bobbing contrapuntally. Gavin was over the side of his drunk, what alcoholic fires the last snort of cocaine hadn't dampened, the suicidal assault by the deer blew away, leaving him attended by only the cold voices of his craziness and cancer.

—We didn't see all this coming, did we? We're like the Indians were, now. They never caught on in time either. Never were aware when their chances went. Fucking deer falling from the sky. Comets, bombs, satellite debris, deer. Death reigns, death rains down. Who guesses for deer? Voices come from nowhere, admit nothing. Dumbfuck buck out to commit suicide in a Cadillac. True-ass Texas deer. Picks a fucking Cadillac! True-ass Texas suicide. No fingers, couldn't get a shotgun to kill himself. Why *not* pick me?—

The Cadillac reached the top of the hill, the *Adagio* scaled ever upwards still, in ever-mournful layers above this small plateau, a grass-tufted level in the center of which was a rough circle defined by limestone rocks. No shadows fell here and Gavin's eye could chase the edges of the sky where he saw color growing in the east. He got out, leaving the door swung open. He tossed down the rest of the beer, threw the can into the floorboards and pushed back the seat. He grabbed the hind legs and pulled. The carcass stretched but wouldn't budge; the antlers were snagged between the seat cushions. Gavin let go and felt sweat breaking across his thinning hairline. He crawled into the back, one knee down on the seat and caught up the deer with one arm and waggled the other antler with his other hand. The head sprang loose, flopped to the side and he slipped out his hand, covered with blood.

Gavin stepped back from the car, holding his gory hand before him like a mirror and measured the heat and viscosity of the shining liquid with his thumb, as if he were testing the delicacy of silk. He drew it closer to his face, saw the purpled sheen of its surface, sniffed its salinity: heavy Gulf waters, pungent springs of memory opening which set his teeth on edge. The hunt. The kick of the .30-.30 on a boy's shoulder, its crack echoing back from a distant hollow, his Uncle Bob by his side, the sweet odor of cowshit and dewy grass from his boots, bacon frying in the deep night that tasted of first whiskey, just before dawn, like now. There, in his hand, he saw a clear picture of the gutting knife, blood flowing down from the trussed animal, spattering into a rust-pocked blue enamel bowl, red pearls leaping to spot his jeans with soft splats.

Somewhere below, a dog barked and Gavin looked away to the carcass. He returned to the back seat and hoisted the deer with both arms, dragging it out from the car. Staggering back on his bootheels, he stumbled, landed hard on one knee and cursed as he srambled to his feet, pulling the dead animal on. In the center of the circle lay a gray firepit littered with blackened broken glass and crumpled beer cans. There he dropped the deer and walked back to the car. It still idled and the *Adagio* took its final, funereal steps into the clouds as Gavin slid across the seat and opened the glove box.

A tiny lamp illuminated the compartment, setting off bright reflections from a chromed Colt .45 with pearly pink grips. Gavin pushed it aside, along with several prescription vials, a small black leather box, a dog-eared paperback edition of *Tropic of Capricorn* and a harmonica to find a small button which he pushed. He heard the trunk open, walked around the Caddy and stood, weaving slightly at his hips, peering into the eclectic chaos: two cases of Wild Turkey, one of which was open and contained only two bottles, a basketball, a moldy water-skier's vest, a human skull, a cracked pair of Charley Dunne boots and some dozen books. Gavin surveyed this trove with a weird smile of recognition. He reached in and pulled out the two bottles. Thinking he might like some company, he tucked one of the bottles under his arm and took out the skull with his free hand. He carried them over to the deer, placing the skull on the carcass and setting the bottles down on a flat rock, he then went to scare up some firewood.

After five trips through scrub oak and juniper, he had managed to build a small pyre some five-by-three feet that stood about three feet at its center. With his face and chest running with sweat, Gavin scooped up the deer and laid it atop the wood. He sat down on the rock next to the whiskey and thoughtlessly wiped his hands over his face. He picked up a bottle and tried twisting off its top, but his strength was gone and his hand shook as he dropped it to his side. He leaned back and reached into his jeans, got out a clasp knife and pulled it open. After cutting around the seal, Gavin pulled the top and took a long, startling swallow, the bourbon leaked from the corners of his mouth, mixing with blood, dirt and sweat. He crushed his eyes closed, put his tongue between failing teeth and blew the fire racing up from his belly and through his throat. He sat and looked at his labors, stretching out his long legs, the tips of his boots touching the bier. He began whistling; haltingly he explored an old tune that came to him from long ago.

The second bottle of Kentucky bourbon was for the deer. Gavin stood and made the ablutions, starting at the head he poured the liquor over the eye, then down the lithe neck with a deliberation that reminded him of his time as an altar boy. The hands of the priest, Father Carlin, pinching his white fingers together, worrying their manicured tips as young Gavin tipped the crystal cruet over them, the holy water tippling down—*Lavabo inter innocentes manus meas,* I will wash my hands among the innocent— Gavin muttered the words, surprising himself, and drew a sign of the cross with the whiskey over the chest of an animal, continuing with a serpentine flourish, soaking the loins and haunches. He tossed aside the empty bottle. He picked up the skull, licked the whiskey that had splashed upon its crown, and held it upright in his left hand, like a puppet.

"Now, Roy," he addressed the skull. "We'll make the blessing for the dead....We're gathered here to commit the spirit...send the soul packing, of this noble buck deer who has sacrificed his life on the altar of Detroit. Whether he was out to kill himself, or me... he fucked up... bad, Lord. Maybe it was just a miscalculation on his part and he just wanted to get to the other side of the road. Urgent business in the deer world."

The skull turned to face Gavin, speaking in a voice like Walter Brennan. "Shucks, son. I think the varmint was out ta getcha! It was hoo-doo. Injun mischief."

Gavin peered into the eye sockets of the skull.

"You might be right about that, Roy. But the sucker's dead now for sure."

Roy rotated on Gavin's fist, scanning the perimeter with sightless holes, then grinned back, drawing closer, confidentially. "Well, kid, you best keep a lookout. This country's crawlin' with hostiles."

"Yeah," said Gavin. "But they won't attack before daylight. John Ford said so. Forget that shit, we got to send this deer back where it came from."

Gavin looked up to the diminishing night, the skull following suit.

"Lord, we ask You to take back this broken deer. Catch it in Your big mouth and swallow its soul. Keep it from further harm. Wise it up, make something of it. You wanna make something of it?"

Roy looked to Gavin. "Watch yerself there, Gavin. Don't be fucking with the Deity. Keep yer drunk mouth on biness."

"Okay, Roy. Into Your hands we commit this spirit. *Benedicat vos omnipotens, Deus, Pater et Filius, et Spiritus Sanctus.*"

As he spoke, Gavin held out his right hand, stiff as a blade, and sliced the air over the deer with two strokes.

"*Dominus vobiscum.*"

"*Et cum spiri-tu* two-oh," croaked the skull.

The dog barked in the distance as Gavin set the skull on the rock next to the whiskey. He looked to the sky while fishing in his pockets for matches. The stars still held their places directly above him, but had vanished in the east. Tender pinks and lavenders were appearing there beneath great slate clouds sailing in from the Gulf. Gavin slipped a book of matches from his jeans and turned to the pyre. He went down on one knee, ready to strike a flame, when he realized there was no way for a fire to catch without some paper. He didn't want the alcohol to burn off the deer before the wood caught, so he got up and went back to the trunk where he grabbed a half-dozen books and returned. Casting a brief eye on the skull, he drawled. "Well, Roy, looks like we go from the sacred to the profane. We're gonna burn us some books."

Gavin sat down in the dirt, crossed his legs and picked up a book: *In A Narrow Grave*. "How goddamn appropriate! We're gonna lead off with a portentous title of McMurtry's. Sorry, Larry, I've never burned a goddamn book in my life. But given the circumstances, this ritual might well use some sacrifice of the Texas muse, right, Roy?"

The light seemed to come from everywhere at once, objects gave off their own luminosity and the skull shimmered in Gavin's eye. He ripped the first twenty pages from the book, wadded them into a ball and stuffed them beneath the brushwood. After finishing the McMurtry, Gavin went on to *A Field Guide To The Birds Of The Western United States, Lost Highways,* Herrigel's *Zen And The Art Of Archery,* a collection of Keats and was halfway through *The Confidence Man* when a squad of quail trooped past him on his right. He stood and the birds exploded from the ground, he could feel the fury of their wings as they flew by. He tossed the remaining denizens of Melville's riverboat purgatory onto the carcass.

"Truly fitting. And so, here we go."

Gavin struck the match and touched the literary kindling with its flame. It crackled orange and black in the blued atmosphere. Gavin stepped back to the skull and whiskey, picked up the bottle and took a long pull. The fire reached up through the tangle of wood, igniting first the juicy cedar before finding the alcohol-laden hide of the deer. The corpus was suddenly enshrouded with veils of cold sapphire. Gavin saw its hair evaporate beneath the heat, *The Confidence Man* curl in a singular island of fire becoming a black flower which twisted and flew away in charry petals that dissolved in scattering ascent from the pyre, now a blaze flowing with smoke redolent of flaming juniper and cooking flesh-sweet, popping fats from the belly, hard, gamey under-odor from thin, burning muscle. Gavin took in all the stink as he moved unsteadily through the primal vapor, the bottle swinging from his hand, toward the car.

He crawled across the front seat to the glove box and scooped out the black leather box and harmonica. Resting on one elbow, the bottle down in the floorboards, he opened the box. Inside were two plastic vials—one empty, the other half-filled with cocaine—and a little silver penknife which he opened with a flick of his thumbnail. He popped off the vial's cap and shoveled two hefty dips into his nostrils with the blade. The coke chilled the ache in his head, gave it distraction as he closed up the works and settled it back in the compartment.

Alternating between the bottle and harp, Gavin sucked and blew his way around the burning deer for several circuits before finally sitting on a rock where he could view the conflagration and, through its topping flames across the hills to the city, his eyes running with numb tears, the glowing pink cocktip of the sun as it rose on this final Friday of August.

Gavin put the harp to his dry lips, blowing gently, wandering out on a shaky plaint of the lonesome cowboy, the lost immigrant in the West, strung out on America, hanging his heart on a mournful song...

"I ride an old paint..." He broke the song with a graveled whisper.

"I lead a dun... goin back to Montana... for to throw... the houlihan... Old Joe Clark... had a daughter and a son... one went to Kansas... the other went wrong... his wife, she died... in a poolroom fight... now Joe just sings... from mornin' til night... Ride around, little dogies... ride around slow... both my Fiery and my Snuffy... are rarin' to go...."

Gavin choked the harp with sorrowed moans and his voice grew stronger as he sang into the flames where the bones of the deer burned yellow under the morning sun.

"Ride around, little dogies... ride around, slow... both my Fiery and my Snuffy... are rarin' to go...."

If I Should Die

Tamara Stanfield Fish

When I was young, I took great comfort in the few irrefutable facts of life. And at age six there was no truth more simple and irrefutable for me than the presence of God in the universe and His benevolent intervention in my daily affairs.

Ours was a half-religious household; that is to say, Mama was an ardent churchgoer who taught Sunday School, sang in the church choir, and took an active part in the various women's circles. Daddy, on the other hand, was an embarrassment. He was on the membership roll and contributed his tithing so that one Sunday a month his name would appear in the church bulletin under "Ushers Next Sunday"; but next Sunday would find my father a comfortable sinner, unshaven, feet propped smugly on the living room table while he sipped his coffee and read the morning news. At church, meanwhile, the head usher for the month, Mr. VanDerCamp or Mr. Patterson or one of the others who regularly landed the job, would finally concede that Daddy had stood them up again, sigh, and step silently to the end of a pew where he'd surreptitiously persuade someone to take his place.

Still, Daddy was of the "do-as-I-say" school of discipline, and he did his part around the house to make ours a home where the presence of God was felt. Each week he packed us off to Sunday School and to church with Mama, deaf to my brother's protests and claims to the Inherent Right of the Male to stay home. We said grace before meals whenever someone remembered to suggest it, usually on Sunday unless the Lions were on TV, and always on Christmas and Easter and especially on Thanksgiving.

Kathleen Thoma

Though I never saw my father pray away from the dinner table, he and Mama visited us regularly at night before bed to hear us chant the bedtime prayer we'd been taught as soon as we could talk. It was a variation on the traditional "Now I lay me" theme. Only Mama, firm in her conviction that the part about death was morbid and inappropriate for a young, impressionable child, insisted upon a revised version that got them blessed in the bargain. It went:

Now I lay me down to sleep.
I pray the Lord my soul to keep.
Bless Mom and Dad in every way,
And all our friends on this lovely day.

And we finished with a great "Ay-men!" as a trio, in two-beat-sustained syllables, a shared effort to signal God we were through.

My picture of God was a composite portrait drawn from scattered conversations with these very unlike parents in turn, and not greatly interfered with by the Presbyterian Church Sunday School, where teachers, mostly mothers themselves, resisted tackling the nature and character of God, preferring instead the memorization of Bible verses and the singing of Happy Children songs. Mama's God was the Great Provider and Creator, the force that put money in Daddy's pocket and dinner on the table-a God to be thanked for all the good things that ever came our way. Occasionally ignited to moments of religious ecstasy, I would remember to thank God for a new toy, for my dog, for ice cream, for grandparents on Christmas—but I drew the line at my brother, for whom Mama frequently intimated I should be thankful.

Daddy's God was a quieter God, God the Protector, a God he remanded me to on those nights of uncontrollable terror or dismay when I lay tossing and turning in my fear of a shadow that moved, or of the deep and rolling spring thunder that rattled the windows and shook the house to its very foundations. On these nights, I called out of habit for Mama, but it was Daddy who appeared and stole quietly into my room, slippered feet padding softly across the bare, hard wood of my bedroom floor. He would sit lightly on the edge of the bed, straighten the covers, and brush back the hair from my face. "What's the matter, Punkin?" he'd gently inquire, and when I had held his hand and cried and told, he would whisper just loud enough to be heard, "There's nothing to be afraid of. Do you remember who's always watching over you?" That was as close as Daddy ever came to mentioning God—at least in a reverential sense—and it worked; I would fashion a naive, impromptu prayer in my head and, in no time at all I would drop back into a protected, peaceful sleep. The same procedure later got me through my fear of snakes and dogs and bees, and through the trauma of the sixth-grade bully who threw tomatoes at us girls from his perch in a tree as we hurried home from elementary school.

That anyone could *not* believe in God was a circumstance that left me shaking my head, incredulous. To my six-year-old mind, the evidence of God was all around us; simple logic would lead any reasoning soul to an acceptance of the fact and existence of God. One morning, as eight girls sat gathered around the pint-size Sunday School table, waiting for our teacher to arrive, someone breathed the rumor that Danny Morris was an "*ay*- theist." We had recently learned that an atheist was a person who didn't believe in God, and we used the label in proud amazement at the slightest provocation. That Danny Morris should be one of them came as no surprise to me, given that he was stupid and dirty and had flunked the third grade twice. But surely even Danny could be made to see the light if only I could explain it to him in the way that made so much sense to me.

"How could *anyone* not believe in God?" I presented. All around the table pigtails and umbrella barrettes shook back and forth in questioning disbelief. "I mean, all they have to do is look around. Who do they think *created* all this stuff?" The conclusion was self-evident, and with a choral "Sheesh!" Danny was unanimously dismissed as a hopeless dolt. It was this same conversation that produced the pact, sworn on the Bible, that if the Communists ever lined us up and asked us whether we believed in God, we would die before any one of us would say no. Such was the confident faith of a pious six-year-old.

Of course, even at that age, I had a sense that the obviousness of things was not sufficient argument to convert a communist or an atheist, so I had ammunition—solid evidence that God had intervened directly in my life, and on more than one occasion. For one thing, there was my birthstone ring. My parents had given me a genuine ruby birthstone ring for my sixth birthday, or, at least, I imagined it was genuine since they had given it gravely, carefully noting that it had been very expensive and making me promise only to wear it on special occasions—and if I lost it, to be prepared to die. I wore it only to Sunday School and church, where I showed it off proudly to the envious praises of everyone there and, one unforgettable Sunday, I had passed it around my Sunday School class for all the girls to try. In the midst of the ring's slow circuit, Mrs. Densmore, Director of Music, materialized at the door to let us know it was time to sing. Aspiring choristers all, we arose in one eager body and, in the shuffle of changing rooms and the competition to get piano-side seats, the ring was carelessly neglected. Later, in the midst of the morning church sermon, where I normally passed the time by twirling my ring around my finger, counting the revolutions, I reached for the birthstone and found it gone. It was almost more anxiety than a child could bear to wait until the service was over to go in search of that precious ruby grail, though I knew it wouldn't do to get up and run out, and I fidgeted and squirmed, no doubt to the irritation of everyone who sat nearby, until I thought that I would surely burst out in tears. The only hope I could imagine was in prayer, so I began a silent litany: Please, God, let the ring be there. Please, God, let the ring be there. . . . Please, God . . . Please, God . . . Please . . .

The instant the pastoral benediction had finally ended, before heads lifted and the organist could begin the postlude, I dashed from my front-row pew and down the hall of the Christian Education Building, now muttering aloud the prayer that had shortened to a desperate "pleeze—pleeze—pleeze!" I burst in at last on the deserted room—and there was the missing ring, poised like the Crown Jewel atop a Bible someone had thoughtlessly left behind. God had indeed come through; I asked and had received, and I promised Him solemnly then and there to be His faithful servant and to mind my parents for the rest of the day.

Most convincing, though, was the Bible cupboard incident. The Bible cupboard stood in the chapel, a tall, narrow cupboard with upper and lower accordion doors. The cupboard stretched nearly to the ceiling, or so I remember it now, an item so top-heavy as to render it unstable, so the cupboard had been fastened to the wall. After Sunday School and before the church service, Sarah Hawley and I always stored our Bibles here, preferring the more adult pew Bibles to the ones that marked us as common Sunday School youngsters. When the chapel was redecorated, in the summer between my first and second-grade years, the cupboard was unfastened from the wall and left freestanding so the paint on the wall could dry—creating a hazard the likes of which we youngsters, with our faith in the stability of things, could not imagine.

That morning, I followed Sarah to the Bible cupboard and waited while she, an enviable three inches taller than I, reached for the handle to the upper door. Suddenly, as in a slow-motion nightmare, the entire huge cupboard began to tilt forward, forward—and Sarah and I stepped back and back, not grasping, at first, what was happening. When at last it dawned on me that the cupboard was falling, I thrust out my arms in an awkward and foolish attempt to prevent it, and later would discover scrapes and bruises the length of my inner arms. But poor Sarah's fate was more horrifying still: When the cabinet had finally done with falling and lay in all its heavy length face-down on the floor, it came to me that Sarah had not jumped back in time; and now she lay only half-exposed, windless, speechless, and terrified, the monster cabinet trapping her from the shoulders down!

I began to scream, but the noise created by the fall had already brought running the entire chancel choir, which had been robing in the adjoining room. First to arrive was prim and tiny Mrs. Richter, Reverend Richter's wife, and without so much as a grunt or a strain, she somehow managed to hoist the cabinet and simultaneously extract Sarah from underneath. All I could hear, for endless seconds, was the sound of wind rushing from Sarah's lungs, and then Mrs. Richter commanding in a voice much bigger than she was: "Get Dr. Higgins, fast!" Somebody asked me if I felt all right and suggested I lie down on the floor, and then people crowded into the room until the silence became a great din. While Dr. Higgins examined Sarah, Reverend Richter quieted the throng and led the body in a prayer and, at last I could hear Sarah gasping and crying like a baby newly come to life. Miraculously, she had survived with only the wind knocked out of her, though Doctor Higgins, announcing that she'd indeed had a close call, directed her home to bed and proclaimed that her ribs would be sore for a week or so. It was a miracle, sure enough.

The other miracle, of course, had been Mrs. Richter's heroic strength and, before ten minutes were past, the rumor had circulated throughout the church membership as though on a breeze: A surge of superhuman strength had given Mrs. Richter the ability to lift the Bible cupboard and save little Sarah Hawley's life. "It must weigh eighty pounds!" Elder Broadman had proclaimed, retelling the story with baritone gusto. "Can you imagine? That little woman? It took three of us men to lift it back up to the wall!"—where it was promptly secured. I was permitted to stay through the service, an examination revealing only minor external bruises, and was given celebrity status for the day. During the service Reverend Richter offered special thanks to God for saving our two lives; God protected His children, he reassured. And if *that* wasn't proof enough of the existence of a compassionate God, I thought, then there simply was no hope for a person in this life.

Clearly, from all I had seen and learned, the God of my youth was a benevolent God—a generous, fatherly sort who wanted to keep kids out of trouble and make life as pleasant as it could be with people like Danny Morris in the world. And clearly, too, God was not responsible for Danny Morris. He had created Danny, that much was apparent; but Danny *chose* to be what he'd become from there. Perhaps he couldn't help it that he was stupid; maybe his parents were. But it seemed to me that there was evidence to suggest he might not have needed third grade three times if he had only known how to pray.

By age eight, however, life's sure realities felt increasingly less sure. It requires little in childhood—a conversation half overheard, an incident misunderstood—to dislodge the pillars of what only moments before had been a solid foundation of faith. There were, I began to understand, pieces that didn't fit into my scheme of life, realities I had not accounted for. Death, for example, and an afterlife. Perhaps, because Mama had excised it from our prayers, and despite my close brush with the Bible cupboard, I had not much considered the questions of death and an afterlife. Oh, I knew that people eventually died, and Mama said Presbyterians all became saints in the next life, so I imagined heaven as a place where we'd all get to see Great-Grandma again. But I had never considered the possibility of an early death—not *really*— and had certainly never connected God with punishment after death. I credit Aunt Louisa with bringing to light my omissions.

Aunt Louisa was short and thin with deep, dark rings beneath her eyes—Mama said from the cigarettes she chain-smoked, lighting one off the end of another. She was not a blood relative, having married my father's brother, and she came from a family that had produced a number of notorious hoods and thugs. Aunt Louisa herself had dropped out of school at age fourteen to marry Uncle Joe, who was considerably older and the black sheep of Daddy's family forevermore. Mama said she remembered thinking Louisa might just as well have dropped out of school; she was never there anyway, but was always sitting in the park smoking cigarettes with the boys. Now Aunt Louisa always had a houseful of kids—six of her own, and any number of nieces and nephews and neighborhood children for whom she babysat or who came to play. The house was always littered with toys and baby paraphernalia, and it smelled of omnipresent dirty diapers. Six kids had settled her down somewhat, Mama said, but Aunt Louisa had "strange ideas," and, even though we lived only a couple of blocks away, we spent far less time in her home than in the households of our other, more geographically-distant cousins.

Aunt Louisa never went to church that I knew of, but she professed to own a personal brand of religion that was an integral part of her daily life. She prayed out loud as she walked around the house, a baby on each hip and a cigarette between her teeth, and her ordinary speech was filled with confident proclamations like "It's the will of God," and "God never intended it that way." There was one thing that Aunt Louisa's religion absolutely prohibited under her roof, and that was swearing—not just taking the Lord's name in vain, but cursing in the four-letter fashion. We all knew this, and mostly it was no problem, for we still cringed at our own fathers' lapses into profanity, grounded as we were in the Ten Commandments, and we would never have dared curse aloud at all, much less in Aunt Louisa's presence and hearing.

But Billy Kibbey did not know about swearing and Aunt Louisa, and his ignorance cost him great suffering. To begin with, Billy was a holy terror, a short-and-mouthy brat who spun around rooms like an overwound toy. Billy wore a white-blond crew cut that made him look bald. His face was spotted with dirty-looking freckles and usually with dirt, as well, and his nose ran a constant, slippery stream which he constantly licked and occasionally wiped with the back of a grimy hand. And Billy cried at the drop of a hat.

The only person on the planet who I knew liked Billy was my crybaby cousin Sam, Aunt Louisa's youngest son. Sam had met Billy in kindergarten and, since Sam shared Billy's tendency to hyperactivity and his propensity for tears, the two had become fast friends. When Aunt Louisa threw an October birthday party for Sam and Loreen, her daughter my age, Billy was invited, much to everyone's dismay.

That Billy wound around the room like a helicopter gone wild seemed not to bother Aunt Louisa in the slightest. Sam, too, was acting like an animal, and most of us who were there for Loreen, two and three years older than Sam and his repulsive little friend, were having quite a miserable time. But then Uncle Joe brought out Pin the Tail on the Donkey, and the tone of the afternoon was altered forever.

To give Aunt Louisa her due, she knew how to throw a party, and the donkey on which we were to pin the tail was not the ordinary makeshift or home-drawn variety so common at birthday parties then. This donkey was the envy of everyone there—a full-size, living-color portrait of an honest-to-goodness donkey with some velvety fabric on his ears and mane and on the tails that we all held tightly in our sticky little hands. The picture was mounted permanently on a piece of plywood the size of half the living room wall and, since the plywood was unyielding to pins, Aunt Louisa supplied thumbtacks to each player in turn, helping the blindfolded contestant to press the tack firmly into the board. Those of us who had played the game before knew to feel around on the picture before stabbing in our tail, for Aunt Louisa would try to throw a player off track by spinning him around and around and landing him someplace far from the donkey's hind quarters; but the spot on the rump where the tail belonged was so well-poked as to provide a braille-like clue to the proper location for one's own donkey tail.

Billy didn't know this and, having taken his turn impatiently early on, he had aeroplaned his tail, without any ado, directly onto the donkey's nose. Children hooted and hollered, and Billy, temporarily embarrassed by his lack of finesse, had lost himself in the crowd to take the attention off his error. Now he watched in rare and blessed silence as Aunt Louisa spun Linda Holloman around and around and guided her toward the middle of the donkey. But Linda, a neighbor from next door and an old hand at the game, was feeling her way toward the donkey's behind and was just about to stab her tack directly on the appropriate spot when Billy, impressed with this act of apparent magic, let fly a distinct and audible "HOT DAMN!" The curse was not whimpered or tentative, but was spoken right out, as if Billy cursed so every day without fear of spanking or a mouth washed out with soap.

He might better have killed someone in Aunt Louisa's house. Everywhere in the room activity ground to a halt. Linda Holloman let drop the perfectly-guided tail and pulled the blindfold down around her neck. Cousin Loreen blinked and stole an apprehensive sideways glance at me. All eyes grew wide and voices hushed till the room was as still as a windless pond. Sam looked as if he might pucker up and cry if Billy didn't, and everyone turned in one tense body to see what Aunt Louisa would do to the perpetrator of the crime. Silently, I wished that she would wallop him and send him home so I could have my turn at the donkey.

But Aunt Louisa appeared to have no such inclination, nor did she head for a bar of soap. Instead she shook her head as though in sadness and disbelief, and then, in two firm steps, grabbed and drew to her a kitchen chair in one hand, and Billy Kibbey in the other. Billy, unsure exactly what he had done but beginning to suspect it was something untoward, was turning red in the face, his white crew cut poking up from a scalp that made me think of a McIntosh apple. There was no question that Billy soon would begin to cry; and, sure enough, when Aunt Louisa swooped him up, all unsuspecting, and settled him firmly and unhappily on her knee, Billy whimpered and the tears began to make muddy tracks from his small, sad eyes to the corners of his ice-creamed mouth. The rest of us crowded around the back of the chair, straining and shoving to see what would happen next, but too intimidated by the wrath of Aunt Louisa to settle directly in her line of vision.

"Billy," Aunt Louisa began in a tone she reserved only for the most major offenses, "do you know who God is?"

Billy let out a low, quiet, whining cry that sounded for all the world like a sick cat, and throughout Aunt Louisa's intense explanation there was the background rise and fall of this injured whine, broken only now and then by a snuff that temporarily tempted back the ever-present slime from his upper lip.

She didn't wait for him to respond before she plastered him with another question:

"And do you know where hell is?"

I had the uncomfortable feeling that we were now teetering on the verge of Aunt Louisa's "strange ideas" of which my mother so disapproved, and I felt vaguely as if I should go home. Also, hell was on the list of prohibited words in *our* household, and I'd had no indication that my mother believed in any such place; that's what Jesus had come for, I'd thought, to save people from that place, and now when people died, they simply went off to heaven and turned into bodiless spirits who were always happy and wore white robes and lived in holy harmony in a golden castle with Jesus and God and all their friends and relatives.

But Aunt Louisa was rolling, and I couldn't seem to bring my feet to budge.

"Billy, hell is a *terrible* place, a place that's worse than anything you can imagine here on earth. There's nothing there but fire that burns forever, and the devil, and all the bad and evil people from as long as there have *been* people who have stolen and murdered and broken any of God's commandments."

Fourteen sets of eyes grew wide and fearful behind Aunt Louisa's head; clearly this was news to some of them as well as to me. Mentally I checked back through the preceding week to see if I could remember breaking any commandments. The one about honoring parents came hauntingly to mind, though I couldn't remember anything more than a sort of general state of disrespect. I suspected I might have coveted Christine Hoyle her rainbow petticoat, though I wasn't positive I knew what "covet" meant.

"Billy," Aunt Louisa continued, crouching some to try and meet his streaming, downturned eyes, "have you learned the Commandments in Sunday School?" Billy simply moaned.

"He's learned 'em," offered Mikey Simms. "He's in my class—when he comes."

Everyone glared at Mikey as though he'd cast the killing stone.

"There's a commandment about swearing," Aunt Louisa went on, oblivious to Mikey's remark. "God said, 'Thou shalt not swear,' and people who ignore His commandment and go around swearing anyway end up in hell, in the fire. Now you may not think you're gonna die for a long, long time, but you could be hit by a car on your way home today, and if you hadn't told God you were sorry for swearing, you'd go directly to hell."

I wished she'd quit using the word. I also wished she hadn't said what she did about dying, for now I began to fear that *I* would be hit by a car while walking home, in punishment for some evil done and long forgotten, or committed without my conscious knowledge. Hoping it was not too late, I launched a rapid prayer for all time in my head: God, please forgive me for all the bad and evil things I have ever done in my whole, entire life....

Billy squirmed and wiggled, but Aunt Louisa had lots of practice and she held him fast.

"On the day you are born," she continued, "God writes your name in a big book in the sky, and He keeps track. On one side of the page, He writes down all the good things that you do. On the other side, He writes down every time you break a commandment—and when you tell God you're sorry, and you're *really* sorry in your heart, not just saying it so He'll think so, He crosses off the sins. But He also has written down the very moment, the day and time, when you will die. And if you die while there's a single sin left on the page—well, then it's just too late. He'll throw you down to hell."

I couldn't tell whether Aunt Louisa was having any effect on the degenerate Billy, but she appeared to have made an impression on everyone else in the room, for behind her fourteen mouths gaped like fish mouths, and the silence was unlike any I'd heard in Aunt Louisa's house. I, for one, was busy turning over new leaves like pages in a Christmas toy catalog, determining to be a perfect child from here on out. This new image of a score-keeping God, like a Santa Claus keeping track of adults and children alike, was frightening; equally unsettling was the idea that God had already decided when I was going to die.

At last Aunt Louisa finished with Billy Kibbey and, satisfied that she had made a sufficient impression on Sam's sniffling, snotty friend, she set him, red and wriggling, down firmly on the ground where he made a hasty exit through the front door, wailing like a siren. I watched him go, wondering if I'd ever see him alive again.

When the party at last resumed at the donkey, it seemed to have lost something of its vigor, and I'd never seen children trying any harder to be good.

For weeks I kept Aunt Louisa's counsel, pondering it silently in my heart. Many times I came close to bringing it up with my mother, but I suspected she would scold me for not leaving when Louisa mentioned hell—she had been reluctant to let me go to the party at all—and anyway, I didn't know how I'd tell her without saying the forbidden word.

Still, my life began to change. What if God *was* a frightful disciplinarian? I thought of Mr. Seldmeyer, the mean old man who owned the dime store and yelled at us when we tracked mud into his store, and I tried to imagine anyone even worse. It was then that I began to add greatly to my bedtime prayers; when my parents left nights and the lights went out, I appended silently the forbidden verse "If I should die before I wake, I pray the Lord my soul to take." I followed this up with the Lord's Prayer in both the "debtors" and "trespassers" versions, in case God was a Methodist, and then with any Bible verses I could call to mind.

And, nightly, I tacked on a list of people and things for God to bless that always ended with my brother, just in case.

Gone Iguana

Russell Smith

Most nights, I'd have been on the street an hour ago, but tonight my energy fails me. I sit in my room drinking beer and listening to the TV downstairs. From the window of my dark room, I can hear TVs all over the neighborhood—pre-recorded laughter, the hortatory, choral mania of commercials, gunfire, car tires screeching. By this time of night, you get the feeling those TVs are the only things alive on this block and they're talking to each other. The humans are all sleeping or dead, leaving only electronic devices to exchange liquid bursts of obscure machine language. The smell of food is in the air, as always—every time one of my brothers or sisters comes in from work, you can smell smoke from the kitchen and hear the water pipes moan in the wall. But, except for the TV, there are no voices at all.

I push the screen out of my window and step out onto the roof. The air is thick with the metallic smell of approaching rain. Onion-red city sky shudders with lightning like a dying fluorescent lamp. Me and my friend Felix Terrazas used to smoke joints up here; it's a good place for that because there's a big flat landing under the window where you can sit and lean back against the descending slope of the roof. From up here, you can see almost all of what the homefolks ingenuously call Meskin Town. You are, however, invisible to observe neighborhood life at your leisure.

When Felix and I used to come up here together, he always enjoyed watching the people in the building across the street. Because most people around here leave their windows open in the summer, you can

Kathleen Thoma

see everything that happens inside. Even when there are curtains, they're so thin that with even the faintest light in a room, you can see through them like water. This excited Felix. He liked to watch chicks walking around in panties, putting in tampons, shit like that. He'd grip his dick saying, "Put this in there instead, *mariposita*, feel so much better. Mmm!" Even if no women were visible, he liked to see whatever was happening in those houses, no matter how achingly mundane.

I found this incomprehensible: one poor meskin held in voyeuristic thrall by the sight of other poor meskins performing the sad, absurd daily routines that demonstrate only what losers they are. Meskins with their fat arms buried in tubs of wet masa flour. Meskins crying and fighting with each other, shouting, making bullshit threats. Meskins preparing for masses in which they'll hear how all the shit they're eating in this life is buying them peace and satisfaction beyond the grave. Watching those people filled me with shame. Even if the soul persists after death—a proposition I instinctively believe to be true—how debased that soul must be in my angry, haunted people.

I'm Meskin too, in case you were wondering. Not one of those suit-and-tie *tio tacos* who pontificate on TV about "issues that strongly impact the Hispanic community," but a real greasy-faced *mojado* with sweat soaking through my shirt and a big stomach and chest and reedy little legs too short for my body. More than death itself, I dread walking into public places with mirrored walls; in such surroundings, you are confronted with the stone, no-smoke truth about yourself. You not only see yourself, but also how ridiculous you appear in the world around you. I feel like a monster at such times...my mind and heart race, I sweat too much, my eyes are wild, my long hair oily, my clothes don't fit my body properly—always a pant leg caught under the tongue of a shoe or a belt lying outside a loop. People are embarrassed for me. I feel the organs of my body as they work, grumbling and popping.

I especially hate to walk the street during the day, because I look precisely like an ape. In fact, *El Babuino* is my nickname since I was a kid. Pretty funny, right?

So instead of walking, I drive whenever possible. Fortunately, my job driving a bread delivery truck allows me to stay behind the wheel most of the day. My route is long; I cover the whole northwest side of the city and spend the better part of my days getting on and off the freeway system. If you ride that route for even a day, you get the whole story of this town. From the very top layer of the freeway, the outer ramps of the cloverleaves spiral down into all the different neighborhoods of the city. It's like descending from the clouds with a parachute. You start in the bright sunlight of the top level, then drop down through the echoing, shadowy levels under the freeway and finally come to earth in a place where the sunlight seems bled of its brilliance.

In the rich white neighborhoods the roads are wide and smooth, the color of pencil lead. Trimmed trees blow in fresh-smelling air—no smell of cooking at all (when do these people eat, anyway?). Their stores are made of dark brick or smooth crackless plaster painted cool pastel colors—pink, azure and yellow. Their cars are small and tight as cockroaches with leather covers stretched across the front grilles and rubber coating on the bumpers. Bumper sticker action: "I'm a Mustang Mom," "Support Your Local Hooker—Play Rugby," "K-108: Jazz Alive!". I come in, I drop off my loaves of bread at the loading docks of the big HEBs and Tom Thumb Pages, then I slip back out again, unnoticed.

My uniform marks me as a nonentity. Even as colorful as it is, with its lizard-green stripes, gold slacks and gold cap, its true, paradoxical function is to make me invisible, one whose existence need not be acknowledged. This is a comfortable condition for me; invisibility is one of my specialties, an ability I've perfected through trial and error. You'll learn more about this later.

After I run my suburban routes, it's back up the spiraling ramps and south on the expressway, listening to the whining and thumping of my tires as they pass over grooved pavement and steel reinforcing bars—NYAH-THUFF, NYAH-THUFF, NYAH-THUFF. Billboards on 60-foot standards peer over the top level of the highway, piercing into the glassy, hypnotic sunlight to advertise motels, lite-rock FM stations, credit cards and real estate. It's 3:00 by now. I'll have bought a beer at a 7-Eleven just before getting on the freeway and, in the time it takes to drink it, I'll make it to the Furlow Boulevard exit.

Furlow is familiar to anglo gentry as the place to go for real ethnic "cuisine" and good buys in cheap rental property. Bring your wife here and watch with satisfaction as she nervously eyes the black kids checking out your car ("Honey, I left my purse in the front seat..."). You just smile and keep eating your cornbread and beans, pleased because you're secure enough to appreciate its authentic flavor even as a pack of shady-looking spooks case your Audi.

Furlow runs for maybe 20 blocks west of the Interstate in a mile-wide strip before blending into Meskin Town. The transition from one neighborhood to another is sudden and goes deeper than the brown faces and the appearance of panaderias, palm-readers and Mexican record stores along Canales Street. There's a kind of wild, aggressive sociability in the black streets. Everything happens right there on the sidewalks: shouting, sexplay, anger, hilarity, violence—the things my people keep indoors until we're freed into drunkenness or rage. The monotonous thump and clap of funk music moves in an endless wave along the street, washed onto the sidewalk from open-doored bars and replenished by rock boxes, car stereos, live deejays. Teenagers in big, slow Pontiacs and Oldsmobiles prowl the narrow streets. Midblock conversation stops as sidewalk cruisers draw honks from backed-up traffic.

Cross the no-man's land of the old railyard and Furlow's street scene vanishes. Completely. I do not exaggerate. Come feel for yourself how the tough, restless energy of Furlow dies in the air as soon as you hit Canales and Meskin Town. Come see how the streets grow wider and see how, as the distances between sidewalks increase, so do the distances between the people. You always hear about my people's fierce sense of community and neighborhood, but that's only true of our response to outsiders. We notice someone who doesn't belong, and we'll band together to resist aggression, but brother, we're as isolated from each other as a jar full of dry seeds, each with its hard airtight casing. We have reverence for the idea of turf; our gangs fight over that. Style, attitude, prestige, recognition—these things also matter deeply. But neighborhood? No way, man. When I look out from my roof, what I see is a lot of houses and a lot of Meskins, but I see no *barrio*.

At the end of work each day, I return to my room. I'll cook my meal on a hot plate, sit and read, drink beer until night comes. Then, I will drive the streets until the need for sleep overtakes me. I drive at random, intoxicated by the black glass shine that streetlights impart to sidewalks, streets and windows. I roll down my windows to absorb the astringent coolness of the night air, my foot relishes the smooth, worn surfaces of my accelerator and brake pedal. The temporary muteness that night brings to the city's harsh daytime voice gives me comfort and respite. If I have not traveled too far, I will return home before dawn, though sometimes I sleep in my car until it's time to go to work.

Tonight, my energy fails me. I hold my beer bottle against my cheek; I press the cold glass against my tired eyes. In my pocket, my hand turns over the finer glass of the little pendant. I take it out and let the chain trail across the soft skin of my wrist. The gold is worked thin as thread. The links are tiny, lovely and delicate like the patterns on a dragonfly's wing. A different hand formed the ornament itself—a rougher hand, more ancient, more vulgar. Tarnished silver of uneven thickness forms the setting, which is about the size of a child's palm. Its outside edges are flat and engraved with primitive images of terror and wonder. Two fearful-looking stags in flight...a field of stars...a sharp-pointed cross inscribed with obscure symbols...an ecstatic woman with flames rising from her head and arms. In the center is the source of power—a smooth amber stone, round, with a small shallow depression in the middle. The depression is the size of a thumb, and it's where you rub the stone to bring it to life. The longer I have this stone, the more closely my thumb matches the worn spot, and the greater my power becomes. These powers I have taught to myself, employing only the force of my will.

That—the power of the will—is the key to accomplishing anything. Rulfo Quiroz told me that 18 years ago when he gave me the amulet. I found it one day when I was looking through his junk store on the way back from school. For a queer little loner like I was, Rulfo's store was the ideal refuge from ridicule and humiliation. It was housed in a building that looked small and narrow from the outside, but whose length and dim lighting suggested great volume once you walked through the doors. I liked to walk to the deepest, most remote part of the store, relishing the brush of clothing against my arms from both sides of the narrow aisles; the odd, archaic look of the tableware and utensils and woodwork; the sour, dusty-smelling air. I'd spend hours at a time looking at old postcards that Rulfo sold two for a penny. I loved them for their rich, extravagant colors and for the unimaginable life and geography portrayed on them ("Fishin' for Croakers at Bountiful Caddo Lake"; "Menlo Park, Cradle of the Electronic Age"). I also liked to read the things people had written on the backs, the communications that breathed the smell of lives that were real, but hopelessly beyond my grasp. Lives now spirits, slipping like silent streams of atoms through the air of Rulfo's store.

I found the amulet hanging around the neck of a large, lifelike doll that sat on the sill of a painted-over window. The doll was made entirely of rough white cloth, but was cleverly shaped and painted so that it looked real at first sight. The red hair and green eyes were especially realistic, so much so that fear weakened my legs when I first noticed her in the window, so beautiful and impassive. Minutes passed, then I dared to approach her, touch her dark green dress, grasp the big silver and amber amulet around her neck.

"It's interesting isn't it, *amigo*," Rulfo said. "You wouldn't think the amber and silver would go so well together, but somehow it's perfect."

Startled, I cried out and jerked sharply around. I found myself facing the old storekeeper, who stood in the center of the aisle no more than four feet behind me. I hadn't heard him come up behind me, hadn't expected it; Rulfo seldom emerged from behind the counter.

"I've had the doll for quite some time and I don't intend to sell her," Quiroz said, twisting a cigarette into a black holder and putting it into his mouth unlit. "I just brought her out to properly display the amulet. Wanted the right kind of person to be drawn to it."

Still rattled, I had no reply.

"The thing about the amulet, you understand, is that it won't do a damned bit of good for 999 of the next 1,000 people who walk in that door. They won't have the will for it, so it'll be useless. To make it work, you have to be able to imagine something, then you've got to direct your will and be able to direct it through the amulet."

Rulfo pulled a big Zippo lighter out of his brick-red wool pants and lit his cigarette, then studied me while he took his first deep draw. His smooth, dark-brown face shone even in the dim light, partly from sweat (the store was always very hot in the summer and Rulfo wore a wool coat and jacket at all times) and partly from the way his tight skin reflected light like a mirror. He must have been 65 years old at the time, but his eyes betrayed none of the spiritual fatigue you often see in men that age. His long, oval-shaped head was still covered with thick black hair that he pomaded and brushed straight back. His mustache was wide but closely trimmed and he had a small triangular patch of beard on his chin. The old man's dandyish appearance, bachelor status and slightly effeminate mannerisms gave rise to widespread rumors of homosexuality; most boys in the neighborhood had been warned to avoid him, but I had never feared him, simply because he had never before uttered a word in my presence.

Rulfo ejected smoke briskly from his big shiny nose and ran his handkerchief over his face. "You're Rosendo Herrera aren't you...you're an interesting kid," he said, smiling. "You come in here every day, you behave as if you were in a shrine of worship, then you leave without a word. Such a strange little fellow. You remind me of myself as a kid. I was avoided and ridiculed like you—I've heard the things your young friends yell at you—but there is a dignity and strength about you. You feel very alone, but I suspect I know many of your thoughts."

Rulfo's kind words, spoken in a quiet, dispassionate voice, appeased my fear. "This is not pretty, but I like it very much," I said, holding out the locket. "What is it for?"

"It's just a tool," he replied. "The parascientific and magical disciplines are not my metiér, but I'm informed that it gives you nothing you don't already possess. It focuses the will much in the way that a convex lens focuses rays of light, yet supplies no motive power of its own. You can, I presume, alter the nature of matter. That which is imaginable can be made actual. Do you want it?"

Quiroz watched with an amused smile as I stood dumbly, glancing first at the pendant, then back at him.

"Here," he said, laughing softly and removing the necklace from the doll. "You can wear it home." Rulfo knelt and placed the thin chain around my neck, pressed it to my chest with his palm, "That which you can imagine, *amigo*," he said, grinning at me through a white cloud of cigarette smoke. Then he rose and returned to the front of the store.

Immediately upon leaving Quiroz's store, I slipped the pendant under my shirt; my possessions were often pilfered by older boys who I'm sure would have considered this new item a rare piece of plunder. Once home, I pulled the instrument out and examined it more closely. I held the amber stone against a naked bulb and was startled by its density. Light hardly seemed able to pass through it at all, though its color seemed deep and rich—a dirty, uneven gold that satisfied none of my eye's requirements for beauty but compelled my touch. I slept with the pendant clutched against my smooth brown, stomach and for most of next day, it seemed that my body's heat was retained—even intensified—in the metal and stone.

Of the remaining years of my childhood, there's not much worth my telling or your hearing. I graduated from high school, accepted a college scholarship offer, but quit after a year. Gradually, I grew away from what few friends I had until only Terrazas remained. Then, he was gone too, first to girls and then to the army. Once I was alone, my life assumed the shape I suppose I'd always considered ideal: a comfortable daily procession between small sealed chambers. My room, my job, my car, the night, and then sleep. All the while, my real work—the disposal of my physical substance—has progressed at a gradual, satisfying pace.

The beginning was frustrating, and would have been impossible without Quiroz's offhandedly bestowed gift. It was the instrument I needed to consummate my only lifelong passion. First steps were fleeting accomplishments that were hard to verify—minute, transitory changes in the pattern of lines in my hand; a barely detectable lengthening or shortening of bones in the face, the momentary transparency of the body observed in a mirror.

Shape-shifting was the first breakthrough. In the early stages, Terrazas was my cohort, merging his will with mine and directing it through the stone as we reformed the stuff of my body, then his. As evening swallows, Terrazas and I raced and wheeled on cold walls of air. As insects, we saw the world in jeweled multiplicity through flawless compound eyes. As jaguars, we made love to each other beneath my dark window. His departure brought momentary weakness to my spirit, but in the end, total isolation has brought greater purity of intent, thus greater power. Eventually, I felt that I had the strength to move from transforming my substance to obliterating it entirely. My success has thus far been only partial, yet, each day seems to bring progress. My periods of actual invisibility are still brief, seldom more than a half-hour, but in the interim periods, my substance feels as light and brittle as crystallized sugar. If I am seen at all, it is surely with the sketchiness of objects glimpsed out of the corner of the eye.

Even the physical weakness I now feel may indicate the further breakdown of my material structure. More evidence...my old fascination with driving has become progressively less urgent. Except for the daily trip to work, my car has been parked for three days. For what do I need it now? My explorations have served their purpose. Still, there have been moments of deep satisfaction. I remember the pleasure I felt when, cloaked in invisibility, I cruised slowly through the rich white suburbs on the north side, free to gaze in amazement at the safe, orderly world these men had built for themselves and their families. My resentment of their privilege, which still afflicted me during my work hours, seemed to fall away with the burden of my visibility. I was now free to admire them for their optimism and the power of their will. This last virtue is the one whose absence inspires the disappointment I feel for my own people. I will never feel that shame for myself.

As I mastered my art, I became confident enough to explore inside these houses. I was cautious in my early explorations, hiding in shadows and listening through doors. But I soon became bolder, and began to walk freely through the houses, even standing quietly in rooms where conversations were being held. I drank their water, used their bathrooms. The knife that I had earlier carried for protection was left behind.

This activity amused me for some time, but two recent incidents have caused me to abandon the practice. The first episode happened as I perused the upper floor of a big two-story house in Briarcliff. I had believed the house to be empty, but when I entered the big second-floor bedroom I heard the soft hiss of a clock radio tuned between stations. At the foot of the bed sat a man, about fifty, smoking a cigarette. The light was dim, but I could see that he was well-groomed and wore eyeglasses. In his left hand he held a cocked pistol. When he finished the cigarette he rose—still carrying the gun—and carried the ashtray into the bathroom, where he flushed the ashes down the toilet and drew himself a cup of water. He then returned to the foot of the bed, sat down and, without hesitation placed the barrel of the pistol between his eyes and pulled the trigger. There was a loud, flat pop and the small gun spat out a shell casing that glanced off a mirror and skipped, ringing, across the tile floor. The man dropped the gun, sighed, fell backwards on the bed. His facial muscles relaxed. The fingers of his big hands opened and closed gently in the air like a newborn baby's. And then he was still.

Astonished by what I had seen, I stood for a long time in the gunpowder smell, my ears ringing. After several minutes, I knelt beside the dead man and used a towel to wipe the pooling blood from his face. His smooth-shaven, perfumed skin was still warm to my touch, but as lifeless as vinyl. The handsome body, life blasted out of it, seemed a skillful, diabolical artifice.

"You blew it,*vato*," I said at last, lifting the body off the bed and carrying it into the bathroom., where I deposited it in the shower. "You should have talked to me....I'd have told you the consciousness isn't the problem....You fucked up."

After I stripped the sheets from the bed and stuffed them in a corner of the room, I laid the man back on the bed with a bath towel folded behind his head. When I heard the neighbors breaking the downstairs window, I pressed my hand against the man's face for a moment, then left.

About a month later, still troubled by the suicide I had witnessed, I returned to the dead man's house. Two women—wife and daughter—sat at a table talking. I stood nearby and listened to their conversation, which contained no references to the dead father. Eventually, the younger woman rose and left the room. A minute later she called to her mother that she was leaving and would not return until morning.

I followed the mother into the kitchen. She ground coffee and placed it in a percolator. As I stood watching her in the bright, spacious humming silence of that kitchen, I realized that my power was reaching a peak. Never in my life had I felt the stuff of my existence to be rarer, more permeable. My transparent substance swelled beyond its boundaries, filling the room like the brightness of the light. The warmth retreated as cold, light particles swirled around me like flakes of snow and sleet, stinging my skin. I seemed to fill the room, then recede again in immeasurably-swift increments of time. I experienced in that moment the ecstasy of physical existence with a keenness that was in no way physical. The woman making coffee was alternately inside, then outside my body's boundaries as I stood an arm's length away from her. I began to laugh out loud as I breathed in the cold points of light and felt them race through my chest. My laughter screeched and whistled from my frozen lungs.

The woman screamed. Shit! She could still hear me! The frost on my body vaporized as I instantly became fully visible. All traces of euphoria vanished and I stood, panting, in front of a small, wild-eyed white housewife in a pink tennis outfit. "How did you get in here?" she demanded in a voice that contained equal parts of terror and indignation. "All of the doors were locked." Her hand crept down below the cabinet level and grasped a drawer pull. As she yanked the drawer, I rushed forward and pushed her hard against the wall. Metal and wood showered to the floor as the knife drawer fell. The woman struggled for a moment, but I was able to hold her.

"I didn't come here to hurt you," I said, breathing hard. She jerked again and almost pulled away before I grabbed her around the waist and pinned her arms to her side. Now what?

Now I was fucked. I knew that in my panicky state, I would be unable to achieve invisibility and would be caught before I could make it home. In the glass door of a microwave oven I could see myself—puffy-faced, sweating, long hair clinging to my face, greasy shirt and jeans, eyes full of fear. I felt as trapped as a specimen on a microscope slide. A moment earlier I had filled the room; now the kitchen telescoped outward in all directions, dwarfing me. I was held in suspension like a bacteria in a drop of jelly.

I turned from my reflection to the woman. Her eyes, inches from mine, were staring directly into mine, assessing me. The terror had gone from her face, replaced by one of calm, intense calculation. I became aware of the heat and mass of her body against mine. In the struggle, her blouse had been pushed up and my big roughened hand pressed the smooth skin at the small of her back. Her breasts rested softly against my stomach. I could smell almond cake frosting and coffee on her breath.

Then—*milagro!* —a hardon. My body, ether and air a moment earlier, was now fluid-tormented tissue straining for a spasm of release. The woman's eyes widened as I tightened my embrace, but her expression did not change. As I moved my hand across her back, caressing her warm skin, her eyes never left mine, never ceased their patient search for clues. I raised her skirt with one hand, stroked her thigh with the tips of my fingers. My hands were cold and trembling, my breath absurdly deep, raspy. Once, during the airless silence of our embrace, my stomach growled, a fluting, skirling plaint, and the woman giggled abruptly. Laughing, I pulled her to me and kissed her with a gratefulness and passion I'd never believed myself capable of. Her response was warm but restrained, a cunning performance clearly aimed at survival. Yet there was understanding in her return of my kiss, something of recognition. I kissed her joyously, my hand cupping her small neck, pressing her thin shoulder blades to my chest.

Then I was in my room with a mind red from pleasure and a body as substantial as an ocean. For many hours I read magazines and drank beer. Then I stepped naked onto the roof and lay drunken in the night air until dawn. For two weeks thereafter, the silver and amber pendant lay untouched in my bedside drawer.

I have, of course, no illusions about the authenticity of my experience with the woman. Nor has my campaign against my own corporeality been more than briefly delayed. In a month, in a year, it will be complete—something will happen. Whether I'll feel it as a charismatic rapture (as I'm sentimentally prone to imagine), whether my awareness will die with my body, whether the change will be noticeable at all is anybody's guess. Regardless, I'm sure that many ancient philosophical conundrums will be solved in that instant. It's a shame that no philosophers will actually be there to see it.

In my moment of passage, anything could happen. It will be no baptism, no confirmation. I haven't speculated about any possible spiritual benefits, and I take no speculative cargo of faith to my new country. As the gutted framework of my substance—the joists, girders and stripped wires—are swept away, I will retain only one souvenir from what I have been for the past 32 years.

It will be love.

June Bugs Circling A Light Bulb

Nan Cuba

I thumped one of my paralyzed legs, laughed out loud, and then mashed the accelerator with my thumb. I loved careening down the empty street in my secondhand brown bomber. The fact that it had been Gran's old Plymouth and drove like a bus gave it character. And the makeshift hand controls next to the steering wheel weren't even noticeable unless you moved in close. Sitting high, plowing low and fast, I almost felt normal.

I was on my way downtown to the small business district of twelve blocks. It was Anne's birthday. My wife had been loose and worshipful when we met. I liked that. She was the waif and I was the nurturer. I've always loved to pamper and be appreciated, and Anne gave the perfect response. She had a great build, but was actually rather plain: bleached blonde, fair-skinned, big gums, glasses when she didn't make the effort to replace them with contact lenses. But I enjoyed her—her simple pleasures and her acceptance of life's unpredictables.

Just as I passed the antiquated memorial auditorium on my left, I noticed a parking space to the right between Winn's Department Store and Zales Jewelry. I pulled in, thinking Zales might have some trinket Anne would love to flash.

It takes twenty minutes for me to get out of my car, and I'm strong—even stronger since the accident. Pulling dead weight is tedious, hard work...and when you have an audience, the experience can only be compared to the feeling a dog must have as his nose is rubbed into his own excrement.

K. Thoma

Sweating, biceps quivering, I finally loaded myself into *the chair.* It was an obnoxious contraption, all steel and spokes, which created fear in any observer like some weird Stephen King movie. In an attempt to diminish its demonic powers, I had defamed it by painting an unnaturally busty, naked woman the size of my palm on the chair's left arm. Besides emasculating the satanic chariot, Shirley (my handy lady-friend) served a higher purpose. At every opportunity, I casually "exposed" her during an irritating conversation with a particularly sympathetic person. No one ever dared to criticize me for that or anything else anymore...gee, I was just poor Luke now, so I got away with murder. I loved to test them though, see how far they'd let me go before they'd withdraw quietly, but devastatingly disgusted. It was one of the few pleasures I had left.

However, at that moment, while facing the store entrance, my mind was focused on the expected pleasure of choosing a gift for grateful Anne. I threw the heavy glass door open with a bang, and shot my chariot into the store's coolness. Immediately, three shoppers at a distant showcase, a woman trying on a bracelet, and the attending clerk looked in my direction. And then they kept on looking, pretending *not* to look...as if to say, I know I shouldn't, but I can't help watching that freak; I wonder if he's going to drool or wet his pants. I resisted an urge to fake a seizure.

Forcing a calmness, I rode up to the counter to inspect the merchandise. The woman with the bracelet leaned across the counter to the clerk and shouted a whisper, "Go ahead and help that pitiful young man. I'll just wait here." I was tempted to respond to Miss Sanctimonious, but decided that she would be too easy a victim. I liked a bigger challenge, and he was conveniently walking my way.

The clerk peered down at me, looking like the pious director of a funeral parlor. "Can I help you," he screamed, exaggerating the enunciation of each word as though I were deaf and didn't understand English. Oh boy, one of those, I thought.

"I'm looking for a gift for my wife," I said, causing the clerk to appear stunned, either because I had a wife or because I knew how to talk.

"Do you have money?" he yelled haltingly. What a moron.

"No, I came to rob the place, complete with my own get-away car."

His face contorted, but his eyes stayed firm. "I beg your pardon?"

"Just show me that small pendant in the front, please."

He sighed, reluctantly pulled it out, then persisted, "But who will pay? I have other customers waiting who have sympathetically allowed you to go first, so let's not waste their time, shall we?" Then he leaned across the counter and barked into my face, "How much money do you have?"

The other customers were staring at us, solicitude and disgust registering on their faces. To my horror, the bracelet lady looked as though she were contemplating coming to my defense. It was definitely time to strike.

"Why Jerry, you of all people ought to know how much money I have. It was only yesterday you brought me the usual pay-off...you know, so I wouldn't let it leak that you have been sneaking just a few little items from the store and selling them on the side. As a matter of fact, do any of these people know about your reduced , private rates?" My friend across the glass looked like he might be headed to a funeral parlor after all. "What about it folks... Has he shown you any of*his* stuff?"

Bracelet lady couldn't resist this. "I want you to know, the owners of this shop are friends of mine. Now, are you saying this clerk has been stealing merchandise?" She had to be the president of the local D.A.R.—French twist, stout sagging chest and fat legs. I loved her predictability.

"Now really, madam...," the clerk began, only to be silenced immediately by my haughty ally.

"Oh, yes ma'am," I chirped, trying to appear the squeaky-clean innocent. "But he didn't mean any harm, and he's been very generous with his payments to me. Why, he even took me to have this pretty picture painted on my chair." I raised my left arm slyly and introduced her to Shirley. "Don't you just love It?"

Some people enjoy a film's rapid display of an awakening rose blossom. Others prefer watching a developing sunrise or sunset. Not I. Give me the poetry of Mrs. D.A.R. exploding her capsuled moralisms any day. Even now, when I close my eyes, I can relive its full beauty in slow motion. The clerk didn't stand a chance. My only regret was that I had to make my exit before the scene had played to its end.

Parked on the sidewalk, I had just decided to give up on the shopping venture and head for home, when a streak of red drove past, then came to a sassy halt. "Hey Luke...you going to just sit there being useless, or are you still man enough to take a ride with me?"

It was Corinne. Naughty, noble Corinne. At least I was still able to enjoy looking at such a fine woman. I've always been a sucker for long hair, and hers was black and curly. She had biscuit-brown skin and, in spite of her average size, there was an impression of delicacy.

Her thick black eyebrows and blue-green eyes created an aura of the lusty forbidden. "Hell yes, Corinne. I'm..." and then I howled my favorite Paul Simon tune, "still cra-zy after all-l-l these years."

Without a word, she threw her Ferrari into park and, grinning, ran over and grabbed my chair. She seemed oblivious to the line of cars backed up, some even honking, as she loaded me in with firm, tiny hands. For the first time in months, I began to look forward to what would happen next.

Now bolting toward the Interstate, she drawled, "Hey Luke, that's a nice touch painting the busty broad on the arm of that thing...but, geesh, those wheels must put a cramp in your style. Can you really not feel anything in your legs...not even if I do this?" She reached over and grabbed a hunk of flesh on my left leg and squeezed, searching my face for a sign of pain. I was reminded of the times in high school when I used to dare her to punch my stomach, the momentary discomfort easily worth the thrill of her noticing my taut muscles and undaunted masculinity.

"No, Corinne, I can't feel a thing." Somehow it just wasn't the same.

"I'm real sorry about that, Luke. But you know, if anyone can survive that kind of thing, I know you can. You've always been the bravest, most positive-thinking person I know." Her comment both surprised and buoyed me. I could always trust Corinne to be straight, and just maybe, today she knew something I didn't.

"And stubborn. Lord, you are so stubborn...but, even still, your stubbornness doesn't come close to your cockiness. I think you must have let all those girls go to your head."

"Oh, you do, huh? Well, you never seemed to let them get in your way. Hell, they knew you'd eat them alive."

"And they were damn right, too." I savored her tough, easy talk...and her natural understanding.

Suddenly she was laughing. "Luke, remember the time we colored your hair green and mine pink? We almost got kicked out of college for that one." I remembered, and it was wonderful. "I never could understand why the teachers liked you even though you were always in trouble. There's just something special about you, Luke."

"Yeah, I wish Chuck, the jock, had believed that the time he almost killed me in the school parking lot."

"Well, what do you expect, dummy, when you take on a football captain with two of his cronies, simply because they wanted you to move your car out of Chuck's claimed slot. It seemed like such a silly reason to lose two teeth and gain a black eye."

"But I hated his arrogance."

"And I loved the look on their faces when you finally pulled that tire tool out of the trunk...a golden moment in history." She reared back tossing her mane, and cut loose a belly-laugh. It was contagious, and then tranquilizing.

Now it was my turn. "So what have you been doing in the three years since then? Robbing banks from the sign of this slick machine."

"Almost. Honey, I've found a gold mine and I'm having a blast. You are looking at the highest-paid hooker in Big D. I never knew I could have so much fun and make so much money doing it. Sugar, good times never felt so good."

"Corinne, if there's one thing the world can count on from each of us, it's surprises. You mean you hump strangers for a living and like it?"

"Luke, you're not listening. I said highest-paid. I only entertain the pretty, clean big daddies who've been well-screened. I've got a regular clientele, and I've become quite fussy. After all, I'm the best...and why shouldn't I be? You taught me everything I know." Her candor and self-satisfaction made me remember why she was one of the few people who had my total respect.

We stopped at a pub just past the county line to have a few beers. We laughed and talked, and I told her about Anne. She didn't say much. There was a lousy band playing. I rolled up, casually lifted my arm to expose Shirley, and requested "Do Ya Wanna Dance" just to see the looks on their faces. Corinne about split her sides when the group started honking out the old song. Before I knew what was happening, she pushed me onto the dance floor, and started twirling my chair and whooping. We even did the hand jive. Everybody in the place moved back, and began to shout and clap. Some of them slapped me on the back and whistled when we were through. I hadn't had so much fun since my hair was green.

When we left the pub it was nighttime—no moon, and hot—the smothering heat of south Texas in August. She closed the barroom door behind us and then paused, just standing there holding the handles to my chair. She was staring at the dingy motel across the street and humming, like a little girl absorbed in the abandon of imaginary play.

"Let's go skinny-dipping," she finally said and it was a command not a question, for she was racing me across the highway as she was talking.

Before I knew it, she was standing there beside the small pool naked as a jaybird and starting to yank off my shirt. Then she turned her head and pretended to be occupied with something at the edge of the water. So I began struggling to remove my pants (one leg, then the other), my socks (one foot, then the other), my underwear (one leg, then the other), and the plastic catheter. I maneuvered my chair to the stair railing at the shallow end and then dragged myself to the top step. Corinne was waiting, and smiling. We took a moment to look each other over. That TV commercial summed it up: she hadn't gotten older, just better. The tips of her breasts were floating barely above the water's edge, swaying with each rocking motion like beacons in an undulating tide. I felt her admiring my muscled upper body, but couldn't help wondering if she were repulsed by the thinness of my legs and my sagging parts.

"Is this considered a charitable service, or are you trying to get experience for your next crippled customer?" She didn't say anything, but I could see I had really hurt her. "I'm sorry, Corinne. I don't know why I said that. Just angry about everything, I guess."

Without a word, she slipped both my arms around her neck and pulled me gently into the water. She bobbed slowly along the shallow edge, seeming to relish the shock of the cold. Our faces were inches apart; our thoughts, as always, focused on the moment. She touched my hair, rubbed her fingers on my cheek, and then she kissed me ever so softly. "Luke, you're still the most beautiful man I've ever known," she whispered.

I was settling myself back on the step when she asked the question I hated most: "How did it happen?" Since the accident, I had told a variety of particularly sickening and/or heroic lies, ranging from being run over by a train to being shot in the back while rescuing a child from her kidnapper. I usually hated the people who asked, and tried to select my story according to what would be the most offensive. But now, for Corinne, I eagerly told the truth.

"Sweet Corinne...the worst part about the accident was its senselessness. It was neither honorable nor exciting. I was simply helping a friend repair his roof and I fell two stories onto the front pavement. Whap. Like a bug on a windshield." She winced.

"But you're making it all right, aren't you, Luke?"

"Corinne, you and I are different than most. We're like june bugs circling a light bulb, headed for sure trouble and hell-bent to get there. We have to be in the middle of things to feel alive. But Sugar, my wings are clipped now, and I can't ever get to the light...and you know, I'm just not sure I can do without it. It gets real ugly in the dark."

She understood. I heard a "shit" as she sniffed and wiped her nose with the back of her hand. She was too honest to make some kind remark. "Come on, let's go for another loop around the pool, Handsome."

We slipped back into the water with our arms around each other, and she began singing to the rhythm of our bobbing..."Do ya wanna dance, under the moonlight...Kiss me, kiss me, kiss me all through the night...Oh, Baby, do ya wanna dance..." I began to sing with her and, before we knew it, we were bobbing, laughing, and shouting the song—circling together within the moment's light.

Suddenly we were interrupted by someone's shouts: "Hey, you two, you'd better get out of there or I'm going to call the police!" Corinne could hardly get us to the steps without drowning because of her uncontrolled snorts and giggles. We were both out of breath, and Corinne was now hiccuping between slurred whispers as she scrambled for our clothes and loaded me into the chair. We were both naked, with her bra looped over Shirley's arm rest and my catheter lying on top of the stack of clothes in my lap, as she darted us across the highway. Somehow we managed to dress, and Corinne headed us toward my home.

As we pulled into the drive, Anne appeared in the doorway. She was wearing her pink robe and slip-on house shoes; from her hair to her feet, she seemed the same washed-out color. She drifted toward the car and growled, oozing rage, "Where have you been?"

I reached for Corinne's hand and squeezed. "I ran into an old friend of Shirley's, and we've been out driving." Glancing back at Anne, I observed her stricken face and her opaque eyes fill with water. I was thrilled, exhilarated. What can I say? I love to make them cry.

Golden Throat

Ray Reece

Stanley is certain that trouble and weirdness are breeding like a twister in his house tonight, and he is helpless in the face of the storm. Priscilla is sulking again. She had loomed silent at dinner with the kids, her eyes downcast, had eaten but little of her chicken-fried steak, preferring instead to sculpt a circle of black-eyed peas around her mashed potatoes and gravy. Nor has she spoken in the two hours since, except to murmur "Thank you, no" when Stanley offered to lead the kids in a kitchen brigade to wash the dishes. He had played Mister Pony with the girls while she composed a threatening clatter of steel and glass at the kitchen sink. He knows of course what the problem is, and she undoubtedly *knows* he knows: she is horny this Saturday night, and he is not. He sets his jaw as he scans the sports page, seeking again to follow the spread on the Superbowl, but the words and pictures of gridiron stars keep blurring out of focus: *Whenever Priscilla is horny and I am not then somethin weird is bound to happen no matter what.* He remembers ugly midnights riven with shrieks and accusations, with futile perfumes and negligees and saucers crashing against the wall. He shudders, scrunching deeper into his sofa cushion, wishing he were sex-charged or out shooting pool instead of home alone with a horny wife. He glances left at the corridor leading to the bedrooms, where Priscilla is putting the children to sleep, and suddenly reaches into his pants to seize his penis in hopes of evoking a response. He finds the laggard inert in his shorts and tries to coax it forth, closing his eyes and

Kathleen Thoma

flashing to the luscious *Penthouse* centerfold tacked to the wall at the rear of Walter's Axle and Gear. He peers in his mind at the naked brunette athwart a hammock on the beach at Malibu, her nipples erect and ruby red. He tugs at his pecker and clenches his teeth, gaping closer at the sumptuous breasts aglisten in the sun, but he has no luck: his cowardly button seems to shrink further from the touch of his calloused fingers. "Shit," he mutters into his mustache, withdrawing his hand and crossing his legs in a pique of dread. He plucks a can from the table beside him and swallows some beer and stares bewildered at the sports page: *I hope she doesn't pull that nightgown trick oh Lord deliver us why can't she wait till mornin?*

Priscilla pauses at the bedroom door to study her cherubs asleep in their double bunks, Sharon on top and Karen below, their faces glowing in the wedge of light from the corridor. They had been such sweethearts tonight, requiring only a single story from *Aesop's Fables* before dozing off. They were tired, like Stanley, having traipsed with Priscilla through five different stores at two crowded malls this afternoon, helping her shop for undies and socks and soap and foil, vegetables, veal and flowers and beer. Priscilla fixes on Sharon for a moment, the older girl at six and a half, her freckled nose a pert little beacon above the quilt that engulfs her. She had sensed the gloom descending on her parents this evening, had in fact been wounded by it, and Priscilla is irate. She beams a message across the room to Sharon's brain: *Don't be a fool in marriage, love, be sure he is rich and has such balls he won't go dead at 37 claimin fatigue from overtime.* She bites her tongue to have dreamed such a thing. She blows a kiss at her angel girls and shuts the door, wanting to spit the word *overtime* like icy water in Stanley's face: what does *he* know about *over*time? She wishes for a second that she didn't love him, didn't adore his muscled chest and perfect butt, as then perhaps the old black magic wouldn't be seething in her tubes again. It makes her a monster with a feather in her crotch. It drains the temperance out of her veins and ushers the Antichrist into her heart: *Lord, Lord, what shall I do?* Slowly she walks obsessed down the hall to another bedroom, flips on the light and opens the door to a tall cedar wardrobe once her grandma's. She digs past her dresses to a black silk negligee, floor-length, with a filmy chemise that ties at the front. She wrestles it loose and holds it to her breasts in a mirror on the wardrobe door. She likes the effect, the flash of evil in her oak-brown eyes heightening the slashes of blonde in her hair. But it's not herself the gown must arouse, it's Mister Fatigue in the living room, and he has never *once* been driven to rip the garment from her quivering flesh. She tosses the gown in a heap on the bed and stares at the telephone gleaming red on the nightstand: *Who can I call and where can I go to scare this devil out of my soul?* Perhaps Irene, her next-door neighbor now divorced, a born-again swinger who had told her last week of a new massage parlor out on Highway 35, a reverse salon for women instead of men, where the studs are waiting to stick their prods—she bites her tongue and slaps her cheek to quell the riot of demons in her thighs, to stanch the tears before they ruin her careful eyes. She breathes as deep as her lungs will stretch and spies her breasts, of which she is proud, and then decides: she will get drunk, that's all, may God forgive her—skip the games and fancy costumes, just get drunk and jump her husband on his precious couch.

Stanley wonders where Priscilla is, what is taking so long with the girls. He tilts his can to drain his beer and clanks it down on the table with the lamp and the telephone. He is still thirsty, would love a second arctic brew, but he is afraid such an act of indulgence would rankle Priscilla somehow, provide the spark for the holocaust: *She'll be countin them beers this evenin I bet.* He yawns and glances at his wristwatch— 9:45—and decides to catch the 10 o'clock news. He stands from the couch and flexes the aching muscles in his back and circles the coffee table, littered with crayolas and children's art, to the ancient Magnavox, sturdy and imposing as a boxcar. There, atop the console in a white, scalloped vase, he finds a bouquet of fresh-cut lavender flowers that he had not seen before. He sniffs the blossoms, knowing Priscilla has bought them for a *reason* tonight, and he has failed to *comment* on them, and his belly tightens so he can't smell a thing but the sweat in the pits of his arms. He switches on the Magnavox, keeping the volume at zero for now, and turns to sit on the couch again, grabbing his paper for another crack at the sports page. He yawns an epic, face-wrenching yawn and hears her voice from across the room, "Well, the kids are asleep."

She is standing in the corridor, hands on hips in tight blue denims, her cowgirl shirt a blaze of red with yellow checks. "Finally," he says, relieved that she hasn't changed clothes.

"Finally," she says, stepping toward him with a curious bounce. He sees at once that her shirt is unfastened at the level of her bra, disclosing the curves of her Dolly Parton breasts, and he looks away as she reaches the couch and stands beside him, breathing. He gawks at the sports page, sniffing the scent of her Estee Lauder, but faint, not reeking as he had feared.

"Nice flowers," he says, nodding toward the vase on the Magnavox.

"Thanks," she replies, "I was hopin you'd notice." They are both silent for a moment. "What're you watchin?" she asks. He looks at the image dancing in color on the TV screen, a lustrous blonde in an evening gown being waltzed by a fellow in a tux on a terrace.

"Just waitin for the news," says Stanley, hoping the guy doesn't kiss the girl, but he does. Stanley is silent. He hears a clink as Priscilla inspects his beer can, shaking it next to her ear concealed by tufts of yellow-streaked hair. "Want another beer, Stanley? This one's empty." He stares at her disbelieving. "Did I hear you correctly? Did you ask if I wanted another *beer?* " She smiles and giggles, "Well, yeah, drawing up her shoulders like a little girl, "I thought maybe I'd have one myself."

"Oh?" He searches her face for a sign of intent, "That's unusual." He glances at his watch, "Isn't it close to your bedtime, Priscilla?" Her smile fades, "Ordinarily, yes, but I guess I'm not so Godawful *sleepy* tonight." He gropes for mirth, "What about your nightmares, honey? You get nightmares stayin up late carousin and drinkin, don't you?" Her eyes start to smolder beneath her pencil-darkened brows: "I guess I don't remember, Stanley—it's been so long since I've *tried* it." He blanches, turning to the sports page: "Well, hell, pop us a couple of cool ones, then. What the hell."

She strides toward the kitchen with a purposeful gait, her black vinyl flats going *click click click* on the wooden floor, and Stanley watches with a troubled eye: *It's startin now, the weirdness.* He studies her ass, too plump in her Wrangler jeans, regretting the bulge at her flanks once supple and smooth. He can't help thinking as she turns from view that a younger woman with a Cadillac butt could manage to light his fire tonight. He cancels the thought with a wave of his hand: *She could be a rodeo queen a perfect 10 it wouldn't matter I'm tired I guess I 'm growin old.* He hears the snap of beercans opening, gurgle of liquid being being poured. "Shit," he mutters, staring glazed at the TV screen, a pair of awesome big-horned rams colliding head to head. He is glad the sound is off. He hears the click of Priscilla's shoes and drops his eyes to the sports page.

"Here we are," she sings, "Would you clear a space for me, Stan?" She is bearing a copper tray with two mugs of beer that are mostly foam, along with their sweating cans. Stanley is irked at the sight of the foam. He shoves the children's art aside, and Priscilla sets the tray on the coffee table, then rounds the table and plops to his right on the sofa. She sighs, leaning forward to hand him a mug and taking one for herself. "Cheers," she says, saluting with her mug and quaffing enthusiastically.

"What're the mugs for?" he asks.

She wipes the foam from her upper lip, "What do you mean?"

"Why the mugs instead of cans?"

"Oh, I just thought I'd fancy things up a little." She takes a can from the copper tray, filling her mug to the top again.

"Did you chill the mugs?"

"Why should I chill the mugs, Stan? The beer's already ice cold."

"That's *right,* Priscilla. The beer is cold till you pour it into a mug that's warm. Then the mug gets cold and the beer gets warm. The mug steals the cold out of the beer."

She glares at him, "Shall I get you another beer, Stanley?"

"No," he mutters, "thank you." He sips his foam and ogles the sports page, seeing nothing, hearing Priscilla slurp at her beer and refill her mug.

"Well," she says, "I wonder what the movie is tonight." Stanley is silent. "The late-night movie on the tube." Silence. "You wouldn't know what the movie is tonight, would you, Stan?"

"First off, Priscilla," he says, annoyed, "there isn't just *one* movie on TV tonight, there's several. We have cable. We have 36 expensive channels. We're modern."

"What's second off?"

"What do you mean?"

"You said, 'First off,' we have this and that. What's second off?"

"Second off, there's a TV section in the paper here that you can read as well as me." He tables his beer and rummages through the newspaper on the cushion between them. He cannot find the TV section. He scoops up the paper and dumps it on her lap and grabs his mug for a gulp of foam.

"Thanks," she says, tilting and draining and sucking at her mug, "Here's lookin at you, Stanley—can I get you another beer?" He stares at her, astonished, unspeaking, and she rises, spilling the newspaper onto the floor, and marches to the kitchen. Stanley hears the snap of a can being opened. He sniffs the acid of discontent beneath his arms and stares at the paper as Priscilla returns with a clicking of her busy flats. She stops at the table just to his left and switches the lamp to its lowest setting and sweeps round the sofa to sit beside him closer than before. She pours herself a mugful of beer, slurping from it and leaning her head against the couch, "Stanley?"

"Yeah?"

"Isn't it nice and peaceful with the kids asleep?"

"Peaceful?"

"Here we are, just the two of us. It's Saturday night. We're sittin on the couch. The TV's on, but we're not watchin it. We're just sittin here enjoyin each other, like we used to do when we were first married—remember?" She chugs and swallows from her mug.

"Hadn't you best go easy on that beer?"

"Why, Stanley?" She empties her mug and fills it again, dropping the can with a clink on the metal tray. "It's Saturday night," she sings, "It'll soon be *midnight* Saturday night. People have *fun* on Saturday night. They eat, they drink, they dance and get*wild* on Saturday night." She swigs from her beer and grins at him, wiping the foam from her nose and mouth.

"Yeah?" he says, "Fun? You're gonna have a Saturday *night* mare if you keep swillin that brew." He is sweating at the base of his scalp.

"Oh yeah?" She empties her mug and smacks her lips and stands from the couch unsteady on her feet. "We'll see about that. Could I interest *you* in another cold *brew*, big fella?"

"No, thanks," he mutters, glaring at the sports page, "I'm losin my appetite."

"That is God's undyin truth." She lurches off with mug in hand, veering left away from the kitchen toward the corridor.

"You goin to bed?" he asks

"You'll see," chimes Priscilla as she vanishes into the hallway. Stanley hears a clank of glass on bathroom tile, followed by the tinkle and splash of his wife on the bowl. "Shit," he mutters, staring incensed at the TV screen, a scene of war in the Middle East, house-to-house combat, swarthy Moslems heaving grenades at tanks approaching on a dusty street, blasting walls to heaps of rubble smoking in the desert sun. Stanley smiles amidst his grief: *She's losin it now like the Middle East. I hope she doesn't blow up the house* . He sips the rest of the beer in his mug and sets it down on the coffee table, mopping his face with the sleeve of his shirt and smelling the ooze of his terror again, like peanut butter gone bad. He hears another can being opened, click of her flats on the wooden floor, and he gasps aloud as she stops beside him switching off the lamp completely, darkening the room except for the flicker of the Magnavox. Then she is suddenly nestled at his shoulder, smelling of beer and Estee Lauder, sipping her foam and purring six inches from his ear, "Now it's just the two of us, Stan, on Saturday night. Isn't it nice and cozy in here?"

Stanley panics and grabs his beer can squeezing it tight, "I thought you wanted to see a movie, Priscilla."

"Later, Stan. I'd rather us make our own movie."

"What're you talkin about?" He slugs at his beer, as does Priscilla, who burps, saying "Oops." She snuggles closer to him, "I want to make an X-rated movie with you, Stan—a dirty picture in our livin room, just like we used to, remember? Boom, boom, boom all over the room." She sets her mug on the coffee table, knocking over an empty can, then turns to face him and reaches for his hair. He is sweating profusely now, staring rivets at the Magnavox, "Come on, Priscilla."

"I *want* to come, Stanley. I want *you* to come, too." She strokes his hair and pops a snap on her cowgirl shirt, then another and still another, pulling the shirt away from her shoulder flaming white. "Do you recall what attracted me, Stan, that very first night at the Broken Spoke? It was your*smell* when we were dancin. You had a smell of *leather,* Stan—like a man who worked with horses and bulls—like the Marlboro Man!" She is pressing hard against him, opening his shirt and caressing his chest, now close to bursting with horror and rage. "You *still* have that smell upon you," she growls, "and I am turned on. I aim to make an X-rated movie with you tonight." She has managed to loosen his belt and starts unzipping his fly. "This one'll even have sodomy in it, cause I aim to mount that wild buckin bull in your pants!" He cracks and shouts,*"Goddammit, Priscilla!"* He shoves her back and jumps from the couch, clasping his pants with a trembling hand: "What the fuck is wrong with you? Have you gone out of your fuckin mind?"

"Yes!" she screams, "My fuckless body is drivin me out of my fuckin mind—you turd!"

"Don't use that language in my presence!" he shouts, flailing his beercan, sloshing his fingers, "And stop that screamin or you'll wake the kids!" He wheels in fury toward the kitchen door, clutching his pants and his near-empty can. The kitchen is lighted by a tiny lamp. He slams the can on a wooden counter and stuffs his shirt end and buckles and zips and towels his fingers on his blue Sears pants. He paws his forehead steaming about his fractured brain: *Oh God oh Christ it's idiot's night sweet love to fight to need a drink.* He opens a cupboard and seizes a fifth uncapping the bottle and sucking a swizzle of soothing fire. Then, hands quaking, he pours a half-pint of bourbon into his beer can, spilling some, and stows the fifth and grabs the can as he leaves the kitchen. Priscilla is slumped on the couch in tears, her pale shoulder awash with color from the TV screen. Stanley pauses, sipping his bourbon. He bends at the lamp and switches it on and settles next to his injured wife, planting his bourbon on the coffee table. He grabs her shoulder and heaves her gently to a sitting position. She jerks from his touch, snatching her shirt back over her bra and glaring at him with eyes gone liquid and makeup-smudged, but volatile nonetheless. Stanley sighs, "Look, Priscilla, I'm sorry. I'm tired. I'm plumb wore out, honey. I clocked 58 hours at the shop this week. That's 18 hours of overtime for you and the kids. I need some rest. Let's wake up early in the mornin and do it."

"I *knew* it," sneers Priscilla, "That's what you always say. And then in the mornin you will have a stomachache, a toothache, a headache, or a cramp in your smelly toe."

"*You're* the who's due for a headache, Miss Priscilla Beerdrinker. Why don't you try to straighten up? Here," he fumes, reaching for the newspaper crumpled on the floor, "Let's watch a movie on the tube."

"No!" she yelps, snapping the paper from his hands, "*You* watch a movie, Mister Mouse. I'm gonna spend some of your almighty overtime money." She rifles through the paper to the classified ads. "On what?" asks Stanley, amused, "An X-rated movie downtown?"

"No!" She grabs her mug for a swallow of beer. "Phew!" she scowls, "It's hot—unlike yourself." She replaces the mug and claps through the pages of the classifieds. "Here they are," she exults: "Massage parlors. I hear they have them for women now—salons where a woman can go for a good stiff fuck." Stanley winces reaching for his bourbon, "Oh? I hadn't heard that." He tastes his whiskey mixed with beer and sees the sports page flattened beside him. He picks it up as Priscilla exclaims, "Here's one! 'Mister Magic, the Massage Master. Treat yourself to a command performance at—"

"Let me see that," Stanley huffs, grabbing the paper from his wife. He finds the ad in a little box and smiles, snorting, "I thought so, Priscilla. Mister Magic is for 'Gentlemen Only,' unquote." He hands her the paper and turns to the sports page, sipping more of the bilge in his can, seeking the shelter of drunkenness. "Hey, Stanley," Priscilla pipes, "Here's an ad that is just your speed. Hah! You don't have to move a muscle for this one. It's a voice on the telephone. 'Golden Throat,' it says—you listenin, Stan?" He doesn't respond. "'Golden Throat, the Queen of the Midnight Telephone. Whisper her your fantasies, and she will whisper your fantasies back. MasterCard, Visa, and American Express.' Hear that, Stan?" No response. "Stanley?" Her voice has weakened, perhaps from fatigue, and Stanley turns to her speaking softly: "Haven't we had enough of this, Priscilla? Why don't you watch a movie on TV?" She blinks, fighting tears, and he faces away from her stripped completely of anything further to say or do. He sucks a deadly swig of his potion, *Goddammit all to hell the girl poor girl.* He stares at the sports page, startled to find it upside down, and he sighs. Priscilla is frozen for a long time. Then she stirs unspeaking beside him, dropping the paper on the couch and rising, walking slowly toward the corridor. He cannot watch her leave. He sips from his vessel another slam and turns to peer at the TV screen, a Chevy commercial on the beach at dusk, a scarlet sport coupe racing the tide with eight fuzzy headlamps instead of four. Stanley shakes his head abuzzing, hears a distant flushing sound and slumps to whisper hoarse, "Goodnight, darlin—I love you."

Priscilla trudges into the bedroom, leaving the door ajar for light, and sheds her jeans, her shirt and bra, and drapes them over a chair near the bed. She finds the negligee black and shining where she had tossed it earlier tonight and smiles amidst her grief, *Why not?* She slips her body into the gown, cupping her breasts still proud in her hands, for warmth, and caresses her thighs and hips still fevered and aching, *Oh Stanley I'm sorry it would've been fun.* She dabs at the tears in her puffy eyes and lifts the covers to sink into bed and soon she is drifting on a smooth dark river of forgetfulness.

Stanley has gotten a lot drunker a lot faster than he had expected, and he wants to commit some raucous unforgivable deed, *Let 'er rip Goddammit and tomorrow be damned.* He tips his can of whiskey to his lips and squints at the woman on the TV screen, a country singer in a sequined gown low-slung at her breasts, which seem on the verge of popping into his open mouth. He swallows, astonished at the heat in his loins. He blinks. He peeks at the hallway, empty and quiet, and turns with stealth to the classified ads on the sofa beside him. He grabs the paper and scans the columns until he finds the ad in question, "Golden Throat, the Queen of the Midnight Telephone." He folds the paper atop his knees, glancing toward the corridor, and pivots left to the telephone sitting on the table with the lamp. Gulping for breath and courage to act, he clasps the receiver to his burning ear and punches the number in the classified, squinting at the ad to be sure he is right. His belly convulses as the phone starts ringing on the other end, and he reaches for his can of liquid damnation.

Well, fuck—there's the Goddamn phone again. She stands from the pot and hoists her panties up over her bulbous thighs and around the marshmallow tiers of her waist. "Got to cut back on those bon-bons," she clucks, trundling into a shabby room where her phone is ringing on the floor near a massive oriental pillow. She descends to the pillow in a lotus position and adjusts her tits, like half-filled water balloons, and reaches to her carton of chocolate bon-bons. She pops a sweet one into her mouth as she answers the phone: "Hello, Darling. Golden Throat has been waiting for your call. What took you so long?"

Stanley gasps at the honey-soaked voice on the telephone, husky and rich and savagely intimate. He is electrified, scalp atingle, and he stammers, "Well, I ah, uhm—"

"Why would you want to torment me so, you luscious man?"

"No, agh," he protests, whispering, glancing at the corridor, "I, ahm—"

"Poor darling. That naughty thing between your legs is limp again, and you want it hot and hard, don't you?"

"Umph," he croaks, his penis stirring, "I, uh, ahm—"

"Have you a charge card, darling?"

"Uhm, ah—yes!"

"What kind, sweetness?"

"Mum, Mumm, Mummah—"

"Mastercard?"

"Yes!" he gasps.

"Read me the number from your Mastercard, darling. Then we'll go very deep and hot, you and I."

"Umph," he sputters, brain stampeding: "How, uh, how, uhm—"

"How deep?"

"How much?" His voice cracks.

"Twenty dollars for twenty celestial minutes, darling—may I have your number?"

"Uhm, ah—yeah! Za secont!" Trembling, fingers clamped in a sweat round the phone, he sets his whiskey on the coffee table, glancing at the hallway, dark and brooding. He claws his wallet from his right hip pocket and cradles the phone against his shoulder, freeing his hand to extract the card from its sleeve. His heart is pounding and his groin is hot, his penis climbing for the woman who waits, who breathes and sucks and whispers tawny on the telephone, *Christ what a stunner ungodly fuck she must oh jungle cat.* He plucks the card from his billfold, lifting his arm to wipe the terror from his seething face, and the telephone squirts like a slippery fish from between his shoulder and ear. He lunges to catch and fumbles it crashing onto the coffee table, spilling a clatter of empty cans to the hardwood floor. He snatches the phone back up to his ear and stabs his eyes at the corridor, gasping for breath, expecting a dreaded light or sound. It does not come. He sighs.

Priscilla shifts on her fluffy pillow, awakened by a noise in the house. She blinks and listens in the semidark, her pulse disturbed, and hears her husband stammering low in the living room, *Am I dreamin is he talkin on the phone?* She rolls to her left, to the phone next the bed, and deftly steals the receiver to her ear, "So that we may come together," intones a smoky female voice, jolting Priscilla from her dreams. "Yes, yes, darling," says Stanley, who seems to be choking for air, "Mumm, mummah card is, *num*ber is 730475981!" He spits out the digits, and Priscilla smiles in spite of her thundering heart. "Thank you, darling," says the siren's voice: "Now tell me—are you comfortable?"

"Well, umph," gags Stanley.

"Is the room you are in quite warm, my darling?"

"Yes, yes!"

"Let's unfasten our trousers, then, shall we? Golden Throat wants to see that rod of yours. I want you to hold it out for me, so that I may touch it and lick it for you—for both of us." Priscilla is astounded. The siren seems already to be sucking on someone's rod, and her voice is alluring even to Priscilla, who tightens her thighs against her crotch beginning to throb anew tonight, in defiance of her brain, *I'm mad insane to divorce and strangle and gouge her eyes.* Stanley is breathing rougher now, and Priscilla hears him thrashing on the couch as he struggles, evidently with his pants. Golden Throat is breathing, too. "I am undressing with you, darling. I am slipping from my black lace panties and my peekaboo bra but I am leaving my fishnet stockings on just for you. My tits are firm as ripened pears. My nipples are pink and taut and tingling with desire for you, darling. I want your mouth upon my tits. My thighs are young and hot with hunger for your stiffening prod, and I am walking toward you." Priscilla is seized with a spasm inflaming her own young thighs, her splendid breasts, her nipples as taut as Golden Throat's, her glands exuding an electric fluid at the mound upheaving between her legs. She touches the wetness through her gown and breathes with Stanley the siren's cadence, "I am stepping closer to you, darling. My tits are dancing in the light. My Venus is wet and swollen with lust—are you hard for me?"

"God-*damn!*'" he cries.

"I am kneeling before you," she moans, "I am licking your cock with my velvet tongue. I am—"

"God-*damn!*'" howls Priscilla, shucking the covers and dropping the phone as she springs from her bed and dashes into the living room. Stanley is angled rigid on the couch, his pants at his ankles and cock in his hand, a towering shaft with balls like plums that dangle over the sofa's edge. His shirt is open at his panther's chest, his muscles gleaming in the jungle dawn, and he stares at Priscilla with feral eyes stunned wide and black, his mouth agape beneath his black mustache. He seems unaware of the telephone stuck to his ear. Priscilla bolts toward him lifting her gown above her Venus soaking hot and thumping with the triumph in her blood. She kneels before him, gown at her waist, and draws his hand from his upthrust cock and licks his balls and sucks his cock protruding stiff and flinching in her mouth. She smells the sap of wildness in his pores. She groans arising and mounts him now and settles slowly atop his pride, his animal knob, a column of heat that fills her body and travels hard through the melting rings and depths of creation, dark and dazzling. "Oh God Priscilla!" he weeps, ungripping the phone and ripping the gown from her quivering breast.

"Oh God Stanley!"

"I smell the flowers!"

"Me too!"

"Oh Jesus!"

"Oh Lord!"

"Oh!"

"Oh!"

Sitting serenely on her Chinese pillow, she ponders the telephone, emitting conjugal sounds in her hand. She hangs up the phone and scratches a titfold, itching with sweat, and plucks from the carton a chocolate bon-bon, crossing herself like a Carmelite in sacred respect for the mystery of death and resurrection. She loves her work.

Kathleen Thoma

An Earthquake in Mexico

Brian Yansky

There was an earthquake in Mexico the day Felt lost his job at the Feed Mill. Reading about it in the paper that evening, he thought, "We're not so bad off. There are others who are worse off than we are."

He was sitting in the living room and he called to his wife, who was in the kitchen doing the dishes. When she came into the room, wiping her hands with a dishtowel, he told her about the people in Mexico. She didn't say anything, so he added details that were not in the newspaper, but that he imagined must be true.

"I know there are others worse off than we are," she said.

He noticed how she was wrapping the towel around her hand, but he said it anyway.

"A lot worse off," he said.

"I know there are others," she said. "I'm sorry for them. I really am sorry for them."

He was about to tell her he knew she was sorry when he realized she was crying. It was the kind of crying that comes out in a rush, and he felt his face tighten against it. She ran into the bedroom, still carrying the dishtowel. The door slammed shut behind her.

Felt didn't move from the Lazyboy recliner. He took another drink from his beer. She had no right to blame him, he thought. He wanted to tell her this, and to tell her she didn't need to worry because he was going to get another job. But he knew telling her these things would not change anything and that they were not what he really wanted to tell her anyway , so he sat in the recliner until he realized it was almost time for the news. Then he knew he could show her what he did not know how to tell her and that, when he showed her, she would stop crying and slamming doors and carrying the dishtowel all over the house. He got out of the chair and turned on the TV.

When the familiar face of the newsman with the smooth voice and the breaths in the right places came on, he turned up the volume so he would be sure he heard every word. The baby began to cry when he did this and, a moment later, Jenny came out of the bedroom and, keeping her back to him, walked down the hall.

He didn't say anything. He waited until the newsman said, "In Mexico today...," and then he walked back to the baby's room where Jenny was sitting in a chair, holding the baby, and he said, "I want to show you something." She didn't say anything so he said, "Please," and he pulled at her elbow, to help her up.

By the time they sat on the sofa, the TV screen was filled by crumbling buildings, and thick, jagged cracks in the earth cutting across lawns and houses, swallowing cars and dogs and people. Although they did not show the earth swallowing people, Felt imagined he saw them falling into the cracks and then the announcer said over a hundred bodies had been found and Felt knew he was right. After the announcer said this, it was night and quiet, except for the wailing and crying of the women. The camera showed the children sitting on the dirty pavement and a group of men who stood in a circle on a street corner, looking helpless and ashamed. The last camera shot was a close-up of a small girl with a dirt-smeared face whose brown eyes stared blankly into Felt's. Felt turned just in time to see Jenny bending over to brush her lips across the wisps of hair on their child's head.

"Now do you see?," he said. "Do you understand now?"

She said she was going to bed and she left him, sitting in front of the TV, drinking beer.

The next day Felt didn't get out of bed until noon. He dressed and went into the kitchen. From the window he saw Jenny in the back yard, trimming a bush her father had given them when they were first married. The bush had had a key on one of its branches, the key to the house where they now lived, with the down payment made and the loan co-signed and only thirty years of monthly payments left.

Felt walked out of the house as quietly as he could and drove downtown to Discount Liquors, where he purchased a quart of Jack Daniel's. He drove around for a while and then drove to the park because he wanted to get out of the car. He walked down a grassy hill to a sidewalk where there were rows of benches. An old man sat on one of the benches, feeding pigeons, and Felt asked the old man if he'd heard about the earthquake in Mexico, and, before the old man answered, he told him about it.

"It was a terrible thing," the old man said when Felt had finished.

"We don't know how good we have it," Felt said.

"No we don't," the old man agreed. "Some of us don't appreciate it, neither."

The man dumped the rest of the seeds onto the ground and said he had to be going. Felt took his place on the bench, the pigeons all around his feet, their heads bobbing up and down, as if they were all agreeing about something.

"No we don't," Felt said, taking a drink, watching the man walk away.

The old man's disapproving expression and erect posture reminded him of Jake, the foreman at the mill.

"I hate to do this," Jake had said when he'd fired him, "but I been bending over backwards for you, boy, and I can't go on with it. I can't have you gettin' drunk on company time, even if you are William White's son-in-law."

Jenny's father had called him that afternoon. He told Felt he'd told Jake they couldn't continue their friendship.

"I lost a good friend because of you," he'd said. "I know Jake. You must have pushed him pretty far."

"I pushed him," Felt had agreed.

"I don't know what's wrong with you, boy. I don't even care to know anymore. You just keep as clear of me as you can. Do we understand each other?"

"Yes," Felt had said, but he had known it was a lie. They would never understand each other and the old men with erect postures and approving and disapproving expressions would never understand that it was only luck that placed them near a fertile earth instead of an earth that cracked open like an egg. They would never know that the pictures on the news were real. That they were as real as the face of their spouse or the voices of their children.

Felt took another drink from the bottle and got up and walked down the sidewalk. He thought of his father as he walked and he knew he was once an erect young man with approving and disapproving expressions and that, if he had lived, he probably would have been like Jenny's father. But he had died when Felt was thirteen and Felt remembered him best as a man without hair, as small in body as a boy, (smaller than he had been at the time), with a starved look, as if he could not get enough to eat. In the beginning, his father did not believe the doctors. But he had had to give in and eventually he gave in all the way and, by the time he did ,it did not seem to matter much to him.

As Felt walked by the concession stand, he noticed a phone booth and decided he would call someone. He wanted someone who would keep his mind from sullen memories and thoughts of old men, so he called Rick Miller.

Rick Miller lived in the basement of his mother's house. He had enlisted in the army when he got out of high school and then went A.W.O.L. After a few months in a mental hospital, they gave him a dishonorable discharge, which he claimed suited him just fine. Since then, he had lived in his mother's basement and stayed drunk as much of the time as was possible.

When Felt asked him if he'd like to join him for a beer he said, "Sure, but I'm broke," just as he always said.

"I'll pick you up in ten minutes," Felt said.

"I'll owe you," Rick said.

He does owe me, Felt thought, just as he owes everybody else he knows. And that is all he will ever do is owe. Still, if he liked you enough and was drunk enough and in a good mood and it was late at night and you had spent all your money buying the both of you drinks, he would discover a five-dollar bill in his pocket and he would stare at it as if it was a gift from heaven.

As Felt walked back toward the car, he thought of how it would be when Rick discovered the five-dollar bill and he thought it would be worth spending all the money he had on him to see it. To see Rick, who was young and did not disapprove or approve of much and who had round shoulders, look at the five-dollar bill and say, "Ain't it a miracle?," and laugh, because it was exactly what he thought a miracle should be—a hidden five dollar bill when everything else was gone.

Jenny waited supper until six o'clock. She ate most of what she'd cooked for both of them and threw the rest away. She left the dishes in the sink, and went into the living room and sat on the Lazyboy recliner. She closed her eyes, but did not sleep. "I knew he was going to miss dinner," she thought. It was the first time she'd known. Other times she'd thought he would, but there had always been, in the back of her mind, the image of him slamming the front door shut and walking in, apologizing and grinning like a boy late for class. But this time she had known and, while it was no revelation, it made her sad, just as finding out sex was not always fireworks and love could not survive everything had made her sad.

When the phone rang Jenny ran across the room, hoping to get to the receiver before the ringing woke the baby.

"Hello," the voice said. "Jen? Hello."

Before she could stop herself, she'd slammed the receiver down. She was a child again and her mother asked her why there were two C's written beside Math and Science on her report card.

"Because I hate Math and Science."

"What did I do to deserve such treatment?"

"Nothing."

"Then why?"

"I told you."

"But why?"

"Because I hate you. I hate you."

She ran upstairs and slammed her door and cried and later apologized and her mother had said, "Someday you'll have children. Someday you'll understand."

She picked up the receiver on the second ring. "Sorry, mother," she said. "The baby was slipping out of my arms."

"Don't rush yourself, dear. You have to be careful with a child that age."

"I am careful."

"Of course you are, dear."

"Well I am."

"Is everything all right?"

"Yes."

"Did Felt tell you your father had talked to him?"

"Dad talked to Felt?"

"He was very upset."

She did not want to cry. Why did she always cry? But once she had started, it was hard to stop and her mother saying, "Jen? Jen?," just made it worse. Why did he have to say, "I won't quit this job until I've got my ten-year pin in my pocket."

"He left a note," she said into the phone. "He left a note taped to the refrigerator saying I was supposed to send his lunch to those kids in Mexico. How can I do that?"

"You can't," her mother assured her.

Jenny held the receiver away from her ear and her breaths became more regular and the tears stopped and she was ashamed. She apologized to her mother.

"I'm just not feeling well today," Jenny said.

"Of course not, dear. You have every right not to feel well. Why don't you and Ann stay over here tonight. "

"I don't think so mother."

"Jen, you can't stay there. He's making your life miserable. Why don't you come home, temporarily? Your father will talk to the lawyer. Everything would be settled for you, Jen."

"I can't, Mom."

"We could get the house back for you. You could start over. You've got to think of Ann. What will he be like in five years?"

"Things might change," Jenny said.

"Things do not just change," her mother shouted. "Jennifer, you have been saying that since you were fifteen. Don't you think I heard you? We gave you everything you wanted and still you said, 'Things might change', like they were so bad you had to wish on a star. You have always had your head in the clouds. You have always—" but her voice failed her, and there was silence.

"I'll call you tomorrow," Jenny said.

"No, wait," her mother said. "I'm sorry, Jen."

"It's okay," Jenny said. "I'll call you."

"Your father has been a perfect terror today. I am sorry, dear. We'll talk tomorrow."

Jenny put the receiver into the cradle. The baby began to cry. For once, she was grateful. She would feed her and rock her and she would become silent and content and it would be as simple as that for years to come.

Felt didn't come home until Jenny was already in bed. She heard him in the kitchen. The sound of a pan hitting the floor. His voice cursing it.

She wasn't going to get up. She was going to lie there no matter how many pans hit the floor, but the baby began to cry and she sat up, and slipped on her slippers and walked over to the closet and got her robe. She opened the door quietly and stepped out into the hall.

"So the baby's crying," he shouted. "I suppose I did that, too. Now you can blame me for that."

She turned around and went to the edge of the kitchen, ignoring the baby, because she wanted to tell him to try to be quiet. He was standing by the stove, leaning slightly, as if the house were slanted that way. His eyes were red, and his hair looked as if he'd been standing in a strong wind.

She watched him break eggs on the side of a skillet. One of the eggs fell onto the floor, breaking open.

"What is wrong with you?," she said suddenly, forgetting what she was going to ask him when she saw the yellow spreading across her kitchen floor. "Just what is wrong with you?"

"What?" he said.

"Forget it," she said.

"You. You're what's wrong with me."

She did not cry. She looked at the egg.

"Are you going to clean up that egg?"

"That egg?," he said.

"Forget it," she said.

He ripped open the egg carton and dumped the eggs onto the floor.

"Don't try to tell me what to do," he shouted. "I don't need you to tell me what to do."

"Stop yelling," she yelled.

He looked at her as if he did not even know her, as if she were not even real. He began by throwing the dirty dishes on the floor and then he opened the cabinet doors.

She ran into the baby's room and picked up the baby and sat on the floor in a corner and held her as close as she could. The crashing of dishes and pans was drowned in the sounds of the shaking earth, the collapsing structures and cracks splitting the house and world in two, until there was the deadly silence of a man falling, as the earth swallowed him up.

K. Thoma

Dot

Isabella Russell-Ides

I have no great hopes of getting to the end of this story. If I get to the end, it will end in a small tent on a California beach. Perhaps in twenty years time, the government will have already purchased every home on the coast and dismantled them stick by brick, sometimes with the help of the elemental water who has, waves down, approved this project. I will be at the beach because the colors there are not surreal and have nothing to do with dimestore palette. No red and yellow anyone could mix has anything to do with what really never is an orange sun, nothing to do with that color on Hallmark Halloween cards. And no one's ever going to convince me that the water is blue or green or grey and neither is the sand any color you can put a name to: it'll resist any poetry anyone could rudely invent.

Meanwhile, I have to live in this large and quite beautiful White House in the middle of a downtown that is scraping up the sky. The French doors, sixteen of them, let in light through the mullion laddered glass and open, when I do open them, onto the sidewalk. Real estate claimed the lawn and some of the monies are federally supporting the California reclamation of the coast project. Mostly, though, I keep the doors closed because of all the little black children who want to get into my white living room and play basketball in their Adidas. They make quite a racket running around in their striped feet, dribbling their orange balls on the oak floors.

Old Jules chases them with a revolutionary musket we keep on the mantle above the fireplace. Old Jules is getting a little dotty and is never quite sure what century he is operating in. Too many movies. But the kids are quick and make the transitions with him. If they are Red Coats, they bop him on the bean with their cannon balls. If they are Indians, they ambush him in the Rose garden. Old Jules complains to The President and gets decorated for valorous conduct. He looks pretty crackerjack sporting his medals. He's a proud man and has been decorated so many times we ought to string him with twinkle lights, let him be the Christmas tree this year. Jules would like that. He appreciates attention and someone's got to keep the kids in line.

Not that they aren't cute. One four year-old is in my dining room right now, tugging at my skirt. This kid has every possible imaginable shape and color of plastic barrettes clipped onto an impossible number of braided ponytails. Her mother, Sister Maybelline, whom I invited to luncheon, is an Excedrin headache, though I suppose it is not her cuckoo fault that she married a Baptist preacher and carries on her cuckoo hosannas over the tea cakes. It's not easy being The First Woman President.

My credibility quotient took a small nose dive in last week's polls, under the confidence of the black community category. So I'll have a few luncheons, pin a few medals, get my white face and some black face on the front pages of the dailies. Dots, that's what they call it. Dots in the newspapers. Dots on the TV screen. Need some Black dots. Need some Soviet dots. Need some Central American dots. Need to cut back on the Mideast dots. Too many Jewish dots. Need some Baptist dots.

When the party boys first approached me about running, I told them flat out, I didn't know shit about running a country. They said not to worry. I had the great American face. I'd make great dots. The divorce was a slight smear on an otherwise perfect media face but it was a quiet no muss no fuss divorce and then my ex conveniently died so he was not about to surprise us with any unexpected dots. Besides, no one has figured out what to do with a First Husband. There was one definite media problem we wouldn't have to deal with. And what are we anyway, but millions and millions of atomic dots. It's a dot situation no matter which way you look at it.

I had great former astronaut dots, consumer advocate dots, ecological dots. I admit I look pretty smashing in my Whole Earth khaki-covered hiking shorts, Sir Argyle knee socks and waffle stompers, with my sun-browned Jane Fonda built body filling out the curves nicely (better than Jane even, I'm not afraid to carry a little weight) and I am cooking fresh trout in the great American outdoors with my two wombees gathering firewood and looking pretty smashing themselves in their camping outfits. It was a Girl Scout postcard anyone could send with love to America and not be ashamed, kind courteous brave and at home on the range. There was no way around it. I made great dots. So I said, why not? I was getting bored with my current cowboy, the kid's algebra problems and the lecture tour circuit. The boys said they liked my on the one hand/ on the other hand lecture style and it would suit the for it/against it policy stands they liked their candidates to take.

We sat around a big oak conference table in the apocryphal smoke filled room when we selected my running mate. There were styrofoam cups filled with cold Maxwell House and Chinese takee outee cartons carrying little loads of Italian pasta and Delmonte sauce across our American dream. I thought about the goldfish I brought home from a carnival when the ping pong ball I tossed plopped in the glass fishbowl and I was the heroine of the school parking lot, carrying my Chinese carton of live gold to a better life and a bigger bowl and a rubber deepsea diver. Goldie and Aqua Man. We passed around eight by ten glossies of my possible future political fiances, looking for someone to balance my meal ticket, someone to make America believe in the chicken in every bucket, a universal Colonel Sanders, elegant southern gentleman farmer to round out my Yankee corners or a Lancelot for the new Camelot I would create. All those glossies and slides projected on a screen...it was just like the movies. Remember that scene in "Darling" where the oil slick advertising mogul picks Julie Christie to be his Cosmo girl? It was like that.

The wombees popped in during one of the breaks and surveyed the American litter on the conference table. Must be art, they say. The wombees are funsters. They say if you can't recognize it or if it looks strange, call it art. They come across a half constructed stairway or some technological debris or any adult behavior that looks deranged and it must be art, that's what the kids say. The wombees think art is a joke or actually The Joke that my generation invented, its favorite euphemism. Don't blame us, they say, blame Pie-casso. You try to tell them that something is art. Big giggle. They say, yeah, right, and the stork brought it.

So what's up, mom? I tell them I am selecting my running mate, my Cosmo boy. They say, you're getting dangerously close to yourself, mom. Heads pop up around the conference table. The wombees are masters of the oblique remark. I shrug my shoulders. Kids, I say.

I give them that look that mothers are masters of that says disappear pronto and I mean yesterday, and poof! they're gone. They're good kids.

I can see the boys are impressed by my highhanded, quick but subtle exercise of maternal power. I've got their attention, so I figure the time is ripe for me to put in my two cents' worth. I've got some suggestions of my own to make. Fire away, Dot, we're all eyes. As I call out the names, someone flashes the appropriate images on the screen and, as if on cue, they shout, face fire! Take two. I finally say, you've got to be kidding. This is the process? They say, Dot Dot Dot, only you can prevent face fire. What about Paul?, they say. Paul who? I ask, a little slow on the uptake. Despite my fantasies, I do my part, make my effort to keep one foot in the door of reality. Newman, Dot, Paul Newman. Now there's a face. There's a ticket. Dot and Paul. Play American Ball. What do you think? Who me? What do I know, I say, he makes great salad dressing and his marinara's not too shabby. Get serious, girl, Paul's worth his weight in... wait, don't tell me, in dots. Right? You've got it.

Okay buddies, let's say it's Dot and Paul, what about my policy? What about the platform we haven't discussed. What am I for and what am I against? That's it, Dot. You're for it and against it right down the line drive. You're checkered. Black and White. Checkered dots? Exactly. Take the bomb. The big one. You're for it and against it. The bomb's your pal Dot, but you hate it. Got it? O Say Can You See. Dot and Paul. Play American Ball.

So that's how it all got started. About my photo opportunity luncheon guest, the Baptist minister's wife, the one whose kid is tugging at my shirt. She's the First Hostess of the LMNOP&Q Club. They've got a national network TV show, that's the Love Message Negro Organization for Peace and Quiet. Lots of dots. So when my black confidence points dropped last week, the boys came up with a real doozy: The President's Bible Basketball Welfare Fund. I asked my party boys if we weren't going to get into a little bit of trouble with this one. They said, naw, America loves ball. I said what about the ACLU cheerleaders and the fans of the Bill of Rights? That's a small fan club, Dot. Not to worry. Besides this was just phase one of The President's Prayer Ball Program. No prob, we'll call it the All-American Bill of Rights Ecumenical Prayer Ball Movement. Cover all the bases. I'd never seen the boys get so excited. They were slam dunking invisible balls through invisible nets, slapping each other's rear-ends, making low whistle noises when they knocked one out of the invisible stadium. It looked like air ball to me. Just like the boys play air guitar when they watch MTV.

Listen up, Dot. We'll hand out little Korans with the ping pong grants, Bhagavad Gitas for the California tennis set, American flags and a Bill of Rights with the baseballs. Or how about this...hit a homer for an omer. It's a whole new concept in welfare, Prayer Ball with a pursuit of happiness twist. I interrupt their World Series and ask about Madalyn and her Atheist pals down in Austin, Texas. Whiffle balls, Dot. No matter how hard you hit them, they don't go anywhere. And it goes without saying, you get your basic capitalist bible with the golf balls. That'd be Adam Smith's "Wealth of Nations?", I ask. You got it, Dot. We don't leave anyone out. The Old Testament with the pigskins (no one's going to argue but that that game's pure Christian). What about the Talmud, buddies? We're working on it, Dot. We're thinking maybe marbles. Marbles? Not to worry. Remember, you're for it and against it. How can I be against it if it is the President's Program? Dot, we love you darling, trust us. Your bottom line policy is always for it and against it.

So talk about sur-reality here, as if this planet weren't tilted enough as it already is, I am about to appoint Sister Maybelline the First Commissioner of Bible Basketball Welfare. You say it couldn't happen in America. You tell me where else it could happen. I admit my spiritual capital is getting stretched a little thin. But think about it. Someone asks you to be The First Woman President of America. You get caught up in it...all those glossies. My cabinet, Oscar material, every last one.

Sister Maybelline is a real eye party herself, with her pink choir robe and satin spiked heels. She doesn't approve of a female President of America. She says all the kings were men: Martin, Elvis, Ali. Praise the Lord! And while she is praising and we are waiting for the TV crew to arrive, her kid is tugging at my skirt, as I said, and bouncing in that bouncy whining way four year olds do. Just now she is saying, tell my mommy, tell my mommy I'm not colored. Everyone wants the opinion of the President. I have been ignoring her. I have been ignoring her through three martinis disguised, not without ingenuity, as tea. So what the fuck, I reconsider to myself and I tell her no, she's not colored. It's not entirely untrue. She isn't any more colored than the water and finally she starts paying attention to the cat in the corner, which seems an appropriate response. However, poetry and politics don't mix so, of course, the hosanna momma is pissed. Damn, it's not easy being the President. I'm not really worried though.

Sister Maybelline will smile when the TV cameras roll in. She needs the dots as much as I do.

Any minute now my own two wombees, as opposed to all the adoptees, will come bouncing down the stairs with their algebra problems. Tutors notwithstanding, they too want the opinions and the attention of the President. The first family is restless and I am just as tired as the kids of over au gratin and fishy stuff in wine sauce and tiny toasts so we're going out to dinner tonight. In spite of the hairy nukeheads pointed at the capitol, we are going to have our burgers. We'll show up in *Time* magazine, looking very American, squirting Heinz ketchup out of little foil bags over our golden fries.

This morning I spoke to Raskalnomoravich on the hot line. His kids don't have algebra problems. They want to be expressionist painters and wear American Levis. Okay Raskal, I say, let them wear Levis. He says I don't understand The Party. So send them to Siberia, I say, with acrylic paints and Levis and fucking forget it. He says, thanks Dot, you're an understanding woman. I say, hey Raskal, nothing I wouldn't do for a friend. I say, I've got to run now, get back to you tomorrow and we'll talk about the hairy nukeheads. Yeah, he says, right. So how's the algebra going, Dot? Not bad. You still slipping the pill in the wombee's o.j.? Hey, fuck off, Okay Raskal? Yeah, right, fuck off, he says.

So that's how the day, no matter what else, kicks off. The hotline call and poached eggs. In the first trimester we discussed Africa, Latin America, the Easteast, the Mideast, the Midwest, the Northwest, the Polar regions. Every morning over poached eggs I got indigestion. We never agreed about shit, me and Raskal. We still don't. I guess it's just more interesting talking about the kids. Neither of us figures we'll be in office long. The glamour's wearing thinner for The First Woman President, despite how pretty me and the wombees look eating our burgers in *Time* magazine. I wonder how much Raskal knows about the little media high- jinks the KGB boys have cooked up for my next electoral bid. I listen to that time bomb tick every night as I attempt to sink my ship of state into the percale ocean of white sheets.

And it's true, I do fuck the key members of the cabinet after the hot call, mostly one at a time, but sometimes we do it *à trois* when we are pressed for time. I realize the public's worst fears (and hopes) will be confirmed when I am posthumous and they publish my diaries. I had good intentions. I wanted to be a saint for future school kids to admire in their history books. I meant to maintain celibacy for the duration of my presidency. I had plenty of good memories to get me through. But you get caught up in it... all those glossies. I took a lot of flak from the press when I appointed my cabinet. All the innuendoes for enquiring minds. I read about what a wonderful time I wasn't even having and all of them, really gorgeous guys, not a face fire among them. So what the hell, I figured. I'll give them dots they'll never forget. Me & Paul. Me & Bob. Me & Charlton. Me & Paul & Bob & Charlton. And I haven't even mentioned the big one, the one that'll knock the faces of the soap stars right off the covers of the checkout stand weeklies for a decade of dots, at least. Yes, I fucked my way into power and I plan on fucking my way into heaven, if indeed that is a possibility.

Apart from that, my interest is only engaged talking about the kids. In the White House I'm still a housewife. Not even a perfect one of those. I get annoyed. Do you know what happens anywhere, to a women's tits when she hears a child cry? They get erect. No matter where or what or whose kid, no matter how you're trying not to pay attention, bullets rise right on your very own chest. Some foreign policy. Should I congratulate the press for being right all along in their suspicion that I cannot conduct foreign policy, that my interest will wane, my attention drift? My tits will tighten into knots.

I cannot even maintain the constituency of my erstwhile ideological sisters, who argue, not without eloquence and academic pedigree, that biology is no determinant. Hell, maybe they're not lying. Maybe it is possible to talk your tits out of their erections.

And speaking of erections, my whole carefully built media image could blow at any moment. My pals in the CIA tell me that the boys in the KGB have some pretty incriminating photos of me and Raskal. It was quite a summit. I got great press. Great disarmament concessions. Headlines. Line drives. Dot hits ball right out of the park. Raskal was the best I ever had. It was Henry the Kiss who said power was the best aphrodisiac and you couldn't disprove it by me. It's true neither of us is about to drop the big one on either of our respective wombees. The KGBs are thinking about leaking the photos to the western press just before my next election and while that certainly would create a lot of dots, Raskal is definitely a major face fire and I'd drop points on the polls faster than the vid kids zap starships off the screen. No one wants a prez who's afraid to drop the big one. Ah well. I have no regrets. Maybe one. Raskal was pretty pissed off when he found out I was on the pill. A lot of foreign guys are like that. They don't necessarily want to raise them, but they like to procreate. I admit, it would be nice if there was a little

Raskalnomoravich percolating in my womb, dividing his little dots, circling my inner circle to some Strauss waltz tune. Former astronaut incubating her own little astrodot/cosmonaut.

Raskal says you can reinvent the past. The comrades have no problem with that. Maybe I should consider thinking about having second thoughts about the diaries. Do a little rewriting. Reality has such a fictional ring. Maybe if I tried being fictional, I'd make better reality. I'm not worried about the kids. No matter what I write, they'll just call it art. Raskal spent quite a few years rewriting history in order to rewrite the future before his party boys made him the star of their movie. That's the problem. You keep getting cast in somebody else's movie. Or you start out swimming with millions of other sperm, carrying your own microscopic suitcase and you've already got a history of heartache packing in the DNA and then you're the one whipping your little tail faster than the rest and you hit the big one, the luminous round cosmic egg and you start making changes faster than you'll ever be able to keep up with. There are just too many dots to connect. And then the bomb drops, squalling in the arms of Ma and Da and takes it first breath, its first bath and is wrapped in Ma's lullabye and Da's uniform. Or whatever is the current or convenient or conventional disguise. In any case, whatever it is, you're already got it on you when you open your eyes.

There comes a time, you just want to wash some of it off. I mean the pool you're swimming in gets pretty muddy after awhile. Maybe I'll burn the diaries for starters. I won't even bother to rewrite. Oh I know you can't outrun the past. But I mean to make it run a little faster than it's accustomed to before it catches up with me. Maybe it'll trip over its own intentions and while it's bent over, bandaging its skinned knees, I'll cash in a few chance coupons with the future.

I'm going to cancel my Camp David retreat and take up Sister Maybelline's invitation to soak in her big plastic hot tub for a week, let her hosanna over me until the day is young, maybe get reborn some. The party boys will have to cancel the facelift they planned for my re-election. There are some dots I'd just as soon not rearrange. The KGBs can do whatever they want with their private collection of negative dots. They'd make great locker room pinups. Paul can be prez, or, if he doesn't want to stay in that movie, they can give the job to Old Jules. He practices his acceptance speech every time they give away Oscars on TV. I'll skip getting my footprints sunk in front of Grauman's Chinese. There are better places to sink your bare foot on this prayer ball. And dear Raskal, after I'm out of office and in case you're looking for The First Woman President of America, I hope you'll find me in a small tent on a California beach and I hope I'll be listening to something like the slap of a wave licking a color of sand no one can name.

Kathleen Thoma

On the Accidental Bombing of an Insane Asylum in Grenada by the United States

John Campion

After the war I had to go mad. One afternoon at the park, I grabbed a young boy by the throat and tried to strangle him. I naturally assumed that he had stopped, not to retie his shoe as he pretended, but to remove and hurl it into our midst. Though glad acquaintances were able to unpeel 10 fingers from around his throat, I still insist, with greater vindication than ever, that deductions concerning his ulterior motives were not farfetched.

Nighttimes, the paranoiac fear that neighbors, my so-called friends, cowled beasts of indefatigable patience, poised in the lurch, prowled the baffling links of alleyways down under the branchworks, waiting for the precise moment when I would drop my only guard, when indeed, I was to be the next victim, that they might feed, gripped my subconscious mind.

The site of the relentlessly placid asylum like a haunting melody to a deaf cobra left me enervated and expectant. I thought maybe in this place I would at least not murder anyone and prayed that nobody would murder me. The first appearance of my fellows, come from beneath the same mantle, reinforced my hope that maybe on this insignificant island, far away, I could be safe and live out a normal existence.

Initially, being strangers, we lived in suspended animation. We hovered about like specters wandering the halls, greeting one another with understanding, with knowledge. Time disintegrated. Gradually we began to trust one another. The ghostly feeling of the place began to vanish; our spirits held up the edifice. We were a family again. Happy. We almost forgot.

Various ones of us boldly struck out into the countryside all glad and dancing. We draped the building with ribbons. I remember a day when light from a triangular window glistened in a fellow's eye and burst round like a wonderful star upon our countenances.

All of us, suspecting a miracle, set up a stage and brought all kinds of fruits and colorful weeds from the wild pastures outside. We gathered leaves from the camphors, where lonely owls fly out toward points unknown seeking their wayward progeny. Made crowns for each and printed words on our palms. Draped the necks of farm animals with sea shells.

We held hands in the daylight, walked to the seawall, and waited for the monotonous waves to lull us asleep. We closed our eyes together and in our dreams did not lose one another in the labyrinthine forest pathways, but walked straight through. We placed a mirror on the ground, laying a fish upon it, and watched it soar through the sky.

With crown tilted at a friendly angle, legs up, I was watching the broomgrass and goatweed thither, when the sound of engines overhead brought a wind that sent them supplicating. Down below, the inmates were holding one another not as before. The chandelier swirled and creaked. A feathered hat flew across the field. The building began to collapse before we heard the explosion. Everything got slow. On the beach I saw the shock troops storm.

Later, a drunken soldiery, victorious under the cratered moon, went scot-free. Unreality lifted its windy head and bulbed out on the sand and rockscape. I felt a little like Mephistopheles in the window, and I felt a little like a hurt puppy, and a clown when the game is blown. The next minute passed.

The gang began to spin as in some bald-mountain ritual of witches. Someone was going to get burned at the stake. The room bounced and tossed. Ogres set up nine pins and began to bowl. A bull's tooth crawled up its nostrils. Paint boiled on the ceiling and, batlike, attached to my hair and denuded my skull top, hotfreezing a small patch, now cold forever. Mouths were open and closed. A pyramid of human form slanted, conglobated lamp bulb teetering on a point swelled and dropped.

Bodies grew gigantic and distorted. Space swallowed a fat elongated arm, five fingers wriggling through mid-air. A top began to twirl. An eyeball lost all hope. Stairs climbed up the wall. The building turned inside out. Guts slid from the cow's belly. A giant raised a knife and cut the roof off.

Rows of bombs exploded and ghosts grew up and stretched their limbs. Maniacal horses lifted their fetlocks and kicked at bombgeists. A child came flying through the air and out the door. A head became a holocaust.

Dogs were set on fire. The sand from the ocean covered us. Rocks pelted the floor. Our lungs were gunpowder. Banisters turned sidewise laddering spooks to heaven. Red faces fell out of their sockets. A toy skidded by.

Soldiers, no doubt misinformed, but who will do anything, riddled the building with rifle fire, scourging the skin off a few stragglers, while I triple-somersaulted through the turning window, lacerating glass tattooing the skin, my spirit barely resisting the urge to join my amputated leg in the hog trough. Walls began to expand as a circle of believers, unable to utter a sound before the spectacle, lost their last strand.

Invisible wires unwound, sprung out like *dementia praecox* in a distortion mirror, as the 37 dove a single word into the echo of a silent scream squatting on steel conduits and were buried alive, just before the explosion, an inverted milky-smoked tornado, vanished in their ears.

Miraculously in the haze, the dark cone reversed pyramidlike from ear hollows, where I saw them come forth astride the backs of fishes and glide straight through tree tops up to the round pearlescent moon.

Kathleen Thoma

Crossing Susie's Heart

Pat Ellis Taylor

my friend
who watches my transformations
like old hippies do for each other
part of the creed we learned
in the desert running together

if you go on a trip into poverty
the friend shares food stamps

when you come home the friend
will take a look at your photographs
yes
susie is there when the medicine
comes on and it's time
to take a walk
around the block

So Susie-my-old-friend calls from San Antonio and invites Leo and me to spend the night at her house for the New Year. She lives in the utmost utmost northern suburb of San Antonio; across from her house woods begin.

Susie is an artist and a transcendental meditator. We met in El Paso, I have known her for 15 years. She was a cartoonist, then a painter; first of large-sized adobe-colored nudes; then women who turned into birds and valleys; then of large canvases of sky and valley only, the women removed. These days her paintings are white canvases with lightly-colored lines drawn by a ruler making horizons and beams of light crossing them. The living room walls she hangs them on are also white. Her living room furniture is white canvas.

Leo says it's okay with him if we spend New Year's Eve with Susie and Straightman, her second husband. Even though they are boring.

Susie has only learned to be boring the hard way. She and Straightman each meditate two hours a day; otherwise they would go crazy with their boring lives.

Some people lead boring lives and they don't know it, so they are somewhat unhappy. But not so with Susie and Straightman. When even two hours of meditation isn't enough to calm nerves shot from too much boredom, Susie will call me long distance, and plead for me to come and see her. I am the only hippie friend she has left. Straightman doesn't have any friends except for the competitive energy-industry sales jocks he works with, so he gets sick with sinusitis, chakras even in meditation no doubt opaque with phlegm.

Susie wasn't married when I met her. I was married to somebody other than Leo and my sons Morgani and Rational were beginning grade school. But Susie's eye crosses a little bit like Morgani's, and then her birthday is the same as his, and these kinds of coincidences have kept us interested in each other.

When I first knew Susie, it was Snakeman she was with, not Straightman. Susie was a black-haired blue-eyed West Texas girl with high cheekbones. She grew up on the high and wide plains running down from the Davis Mountains, her father being the switchman for an isolated piece of railroad track; the only city she had visited while she was growing up was El Paso, several miles away.

Snakeman was a sculptor who was also dealing marijuana. I got my marijuana from him. He was living in an old adobe in the Upper Valley above El Paso making jewelry out of silver and turquoise amid marijuana bales.

Before Susie met Snakeman, she was an art education major at the University of Texas at El Paso, a sorority sister, and a member of the cheerleading squad. But Susie was wild, you could see it in her daft eye and wide and sweeping brush strokes. Snakeman could certainly see it in her.

One day he clung like a spider on the wall of the women's restroom in the art building above the door for an hour waiting for Susie; when she came through the door he swung down in front of her and hung by his toes. She was engaged to the son of a West Texas rancher, who owned a large piece of desert and looked forward to a long life of inherited prosperity under the calmness of large skies and title to large tracts of mountains and plains.

But after the vision was given to her of Snakeman's face hung upside down in front of her nose, she dropped out of school, and stopped going to sorority meetings, and did not cheerlead any more.

She became my friend. Snakeman was already my friend; we smoked marijuana together.

Susie sketched me sometimes. Because she was younger, she asked for my advice about things, recipes, vegetables to cook for Snakeman who was a vegetarian, Susie coming from consciousness where beef had been king of the daily menus, like all of us.

She smoked marijuana. She dropped acid. Her eyes got wilder and she became confused. There were many men who loved her, because she was so beautiful.

There was another El Paso marijuana dealer who loved her. He came and got her out of Snakeman's adobe one time and brought her into town. He put her in a room painted with rainbows and gave her more acid which she ate.

Her spirit went out of her body and clung to the corner where ceiling met wall just like Snakeman had once clung to jump in front of her. She saw her own Susie body incapacitated, the eyes unfocussed and the black hair loose and rich with strands of color, head slightly bobbing in the rivers of smoky air combining hair with walls.

Snakeman came in the room and shook her body. He picked her up and carried her out to the car, back out to the desert, to the adobe. Her spirit followed.

On a day not too much later, Snakeman called her from Las Cruces. He had been busted. He and his partner Alito were in Las Cruces jail.

There were 2500 dollars and 10 pounds of marijuana under the front seat of their VW van. The Las Cruces police took that and the IRS confiscated the van itself for assumed back taxes.

Well, Snakeman had a lot of friends. He was out on bond in no time. The case was eventually dropped because of misplaced technicalities. But when Snakeman came out of jail, he was broke and didn't want to deal marijuana anymore. He wanted to learn how to transcendentally meditate.

And Susie's spirit followed Snakeman's. They learned to transcendentally meditate together. They were the first two meditators on the El Paso border. Susie's wild eyes were taught a mantra and her eyelids given an excuse to slide down in the daytime without sleep covering her restlessness. And she became even more beautiful, eyes clear wide blue when she opened them up after meditating.

Meanwhile, I was struggling through my own first transformations. Susie was like my sister. I was dropping suburbia off my shoulders—dropping my job and my Mexican maid to stay home with my sons while she was ducking her sorority sisters and her rich fiancé. We had gotten our marijuana from the same source. We had split acid tabs.

So when she started meditating, I wanted to meditate, too. And I did get a mantra. I hummed it fairly steadily for about two years. But then other kinds of things occurred to me so that after a while I didn't meditate anymore, at least not in that maharishi-style. But Susie continued it.

And now Susie still continues it. First she meditated fifteen minutes a day. Now she meditates two hours. Every day for fifteen years. That's how long we've known each other.

Susie is really not boring, as you can see from this little bit of background. It is only Susie's present life that is boring.

Because Snakeman finally neglected her. He was very poor when he only meditated and didn't deal marijuana. He made jewelry but never fast enough to get ahead of the bills. Sometimes he did deal just a little bit of marijuana through friends, to get caught up on utilities and such, but that made Susie uptight. Because she was afraid he would go to jail again.

Snakeman had a friend whose name was Straightman, and Straightman was a marijuana dealer, too. By this time Susie was the mother of a six-year-old boy and she had been meditating for seven years, but she couldn't keep a lid on the restlessness anymore. Snakeman had turned to alcohol since both Maharishi and marriage condemned marijuana, and was spending many of his evenings drinking beer and shooting pool at a country cantina, although he told Susie it was actually business, being a good time and place to get commissions for rings. So Susie ran away with Straightman.

Straightman promised he wouldn't deal marijuana anymore. He would learn how to transcendentally meditate, too. And he wouldn't be poor either—he would work at being an energy-industry salesperson and they would leave the border entirely, in fact, to live in San Antonio.

So that is why their life is so boring now. Why Straightman has asthma and Susie has to call me to San Antonio every once in a while.

When Leo and I get to the house early New Year's Eve, Straightman is already in his bed, too sick to talk to us. Susie shows us the home computer set he got for Christmas. She has a yellow canary in a cage that looks green at the gills.

"You should let this bird out of its cage," I tell her.

"Oh, sometimes I open the door, but it won't fly out. It seems to like it where it is."

This bird has had it. Its little shoulders are hunched up and it's kind of panting. Its eyes are half-closed. But I'm too polite to open the door and let it out.

"It'd die anyway outside," Susie says.

Of course she's right.

And flying inside? Not on your life. Black canary turds on white canvas furniture and blonde wood floors?

We proceed to have a quiet boring time together. Susie's son-of-Snakeman is away for the holiday in El Paso visiting his father. Straightman is quiet in his room, never comes out. The ceilings of the living room are high and there is a hidden stereo that plays quiet music. There are glass windows from ceiling to floor so that you can look out into the woods which start at the back of Susie's lot.

(When Susie lived with Snakeman, they lived on the outermost limit of El Paso, in a rambling adobe in the middle of a vast cotton field.)

Susie's paintings stretch across various walls. They are similar to the ones I saw her doing the last time I visited, almost a year ago—the same large white canvases with faint pastel lines crossing to make horizons and beams. But now, some of the thin pencil lines are beginning to open up onto long, dark and flickering shadows in their crisscrossings of each other, at odd points like split seams.

Leo met Susie when he met me, almost seven years ago. He and Snakeman got into a fight after they met each other, I can't remember exactly why, but something about territory—Leo moving in with me and Snakeman being my friend a long time but not knowing the Leo-Stranger. They can talk to each other now, but still aren't friends. And Straightman never got along too well with Leo or me. But Leo likes Susie; he knows she is part of my baggage—my household treasures he began to share when he moved in with me. Leo loves at times to be quiet and not talk. So this is what he generally does at Susie's house.

Susie puts out fruitcake, wine, cookies, apples. But pretty soon Leo becomes tired of eating and drinking and flipping through old magazines listening to Susie and me catch up with who's-doing-what-where—totally boring talk. He has already gone for a little walk, but the woods are too dark at night for an unfamiliar stranger to navigate. So, before eleven o'clock, he is in bed, too.

But I want to stay up 'til twelve at least to experience the dawn of the calendar year and so does Susie.

I have asked her about her work and she has asked about mine, and about Straightman's work and Leo's poetry, proceeding right along in the autobiographical-style exchange of boring pleasantries. I have asked her about her son, and she has told me the details of his education and his involvement in sports.

(I remember when Susie's son was born. Snakeman came knocking on my door at seven in the morning, up all night with Susie and labor and yes! he got to see his own son born. He hadn't passed out, although he of course had been excited, so afterwards he had thrown up. But then he had held the baby and Susie was asleep. So he came to my house for a cup of coffee and for the joy of telling the story to someone.)

Susie asks me where Brook-my-daughter is, and I say she is in El Paso with her father, just like Susie's son.

Susie's son, my daughter.

(Susie had been in Mexico getting turquoise and inspiration when my daughter was born. She didn't visit me at the hospital but when she came back she brought me a rebozo with blue and wine-red stripes.)

Then she asks me how Rational-my-second-son is doing. And I say, "Oh, he is settling down."

She says, "What do you mean?"

I say, "Well did I tell you about the trouble he was having?"

And she says no.

So I tell her about Rational, how he was in love with a Church-of-Christ girl in Dallas while we were living there. They were both in the theatre department of the Arts Magnet High School and they shared a dream of having a traveling puppet show.

"So when we came to Austin, he didn't want to come with us. And the daughter's mother said he could live with them and go to school there his senior year. So he cut his hair short and started going to bible classes on Wednesday nights. The mother refinished houses, so he did carpentry work for her to earn his keep. And the girl was very beautiful, but neurotic. Nervosa anorexic. She started going out with other boys. It was inevitable. She was only fifteen.

"The mother had once been into astrology and such, but she married a drunk who made her miserable. So she divorced. And got saved with the Church-of-Christ people and became very religious. So in her framework, Rational and her daughter had to get married sooner or later because they had had sexual relations with each other. So she wanted this marriage to occur between them. You can see it was a mess."

Susie is nodding. She is a great friend. She puts some more white wine in my glass. She is such a good friend that she doesn't even once remind me of how similar this screwed-up Church-of-Christ woman sounds to my own self in previous lifetimes when Susie has known me.

"So I guess that messed poor Rational up," she says.

I nod. "A couple of nights he got so mad at this girl who had begun to date these other boys, that he stormed out of her house and spent the night sleeping in the bushes near the high school. This is what was funny. The girl had loved Rational when he was smoking marijuana and lounging through life in Dallas-hippie-apartment style. But when he came and lived at her house and stopped smoking and started making good grades in school from doing his homework regularly and attending church every Sunday with her and her mom, she didn't like him anymore. She said he was too boring!

"He wanted to finish high school there, but he couldn't. So he came to Austin to live at home with me again. And he was very messed up. I checked him into Austin High School. He was still reading the bible and thinking about this Church of Christ stuff. But he also started smoking marijuana again with me and Morgani. Then he started freaking out with other kinds of drugs. At the high school, he joined some kind of drug- awareness group and started making these speeches about how he had been addicted to drugs since he was a little boy because he came from a hippie family and then how he hadn't done any drugs now for two years. And he was so good—because he has always been a great actor—that this group wanted him to speak in front of classes. So then he was so good at speaking that the principal arranged for him to speak to all the senior health classes together, about three hundred people.

"But the night before, he dropped acid with a friend from El Paso. They prowled up and down Congress Avenue and all around the Capitol grounds. They climbed the cannon and the bronze statue and rolled in the grass. But then the sun came up and Rational was still higher than anything. He had thought when he dropped that acid that he was going to be down by then. But no! Here it was time for school and he was still going. So then he thought he could get out of speaking, he could get someone else to do it for him, if he said that he was sick. But when he told the teacher, she said that he had to do it. So..."

I take a long swig of Susie's white wine, zinfandel-grape has begun to make the words come out of my mouth like crazy drunk and howling coyote, and Susie is sucking in the story with great slugs of the same juice.

"There he soon found himself—stepping right into some great archetypal hippie horror dream—higher-than-he would-ever-want-to-be-on-acid, standing in front of three hundred strangers ready to hear about the reformation of the drug addict, now a successful, straight and blonde young man. He said he looked out at all the faces. Then he began. He told them that he had been a young drug addict, that he had had a hippie mother and an alcoholic father and that he had begun to take this and that, whatever was around, at an early age. But now, he said, he had been straight for two-and-a-half years. Then he stopped. 'Well really,' he said, 'about one-and-a-half years.' He stopped again, trying to count up how many months it really was; maybe it wasn't a year after all, but so many months, and he couldn't remember how many months it was. So the audience was waiting for him to say something and he looked out at them and he didn't have any words.

'I'm sorry,' he said. He ducked his head, waved, 'I'm fucked-up on acid.' He walked out the door and then he walked out of the school. Then he came home. I didn't know what had happened to him for a long time. He went to sleep and must have slept for 36 hours straight. I finally realized he was sick with something, so I let him sleep. It was three days before he could tell me what happened."

"Well, what did you do?"

"Oh this was last year, right before vacation started. So I called the school and told them what had happened. I told them he had had a nervous breakdown. Which was true. And I told them I didn't know if he was going to be back in school again after vacation was over. He didn't think he wanted to go back. But in a few weeks he felt stronger. Then he went back. Now he's a lot steadier."

It was about ten minutes before midnight. Susie said, "Well, maybe we'd better make some resolutions."

I swing my glass around. "I don't want to make any resolutions. I don't want to stop doing anything."

"Don't you want," Susie says, rocking back and forth, frowning slightly in the way she has that brings her dazed eye in line with the other one, "to improve yourself?"

"I like all my vices," I say, "I don't want to give up any of them."

Guy Lombardo has begun to play on the radio—the cheering sounds like static when New Year's bells begin to bang with the music.

Susie pours the last third of the third bottle into our glasses and we click them together.

Then the polite-and-well-mannered sorority-trained sister Susie remembers that she has neglected to ask me about someone and that is Morgani-my-oldest-son whose birthday coincides with Susie's and whose eye is dazed like her own!—How could she be so rude as not to ask about him?

"And how is Morgani," she asks at midnight, "have you heard from him?"

"Yes", I say with some little edge of resolution left over from New Years past, "He and Moanah are in San Francisco, trying to get their musical act together, calling themselves Mishka and the Barbarian. In the meantime, he is working as a security guard at a go-go club and she is dancing nude behind glass."

Susie sneezes into her wine, breaks into uncontrollable giggles, falls off her chair. Her wine spills over the white canvas.

"Oh Pat," she says, "That's why I have to see you every once in a while. You make me laugh."

I myself do not know exactly what she is laughing about.

In the morning Leo and I wake up in the son-of-Snakeman's room—spaceship models and pictures of Maharishi Mahesh Yogi, Vader robot doll, sword of force, wax wizard that the son has made himself under the guiding hand of his father.

Straightman doesn't want to take a morning walk. He wants to stay and learn how to work his home computer. He already has the instruction manual out when we get up.

Besides, he doesn't like me much. He thinks I always liked Snakeman better. Maybe he thinks I talk about him behind his back.

But the morning sky is bright blue and the rest of us want to walk. Susie leads us into the woods. She shows us the safest paths. She points out arroyos—which way the water runs when it comes through these dry ways. And she shows us where the fault rock comes up and where it stops, how the vegetation is different on the other side of its rim. Susie never says very much. But she points and gestures. She has only been in this house about a year, but she knows these woods.

Leo runs away from us—he wears brown corduroy with a red feather in his straw hat, and bounds like a rabbit. When Susie and I come up over the last rise of the woods, he is standing at the edge of the ridge leaning against a fence post where the woods end, looking over the meadow that runs like a ribbon between us and the sky. He is puffing on his cigar, and the sun hazes his beard. Susie and I stop at the same post. Nobody says anything. Nobody moves. And for a moment, all the intersecting lines of the scene are quiet in their places, like a giant wheel has just come to a stop before starting rolling again in a new direction. The only thing moving is Leo's cigar smoke wisping along the horizon. Then someone steps back and the leaves rustle. It's the first day of a New Year and so good to meet with Susie at this place again.

Calling Home

Claudio G. Segré

The electric clock's red second hand touched eleven sixteen, then crawled on toward eleven seventeen. Jacques sighed. Black, immutable, the phone on the edge of his desk seemed to take on density and weight. If he picked up the receiver, he was sure it would feel like a small barbell or one of those weights that joggers lugged around. Well, unlikely now that the boy would call. Back to tomorrow's "Intro to Mod Eng Lit" lecture. "Yeats for the Yokels"—as if it mattered what he said to the rows of blank faces, particularly on Monday mornings.

But why didn't Philip call? Maybe he was sick. Maybe something had happened. Not likely. The school would have notified him; he was the father. Probably the boy was out playing ball and he'd forgotten it was Sunday, or maybe he didn't feel like calling. How did it feel to be fifteen and at military school? Not good, Jacques remembered vaguely. Maybe he should leave word? No. Jacques remembered how much he hated those "please call home" messages on the little pink slips. "Folks checkin' up on you, Jackie babe?" The sneering, jeering voices of the seniors echoed in his mind even a quarter of a century later. Nor had he forgotten his own futile pleas: "Papa, don't leave messages. I'll call on my own."

But then the phone did ring. He clutched the receiver. So it was still plastic after all—and easy to lift. He needed at least two more rings to compose himself, but that wasn't really enough.

"Hello!" The word rolled out of his mouth like an oversized ball bearing and dropped into the receiver. That was no way to greet his

K. Thoma

son. But instead of an "It's me, Dad" or—since military school—an inadvertent "It's me, sir," he heard simply "Hallo." This was a nasty surprise. "Hallo" and not "hello," authoritative and impatient, almost a snarl, as befitted a quasi-Nobel Prize winner.

"Papa?" Hard words to pronounce, even after forty-three years of practice.

"Ah Jacques, *ça va*?"

Why couldn't he be out walking, as he usually was on Sundays, in his tweedy jacket and matching cap? Or getting ready for lunch with his agent or one of his literary buddies?

"Me? I'm fine."

"Really?" The tone was the same as when the old man's agent gave him advice he didn't like or when a crony inadvertently said something nice about Camus, who, after all, had stolen the Prize from him.

"Yeah, really."

"If you know how I am, why ask?" Jacques muttered mentally.

"I'm glad to hear that." The voice relaxed. Authority and distance faded. In their place, overtones of warm puppy squeals, sniffing, whimpering for a stray pat or two. But there were no traces of warm, milk-fed puppy curves in that somewhat bent and shrunken seventy-year-old body—at least not when Jacques had last seen it six months ago. Nor did the massive head, with the great, tufted ice pack of hair, smelling faintly of lavender-scented brilliantine, invite petting.

"Yeah, I'm fine," Jacques echoed almost defiantly. The burr of his unshaven jowl and the traces of nausea from last night's hangover were nothing to call home about. Nor was a studio apartment, bare of wife, bare of son, bare of everything except a desk, some sway-backed chairs and a rickety table. That's what came of splitting with Nan and packing the boy off to that school.

"And you? *Ça va* ?" The warmth in his voice startled him. So did the flow of French, the mother tongue, still the language that bonded. Still so many bonds—then why was he so relieved a few days ago, on his forty-third birthday, when the old man didn't call? Why did he always feel as if he were fighting off some giant lobster or monster crab clawing around in his affairs?

"*Moi* ?" The old man, of course, took Jacques at his word. To him it was impossible that someone should *not* care. Jacques braced himself for the latest bulletin:

"For seventy, I can't complain. The usual arthritis in my left shoulder, quite close to the blade. Those brigands at the Academie

Française have asked for a lecture on May 14 at four o'clock. Can you imagine, four o'clock? No one will be there at that hour. They pay practically nothing. I'm hardly awake then. I'm no longer so young, you know. I need a little nap. I never finish my work before two o'clock. A man needs some lunch and a little nap. Anyway, it took them twenty years to discover who I was. Twenty years. Idiots, a band of cretins, that's what they are."

Someone was interrupting in the background. "Eh? *Quoi* ? What are you saying, Marie?" From that distance, Jacques felt her voice like a little pin prick. In the same room, he remembered how it sliced like a carving knife. The old man muttered and wheezed about how after two marriages he still hadn't learned what a nuisance women were. He should have hired a maid. "*Mais, oui, oui,*" he grumbled. Muffled over the telephone it sounded like "wah wah" or "nyah nyah", like a little boy talking back to his mother. Suddenly, his voice dropped to a conspiratorial whisper: "The frogs in the little pond behind the house keep her awake at night and so she doesn't sleep enough. I tell her to stuff her ears with cotton. No! She wants to kill them all. She's a ranacidal maniac."

"Ranacidal?" After all these years, Jacques should have known better.

"Well, it isn't homicide. It's ranacide, then, isn't it?" Only fools, of which there were too many in this world, the voice said, could miss such elementary logic.

"You just made it up."

"Ah, my muse is ever fertile," he said gleefully.

Let that one go by, Jacques told himself.

"Otherwise Marie is okay?"

"And why not? She's well provided for. You know, I love women. I loved your mother tenderly—no, how you say in English, 'dearly.' I know you don't believe it. But such a nuisance, the lot of them, always whining and crying and nagging when a man has important things to do, so little time left. So little time left, and she complains about a few lovesick frogs on a spring night."

Abruptly, the long distance lines crackled and whistled faintly, like blood singing in the ears. Jacques felt the instant of nausea, like the sudden drop of an express elevator, the drop into the conversational void. Every week, it seemed, he had less and less to say. One day, there would be only the sound of the long-distance lines. Fortunately with very little prompting, the old man was always willing to fill the space.

"You were saying about your shoulder? The arthritis?"

"Yes, yes, a little arthritis, perfectly normal for my age." The impatience in his voice said it all: this week—unlike last week—arthritis was out as the topic of conversation. "Tell me. How was your birthday?" It was as if he were tearing away at a gift wrapping, ripping into the inner box.

"Huh? Oh, that was fine. Nan and I got together with the boy, had some cake, opened a few presents, drank a little champagne. Now that we're apart, we're more together than ever."

"Ah, *très bien.*." That was good news. The old man liked Nan. She was polite and respectful, a tireless listener to his stories, an avid reader of his books. How could Jacques have a falling out with such a woman?

"And the boy? Is he still so big?"

"Still so big? What else could he be? At fifteen you don't suddenly start shrinking." The scorn in his voice startled Jacques, and he was also a little awed.

Just like that, he'd caught the old man out in the open, really caught him, tripping over his own logic. Here was a classic display of—what would his father call it? Maybe "cretinous clumsiness," or some such expression, well basted in contempt.

Jacques tried to savor the moment. The old rascal had it coming—a little repayment for that "ranacide" nonsense. But, as usual it was a short triumph—one that lasted perhaps all of five seconds.

"Yes, you can be proud of your grandson. Even though it's his first semester, he's already a captain or a sergeant or something, got himself a chestful of medals."

Why couldn't he hang in there? Tear a little flesh? Picking on a seventy-year-old wasn't very sporting, or was it? He had all the insulations of old age and the defenses of a lifetime to protect him.

"*Très bien.*"

But that wasn't what the old man was listening for and Jacques felt his throat tighten as if he were ten years old again and didn't know the answer.

"And you? Are you glad you were born?"

"Am I glad that I was born? Now what kind of question is that?" His fingers tightened around the receiver, clutched the slim handle as if to choke off the voice, but it said calmly:

"Just a question, just a question. You don't need to get excited." Then the usual arrogance, disguised as reason or logic, popped up. "It's a simple question. Answer 'yes' or 'no.'"

"How about 'maybe'?"

"Ah, you shun existential questions at your age." He said it with such relish, as if he'd discovered that Jacques still wet his bed at night.

"Am I glad to be alive? Sure. I don't know what it's like to be otherwise—yet. Not that I conceive of it as a particularly interesting state. I imagine you'll find out before I do."

Victory again—a three second one this time? Or just bad taste. Well, he'd had a good teacher. Like father, like son. That was no excuse. Probably the old man had missed everything. He was a little deaf and most of the time he wasn't really listening anyway.

Like father, like son, but with Philip, there were never any exchanges like that. Jacques was always careful to ask about the food at the school or about sports or even rock bands and computer games. Which made their conversational black holes even more puzzling—and disquieting.

The old man erupted again: "Did you get my present?"

"Yes."

"Well?"

"Well what?"

"Did you like it?"

"It was certainly different." Of course that wasn't good enough, but what was he going to say? "At first I thought there might even be something nice in that little oblong box, something nice, appropriate, like a pipe. Something I might even like? But, after forty-three years of experience, I know better than to get my hopes up."

"You didn't like it."

"I didn't say that, did I? I said it was different." Nothing new in that. His birthdays had always been different. On the one when he was supposed to get a bike—he was eight—instead of a shiny new ten-speed, he got an old beat-up balloon tire. The birthday he was supposed to get a watch, when he was ten and all the other kids had gotten theirs, it was decided that he was too young and irresponsible. He waited two more birthdays, at which time he no longer cared.

"It was a sort of joke."

"I understand." Half-hidden behind a row of books on his desk, the joke stared at him with its blue goggle eyes, its obscene, wiener-chewing mouth and its bulbous red ears. Only once had Jacques squeezed the rubber flesh, watched the eyes bulge, the tongue and ears pop out.

"Did you think it was funny?"

“Not exactly.” Goitered, hyperthyroid little monsters that squeaked "nyah, nyah" weren't his kind of humor.

“It's me, you know.”

“I know, I know.” So the card had explained. *“Mon chèr fils,* since I can't be there for your party, I'm sending this little *poupée* as a proxy” read the scratching on the card. The rest was difficult to make out: “It carries my most affectionate wishes for your birthday. Give it a little loving squeeze and see what it does.”

“Ah, well, I meant well. I thought it was funny.”

“I can imagine.”

The old man's voice lost shape and direction, like a birthday balloon gone flaccid. The phone lines whistled embarrassingly. He had it coming, Jacques said to himself. Then, of course, he felt guilty. Did he expect a mute to sing "Madame Butterfly?" Anyway, was he any better? What had he done for Philip's last birthday? Nan had insisted on a Swiss army knife. Like a sand crab scuttling into the mud, he'd gone along, immediately burying his idea of a poetry anthology for young people, or, better yet, a "Rolling Stones" album. Of course he had his excuse. As Nan said, they might have given the boy a hard time about the book. As for the album, did he want his son to think that he approved of Neanderthal eruptions? Now, from the fountain of guilt, the questions bubbled forth, effervescent with enthusiasm. How was the piece for *The New York Times* coming? Had there been any new reviews of his latest book? Had he been in touch with his old pal Saul—Bellow, of course—recently?

The old man replied with his usual recitation from his agenda. Jacques imagined him peering over his glasses at the blue calfskin volume that the French bank sent him every Christmas: the dinner with the French ambassador in Washington, the lunch with the thieving publisher, the unexpected invitation from...Jacques didn't catch the name. All he could hear was Philip's polite, patient, respectful, “How're your classes, Dad?” and “How's the book going?”

Abruptly, the recitation stopped, as if someone had suddenly removed the tape. Perhaps it was just age. When there was no more to be said at the summit, it was time to continue the dialogue on a lower level, to turn things over to the emissaries.

In one great cascade that threatened to overload the lines, Marie came on to report officially on the old man's health and activities and to extend official greetings to Nan and the boy. If he held the receiver about six inches from his ear, it was all quite bearable, Jacques had learned.

"What did you think of the *poupée* ? I thought it was horrible. He wanted it. He insisted on it. It was his idea."

"It was kind of cute. I got a laugh out of it."

"You did? Oh good. I'll tell him. He was so worried."

That's what emissaries were for. They salved and dulled the cuts and bruises, so that before too long, even by next Sunday, he was ready for another weekly dose.

"I'm so glad you like it. It was nice of you to call. These Sunday *tête à têtes* are really important to him, you know."

"Just trying to keep in touch," he mumbled, realizing that he was both lying and not lying. Should he tell Marie who had done the calling? Why should he? Such misunderstandings sometimes came in handy.

"*Au revoir.*"

"*Á bientôt.*"

Then it was over—for a week, anyway.

He glanced at the doll again. "Goddamn little monster," he muttered. Philip, at least, had gotten his bicycle and his watch on time and his face had lighted up over the Swiss army knife. When he said, "It's me, Dad," he didn't choke on it. Maybe he sounded hesitant, maybe shy and uncertain, especially after this separation from Nan, but he wasn't gagging. Jacques was sure of that. The boy was more patient, polite, respectful. As Nan said, his son was everything that he'd never been with his own father. And be grateful for that.

He glanced at the clock. Eleven thirty. He really must sit down and think about tomorrow's lecture. The yellow pad with the blue lines and the red margins resisted his black scratchings. Never mind. After twelve years of "Intro to Mod Eng Lit" he learned to be thankful, when he glanced out at the sleepy, or bored faces, for the gum chewers, for the occasional twitch of their jaws. Be thankful for the twitch of life.

Maybe a little hair of the dog would help him. Nan was right for the wrong reasons. He should stick to white wine, not because that's what his father did, but because he could never drink enough to get plastered.

Jacques' hand moved from the note pad to the receiver. Chapel, or whatever they called it at that junior West Point, was long since over. Maybe the boy had been trying to get through while he was talking to the old man? Jacques' fingers curled around the receiver. Did he want an earful of those "how're your classes going?" or "How is your book?" His eyes crossed those of the spying, eavesdropping little monster. "Well, what d'you think? Should I? If I did, does that make me like him?"

Abruptly, he snatched the doll off the shelf and flung it in the wastebasket, on top of the torn envelopes, discarded notes, old bills. He reached over and buried it at the bottom. No more little monsters here.

Yet, the yellow pad was no more receptive to his scratching. Nearly a quarter to twelve. Jacques scribbled away. Probably the boy was out playing ball. Anyway, in seven days there'd be another Sunday, he told himself. Monsters need not breed monsters.

Nevertheless, he got up, took the wastebasket around to the garbage can in back of the house. With satisfaction, he watched the doll disappear beneath a mass of soggy old tea bags, coffee grounds, beer bottles and last night's leftovers. Then, he marched back to his desk. Now he could concentrate.

But then he remembered how the boy had stood around at the birthday, so tall and gawky and ill at ease, looking as if the only thing holding him together were all those brass pins and medals and that starchy uniform. Why? Why? The boy had gotten all his presents on time. They talked about sports and computer games and even rock bands. Did monsters inevitably breed monsters?

Sure, in seven days there'd be another Sunday, and another one after that, and another after that, and still the phone did not ring and did not ring and did not ring.

Kathleen Thoma

Unholy Matrimony

James McEnteer

The cable marked URGENT would have provoked immediate curiosity had it arrived anywhere but Claudia Hardwick's office. There, it became just another bit of exotic clutter on Claudia's desk, lost in a chaos rendered more desperate than usual by the ending of the academic year. Claudia was rushing through her duties, reading theses, term papers and final exams, in order to return to her own work—drafting a paper she intended to present at the International Anthropology Symposium in Malaysia, only three weeks away. The State Department had chosen her to represent the United States at Kuala Lumpur. That was the extent of U.S. support for this prestigious conference.

"I guess it's a promotion," she had joked to Beth Chambers, her graduate assistant. "From token woman to token American."

Ethnic Integrities Within The Global Village: Can they be maintained? Should they be? If so, how? That was the symposium topic. Just the sort of philosophical overview based on hard research data that Claudia loved. The United Nations would publish the conference results in twenty-two languages. It was a great chance to influence the haphazard and often cruel ways in which Third World peoples were wrenched from their centuries-old traditions into the modern era. Claudia found it hard to concentrate on regurgitative student reports about the Hopi or the Andaman Islanders when she considered the importance of her project. She must do what she could to offset some of the outmoded concepts and downright dangerous ideas of other social scientists whom she knew would attend the conference.

"Knock, knock." Beth entered Claudia's inner office. "Ready for the latest interruptions?"

"Where would I be without them? Never mind. Shoot."

"Okay. Don Warshall at Communications wants a signed receipt from you for the videotape cameras and the recorders before he'll okay them for travel."

"Just have Don send the receipt with the equipment. I can't run over there now. I'll take care of his precious goodies. After all, he taught me how. Remind him, all right? Tell him I'm just too busy..."

"Okay. And Tommy Coleman is here again. Waiting in the hall."

Claudia sighed.

"Don't you think he's cute?"

"Cute, but lazy. His paper was sloppy. If I talk to him now he'll just bat those big brown eyes of his at me for an hour, and I'll sit here and let him. Anyway, there's nothing I can do. His exam is in. Tell him grades will be posted next week. It's too late for charm. Don't say that, though."

"All right. And Bob Weidemeyer has already called three times today. He doesn't believe any meeting could last this long. I told him you were in a meeting..."

"Good."

"But he says he's going to drag you physically out of the meeting for your own sanity..."

"Quite the caveman, isn't he?"

"But so well disguised as a mild-mannered English prof..."

"At a great metropolitan university. Yes. Well, tell him I'll call this evening. Maybe. Is that all?"

"Yes. Or no. There's the usual mail. But an odd cable came for you... yesterday, I guess... from the... the New Orkney Islands? Ever hear of them?"

"Yes. What's it say?"

"All right. It says: 'Chance Lifetime Marriage Kilburra Full Moon July Guide.' That's all it says. And it's signed, T. Chad. Strange, huh?"

"Let me see that." Claudia took the cable. "T. Chad. I don't remember the name. He might have been at that thing in Madras last year or... Kilburra. What was it about Kilburra? God, I think my memory's starting to go."

"Yeah? How you remember half of what you do amazes me."

"The New Orkneys. Koora International Airport..."

"Where are the New Orkneys anyway?"

"Hmm? Between the Solomons and the New Hebrides..."

"Oh, swell."

"South Pacific."

"Uh-huh."

"Look, do me a favor, would you, Beth? Look up Kilburra for me. Anything you can find. And check the files for this T. Chad. I don't have time now. I'm going into seclusion."

"With Bob Weidemeyer?"

"Ha. Doesn't he wish. I'm going to hide out in my carrel until I can see daylight again."

"What do I say when he calls?"

"Tell him I've decided to enter a nunnery. Tell him sublimation is the higher path..."

"He'll love it."

"And get rid of Tommy, will you , please?"

Claudia filled her briefcase to bulging with papers, then stepped into the outer office.

"You're all clear," said Beth.

"That'll be the day. Don't work overtime. Can't afford it." Before Beth could make a comeback, her boss had gone.

Even when the pace became frenetic, Claudia gloried in the fullness of her schedule. She seemed to know the secret of avoiding dead spaces, those vacant moments that eat our free time and consume so much of our lives. Refusing more invitations than she accepted, Claudia enjoyed her reputation as the most eligible woman on the faculty. At thirty-three she appeared youthful enough to be asked occasionally for identification when she ordered a drink. Men found her desirable, but had trouble keeping up with her high energy as she sped, unwavering, sure of herself, through her day and her life. Her mind functioned at equally high velocity, giving Claudia the air of being at once completely present and terribly elusive.

A respected anthropologist, she was neither bookish nor boring. An enjoyable supper companion, she indulged neither in triviality nor in pretense. She played up or down to no one. Meaningless flirtation did not fit her busy schedule. The men who wanted to be the center of her life but found themselves, when they reckoned realistically, at the edge of it, could accuse her of no fault or lack with which to console themselves.

"You're sublimating your true desire, like some sort of religious or political zealot, Claudia. Don't you think you should ask yourself who you are and what it is you really want?"

That was Bob, who hoped *he* was what she really wanted. She liked Bob a great deal. More than any other person, he satisfied her need for a kindred spirit, a true companion. But as a logician, he was strictly a self-centered lightweight. She sublimated nothing. She had joined her energies to the search for understanding within her discipline, anthropology. It was the sort of marriage Bob was incapable of understanding.

Yes, she smiled to herself, he didn't understand she was married, even if single, and could spend time with men as she pleased without being unfaithful to that marriage. Ideas which inflamed her, such as the effects of acculturation on a global scale, were simply too abstract for most people. That was what deceived Bob and other men, who seemed to cordon off their intellects from the rest of themselves; they were too blinded by their own sexual desires and their egos to understand that her marriage involved neither. Well, maybe it did involve her ego. She was glad to be going to the conference, proud she had the reputation to be chosen.

Claudia emerged from two days in the library with her grading finished and her conference paper roughed out. Beth glanced up when she walked into the office.

"I'm sorry, Ms. Hardwick is much too busy to see anyone at the moment..."

"You sound like a recording. Been busy?"

"Oh, not really. I don't think Bob's called more than a dozen times since your mysterious disappearance. He's really worried."

"I thought women were supposed to be the hysterics."

"Yes, well, I think you should call him. Poor man. I really think he loves you, Claudia."

"Well, I think *he* thinks he does. All right, I'll call. I've got the Malaysia thing going. Soon as I finish the draft I'll need you to type it. Forget this mail for now."

"Kilburra?"

"You remember. That weird cable? 'Chance Lifetime Marriage'?..."

"Oh yes..."

"Well, let's see." Beth leafed through her notes. "Kilburra is a small village in the New Orkney Island group populated by people called the Bundoloos. They worship a mountain god, also called

Kilburra. The god is believed to reside within a large volcano... and it seems the marriage ceremonies are held in the crater of the volcano itself..."

"Ah, yes. I think I remember. But you can only go into the mountain at certain times, right?"

"Exactly. Marriages are performed under a full moon in summer during years when the moon's trajectory precisely transects the opening of the crater. An event which occurs in cycles of four to seven years..."

"I do remember now! Of course, Kilburra. Margaret tried for years to get permission to observe that ceremony. The Bundoloo priests wouldn't let anyone near the place. That was one of her major disappointments. She was still talking about it, just before she died..."

"Margaret Mead?"

"Of course. She opened up the whole Pacific for us. Hell, she opened up anthropology, let's face it. But she could never crack Kilburra..."

"According to the Index, there was a monograph written on the Bundoloo in the early thirties. By an Englishman..."

"Yes, I know. But he never actually got inside the volcano. He just summarized reports of his informants, hearsay really. And it didn't do his career much good, believe me..."

"Well..."

"'Chance Lifetime Marriage... Full Moon July...' Margaret would've jumped at the chance. And so should I. For her sake, if nothing else. She certainly did a lot for me..."

"But..."

"When is the full moon in July? Where's the calendar? Here it is, the sixth. And the conference is... the fourteenth? I could do it, Beth. I could just do it. Leave early..."

"You're kidding..."

"...reroute from Sydney to the New Orkneys, get the ceremony on video tape... Imagine that. Then jet on to K.L. in time for the conference. We're not even due there anyway until... when?"

"We're booked into the Hilton on the twelfth."

"The twelfth. Fine. If I get held up in the New Orkneys, you can always cover for me. You'll have the written speech..."

"Now wait a minute, Claudia. I hope you're not serious about this."

"Why not? It may *be* the chance of a lifetime. Who knows when or if I'll ever get to that part of the world again. Certainly not on government money. And I haven't been in the field for five years. You realize that? I mean, it'll only be a few days, but it sounds exciting, really. Maybe I'll even get something really worthwhile from it..."

"Can I come with you?"

"I don't see how, Beth. Sorry. Somebody's got to cover here and in Kuala Lumpur in case I'm running late. And you're the one, kid. Okay? So book me through to K.L. with a detour to the New Orkneys. I've got to get in gear. And round up all the information you can get on the Bundoloos and their ceremony. I'll have plenty of time to bone up on the flight to Sydney. And I suppose you better wire T. Chad my arrival time as soon as you know it."

"Aren't you being pretty impulsive, Claudia? Heading off alone to some obscure island..."

"Beth, your concern sounds downright sexist. Remember, I did two years of fieldwork in New Guinea, all by my lonesome. And none of the so-called cannibals even gave me a nibble."

Beth laughed, then frowned again.

"But don't you think it's strange? Why are they suddenly inviting an anthropologist to a ceremony they've been guarding jealously for generations?"

"Who knows? Maybe they want their pictures in National Geographic..."

"I'm serious, Claudia. Holding weddings in a volcano isn't the only peculiar thing about these people. I looked through that monograph. The Bundoloo believe marriage is as much a contest as a union, a struggle for dominance, winner take all..."

"How realistic of them."

"I think you ought to read that monograph."

The phone rang.

"I will. On the way to the ceremony. So please rearrange my schedule, all right? Beth?"

The phone rang again. Beth looked unhappy.

"Aye, aye, captain." She picked up the receiver. "Yes? Oh, hello, Bob. What? Hang on a second, will you?" She cupped the mouthpiece in her hand. "Are you in or out?"

"I'll take it in there," Claudia whispered. "You make those arrangements."

"But you don't even know who this T. Chad is..."

"Oh, he's probably one of those Indian anthropologists I met last year. They always use initials instead of names." Claudia headed for the door.

"He's not listed in the Association Directory."

"Could be a she." Claudia disappeared through the doorway, then popped her head back out. "Might be an admirer. I have them you know." She pointed at the phone and smiled, then disappeared for good behind her office door.

On the other side of the world, Twanda Chad crouched in the dirt before a small charcoal fire, stirring the root mash which would be supper, as it had been breakfast. Around him villagers wandered back and forth in front of their stick huts, chattering to one another, rubbing their mud-caked bodies, preparing their meals. Chad ignored them, staring into his own small fire, wondering if he had been what they called a *fool* in English to spend his last money on a cable to the Americani woman he had not seen for so many years. She might be dead. But he did not believe it. He had watched her in New Guinea, young and naive, walking among dangers of which she knew nothing. Clearly, she carried a powerful charm for survival. Good. Such charms were expensive. He counted on her wealth as on her strength.

Bad fortune had brought him here among the Bundoloo. To remain meant danger, probably death. But even if he had possessed the means, he could not return home. He had departed his own village in disgrace, discovered in the act of stealing sacred totems for sale to whites. The elders could have killed him, but chose instead the more subtle, infinitely crueler punishment of exile. Since then, Chad had wandered the tortured path of those whose fate mocks their hopes, falling ever lower in his own eyes and those of the world. Worn out and broke, he had all but abandoned the struggle for life when he was picked up by Jukka, Bundoloo shaman.

Jukka had his own reasons for saving the outcast, charity not chief among them. The shaman cast spells, laid curses and made predictions which occasionally needed assistance to reach fulfillment. It was beneath the priest himself to influence circumstance by means other than magical. But the priest's helper, especially an outsider, exempt from tribal rules, enjoyed great license. Some of the tasks he performed as Jukka's "instrument of destiny" caused sorrow and suffering. He knew the Bundoloo hated him and that only the protection of the shaman kept them from tearing him to pieces. He was lonely and afraid, and much too awed by Jukka to risk an escape. Failure would mean death.

When Jukka told him Kilburra wanted a foreigner to witness Bundoloo marriage, Chad hid his great surprise. He knew no outsiders had been permitted even to enter the mountain. Now the shaman was saying Kilburra desired someone from a far place to know his power. Squatting on his heels in silence, Chad listened carefully as Jukka added that Kilburra would grant any wish to whoever would bring such a foreigner. For days he considered Jukka's offer and thought of the only foreigner he remembered—the Americani woman.

"If I bring someone, I have my wish?"

"What is it?"

"To leave."

Jukka stared at him a long time. Then he agreed. Chad spent all he had saved for ten words at the cable office, words cast into the air, an appeal to the fearless young woman far away. Would she remember him? Would she come this distance to the ceremony? She could help him. She was rich. She would be grateful for the chance to see the Bundoloo wedding. In New Guinea she had paid well to see and hear things. She would reward him well. So Jukka predicted. And Chad believed him. She would help him escape. Or was that an illusion, fostered by Jukka, to make him waste the last of his money that the priest might hold him still more firmly in his power?

Chad looked up from his fire at the approaching figure of the shaman, as if his own thoughts had conjured him. Inwardly trembling, Chad did not shift from his crouch before the fire. Jukka stopped before him. Still Chad made no move. One did not greet the shaman like the others. One waited for him to begin.

"She comes."

"I received no word..."

"She comes." The shaman's confidence intimidated Chad. "You must prepare to greet her."

Chad nodded. Fear kindled in him like a fever, a sickness he knew would remain until he had left this island forever.

"While the Bundoloo have never permitted outsiders to witness marriage ceremonies within the Kilburra crater..." (Claudia was reading the 1931 monograph of Sir Rodney Worth-Peters, University of London.) "...native observers have freely discussed the proceedings with me before and immediately after the event. As the informants consulted in this report have been proved correct in other verifiable matters of social and religious custom, there is no reason to doubt their veracity concerning this particular ceremony. I simply wish to point out the following account is not based on first-hand observation.

"The Bundoloo believe that marriage is at once a union and a clash, a paradox perfectly symbolized by their principal deity, Kilburra, who resides in a mountain at once inviting and threatening, open to receive believers into its breast, but capable at times of wreaking havoc on the land below. As in so many mythologies, creation and destruction are never very far apart from each other in the minds of the Bundoloo. The fact that this belief is recognized in social practices differentiates the Bundoloo from other primitive societies in which such belief is merely ritualized, albeit on occasion with ceremonies of sacrifice..."

Claudia lay the manuscript on her lap with a sigh and looked out the small airplane window at the Pacific, 35,000 feet below. Leave it to anthropologists to render even the most colorful aspects of humankind in dry, factual prose. The best of social scientists - like Margaret Mead - escaped that tendency, as she herself had tried to avoid it in her own work. But the majority of them couldn't make anything sound interesting - birth, death or infinity. Probably because there was too much emphasis on discipline. Keep your distance. The first principle of anthropology. Live among your subjects, gain their confidence, eat their food, yes, but you must never "go native." That would distort your objectivity. You must hold back in order to describe and dissect.

She smiled, remembering Beth's warning to her at the airport about old Harker. Joseph Harker, dean of American anthropology, now in his eighties, the archetypical absent-minded professor. Flying from New York to London for a meeting, he became so engrossed in his work he refused to leave the plane, but worked on through the refueling and a second take-off, not pausing until the plane had landed in Kenya. After great confusion at Nairobi Airport he was placed on another flight to London. He slept awhile, then woke. Unable to endure inactivity, Harker resumed his work. In London, he snapped at flight attendants trying to assist him off the plane. His air of authority made them desist. Not until well over the Atlantic once more did Harker demand to know when they were due at Heathrow. He landed back in New York where he had begun three days earlier, having missed his meeting. Harker claimed that while airborne, he had made significant breakthroughs in his work, due, the old man hypothesized, to his distance from earth, which gave him much greater objectivity.

Claudia had the opposite problem—distraction. She tried to put the upcoming Malaysian conference out of her mind, along with thoughts of Bob and the university and worries about the equipment for which she had signed responsibility and which now lay in the baggage compartment (bouncing? breaking?). She took up Worth-Peters' monograph with a sigh.

"Because the position of the moon is favorable for marriage only at intervals of four to seven years, a number of couples are united at each ceremony. Brides and grooms are prepared separately, by the women and men respectively. Everyone, whether participant or observer, must be dressed and anointed in strict ritual fashion. The preparation consists mainly of advice and "pep talks" given the prospective brides and grooms by members of their own sex, almost as if they were opposing gladiators entering a circus or fighters entering a prize ring. And indeed they are, for while the couple will be united in marriage, only one of the two will emerge physically from the Lodge of Kilburra within the mountain.

"The union takes place within the body of one or the other, regardless of sex. As we have seen elsewhere, the sexual union, traditional basis for marriage in the Western world, is irrelevant to marriage among the promiscuous Bundoloo, who copulate freely and casually with whomsoever they please, children being raised according to a communal matrilineal pattern..."

Claudia blinked and read the paragraph over again. "The union takes place within the body of one or the other... Only one of the two will emerge physically from the Lodge of Kilburra..." What did that signify? She would like to have called Rodney Worth-Peters from Sydney. But, of course, that was impossible. He was dead.

"From their separate locations, the men and women observe the rising of the full moon which commemorates and binds the union. At a sign from the presiding shaman, drumming begins. Musicians, male and female, play throughout the ritual, until the moon has set at dawn..."

Claudia skipped down several paragraphs.

"As we have seen, married individuals enjoy much greater status and privilege among the Bundoloo than the unmarried. They are given the best home sites, and larger, choicer plots of land for gardens. Aside from the material benefits due married villagers, they are considered wiser and more worldly than all other tribesmen except the shaman, since they presumably possess male and female insight, whatever the gender of their bodies. Because of the fear surrounding the marriage ritual and the journey of a soul from one body to another, married individuals are accorded respect for having endured a difficult rite of passage. It is this fear, above all, which keeps the number of married persons confined to a small group of Bundoloo, despite the incentives outlined above..."

"Married Bundoloo constitute the Council of Elders, regardless of their ages, while older men and women, if single, are virtually ignored once their fertile years have passed. Only married individuals are considered fit to make decisions which affect the well-being of the tribe. Among them lies all community policy, all political power. The bi-sexual practices of married Bundoloo are discussed elsewhere in this monograph...".

"Would you care for a drink before we land?"

Claudia turned reluctantly from the monograph to the scrubbed, smiling face of a stewardess. Old Harker had a point.

"I beg your pardon?"

"A drink. It's last call before we start our descent into Sydney."

"N... well, yes, all right. A brandy, please."

"Brandy? Yes, ma'am."

The warmth of the alcohol enhanced Claudia's controlled excitement. Her instinct had proved correct. The Kilburra marriage ceremony—with all its cultural implications—was an important discovery. Margaret could have had a marvelous book from it, maybe more than one. But Worth-Peters' monograph was the only existing literature on the Bundoloo, save a brief mention in a nineteenth century Evangelist missionary index. The Evangelists had spent little time among the Bundoloo, finding them ill-suited to conversion. Would she really be allowed into the mountain herself or would she be restricted, like Worth-Peters, to conversations with informants? Maybe she could slip Don's video tape camera into the volcano with a willing villager. But, of course, that was impossible. The equipment was much too sophisticated. And she would have to pay for any damage. But she would find a way. She trusted her own on-the-spot resourcefulness. She was not above a little judicious bribery, a method that served her well in New Guinea. She couldn't worry in advance about tactics. She would have to deal with problems as they arose.

Incredible, the Bundoloo concept of marriage - union of the sexes within a single body. Carl Jung would have flipped to discover such a perfectly symbolized enactment of the masculine-feminine balance he believed individuals must cultivate within themselves. Claudia scribbled Jung's name in her notebook, thinking ahead to her own monograph on the Bundoloo marriage rites - or was there enough there for a book? Possessive individuals, men especially, might learn a lot about themselves from such a study. Too many men she knew still saw their wives as objects. It made a twisted kind of sense; the American acquisitive ethic gone mad. Love my possessions, love me.

Love my possessions, they *are* me. Even Bob Weidemeyer, sensitive and intelligent as he was for a male, probably pursued her as much to flatter himself as for any deeper reason. Nothing was more foreign to Bob and others than the idea of a true union of opposites, a yin-yang balance that would produce a wisdom greater than the sum of its parts. Yet that harmony was Jung's ideal, and the point of Bundoloo marriage. As Claudia considered where these ideas might lead, the brandy spread its warm benediction through her body and the large plane gave itself to the gravity of Australia.

Busy with customs at Sydney, checking in with the airline and clearing equipment permits, Claudia had no time to read more or think about the Bundoloo. Not until her nearly empty Pacific Airways jet lifted off for Koora International Airport, New Orkney Islands, did she again relax. By then, the lack of sleep caught up with her. She dozed fitfully, waving away offers of drinks or a meal, dreaming about oversleeping her destination. She woke to the noise of the plane descending at Koora. Walking down the ramp into the glittering airport, Claudia had no sense of what time, or even what day it was, or where in the world she might be.

The futuristic structure she was in gave no hint of the primitive world beyond its gates. Brainchild of the late premier, the airport symbolized that ruler's greed, an avarice he imagined could only be quenched by the arrival in his country of as many tourists as possible. The resources of the New Orkneys, never great, had been wholly sacrificed to the completion of Koora International. There was not enough money left to pave a road from the airport to the capital - a city which remained on the drawing boards for the same reason, along with nearby, hypothetical beach resorts. Koora stood alone, the Brasilia of airports, surrounded by a dense, threatening rain forest which kept a full-time crew engaged hacking it back and filling cracks in the runways. With no reason for travelers to visit the New Orkneys except to see the airport, hardly any did.

The huge cubist montage of glass, steel and translucent marble gave Claudia a lunar feeling, its emptiness enhancing her sense of its size. On her long journey to the baggage claim, Claudia felt like Dorothy wandering lost in the palace at Oz. Customs was less an inspection than a ceremony of thanks to her for coming. The uniformed men only nodded at Claudia's expensive equipment and the vouchers she tried to present. Whatever she wanted to bring into the country was all right with them. Politely, Claudia sipped at her Koora Kocktail and accepted her complimentary orchid as she looked around for someone to meet her.

Beth had cabled Chad last week. Had he received it? There hadn't been time to receive a reply. No one stepped out of the crowd to introduce himself. Nor was there a crowd to step out of, save the cluster of customs officials and curious airport employees. The porters fought among themselves for the chance to carry her luggage. Claudia stopped the fiasco by allowing each porter to carry only one piece. Seven of them followed behind her, safari-style, as she set off across the cavernous lobby, uncertain of her destination, amid the echoing roar of shuffling feet.

When she spotted the familiar logo of a car rental agency, Claudia directed her bearers to it and paid them off. The best plan would be to rent a jeep and head for Kilburra. Chad would catch up with her, or she to him. But the agency, like the airport, proved a facade; what appeared to be the tip was in fact the entire iceberg. The clerk informed her no cars were available. As he pointed out, after all, there were no roads. Stunned, exhausted and temporarily stalled, Claudia retreated from the rental desk and fell back in an armchair to fiddle with her equipment and collect herself.

Emboldened by Claudia's pause, Twanda Chad moved cautiously closer. He had watched her from a distance since her arrival. Years of running and hiding had made him a shy man, a furtive man. He wanted to take her measure, after all these years. As Claudia checked out her recording and taping apparatus, Chad recognized the confident girl from New Guinea, but saw too that maturity had added to her stature.

Her good fortune continued. Excellent. The expensive-looking machines proved her wealth, too, had increased. These perceptions began to soothe Chad's nervousness. He wiped his palms on his ragged shorts. The Americani woman would be his deliverance. Poised at last to approach her, he hung back as Claudia returned to the rental desk. Her fury surprised him. The clerk summoned the manager. A long, animated palaver ensued. Chad edged close enough to hear the man agree to rent her his personal Landrover overnight.

Chad hurried outside. When Claudia emerged from the sliding glass doors, trailed by the caravan of porters, Chad greeted her effusively and apologetically, as if he had only just arrived. Claudia was too relieved to be angry.

"Welcome, welcome." Chad bowed deeply. "Happy you come. Happy remember Chad."

"Ah, thank you, Mr. Chad. I did get your cable. But I'm sorry. I'm afraid I really don't remember you at all..." His ragged appearance surprised her.

"Oh yes. New Guinea. Long time, long time..."

"New Guinea?"

"Oh yes. Chad help. Like these men." He indicated the porters still gathered about Claudia's equipment.

"Oh, I see. Well that's... I'm glad you remembered me, Mr. Chad. Incredible, ha. Well, New Guinea. So you're neither an anthropologist nor a Bundoloo. How can you help me see the wedding ceremony?"

"Wedding, yes. Tonight full moon..."

"Tonight? Good God, I thought... I lost a day somewhere. We don't have much time then. What can you tell me about...?"

"Chad speak Bundoloo. Speak English. Tell everything. You understand, yes?"

"Uh huh, sounds good..."

"Chad help you. You help Chad, yes?"

"Ah..." Claudia looked sharply at him. So that was it. New Guinea. He remembered her generosity. Perhaps he had even received one of her bribes. She had had so many porters in two years. Still, she was embarrassed not to remember. "Well, of course. I'll be very grateful if you can get me into the ceremony, inside the Kilburra crater..."

At the mention of Kilburra, the porters looked at one another and muttered unpleasantly.

"They go, madam. They go, we talk."

Claudia dismissed the men, who sulked away, looking back suspiciously over their shoulders.

In his odd, broken English Chad told of Jukka, the Bundoloo priest who owed him favors. Chad had remembered Claudia and her interest in exotic events, guessed she would like to see a ceremony barred to outsiders. Jukka had resisted the idea at first. But Chad had argued forcefully, wearing him down. At last, the shaman relented. He gave Chad permission to contact his friend, the Americani woman. So Chad had sent the cable.

Claudia nodded, paying as close attention as she could, wishing her head were clear, that she had another day to rest and overcome the jet lag that weighed on her like extra gravity. Why did Jukka agree to let her view the forbidden ritual?

Chad shrugged.

"He doesn't want payment? Gifts? Money? Only to repay the favor he owes you?"

Claudia watched Chad shift nervously from foot to foot.

"And what do you want, Mr. Chad?"

"I?" Chad started to shake his head, then stopped.

"Yes, you. As I said, I'm grateful for this chance..." She smiled, hoping to maintain good feeling as they came to the necessary terms. "What is it that you want? Money?"

Chad hesitated.

"I want go, madam. No happy here. Want go America. Work there, plenty. Chad fine worker. Very fine, yes..."

"I see. Well, that's... I can certainly help you with money to leave here. You could always go home to New Guinea..."

"No!" Chad's vehemence surprised her. "No New Guinea. Go America. Fine Place . Work for you there. Work your friend. Chad fine worker. Very fine..."

Claudia had no desire to argue. She had been through this before, the naive longing for America. There was no dissuading many of the world's poor from their belief that America would magically solve their problems. Their America was that of the early Spanish explorers who searched for fountains of youth and lost cities of gold. She assured him things would work out.

Apparently cheered by this vague promise, Chad helped her load the gear into the borrowed Landrover.

"We talk Jukka."

"Yes. Good." She needed all the information she could get before tonight. She felt ill-prepared for the ceremony.

At Chad's direction, Claudia drove along the mud track into the dense rain forest. The futuristic airport dropped from sight behind them, as if they had plunged thirty centuries into the past. Their progress was slow, hampered by the soft, soaked ground and the jungle, crowding in on them from all sides. As they slogged and bumped at ten miles an hour through the primordial morass, Claudia thought, for the first time, that coming to the New Orkneys might have been a big mistake.

In a clearing strewn with crude huts, Chad touched her arm. She stared up at the cloud-crested volcano towering over the island like a judgement—a solitary, forbidding Olympus—Kilburra. No wonder the Bundoloo thought it was the home of a god. Claudia slipped the camera from its case and shot several pictures. Naked children had gathered around the Landrover to stare at her. Claudia smiled at them, aware that the adults in the village were too absorbed in their own tasks to gawk at the foreigner. Getting ready for tonight. She wanted to speak with them, ask what they were doing. But Chad had slipped off somewhere. To find Jukka, she hoped.

With increasing impatience, she watched the afternoon sun decline in the sky. Already several groups of men and women had departed the village, headed toward Kilburra. Should she look for Chad? Just as she decided to do it, he returned.

"We go." He pointed at the mountain.

Claudia drove, exhausted, slightly confused at the turn of events, a prisoner of her own momentum. Along the way they passed groups of men carrying large drums and bundles of food.

"Where are the women?"

"Woman go other side. This man way. Man."

Worth-Peters said the sexes maintained separation before the ceremony. She felt amateurish, crazy. She had so many questions to ask. But there was no point trying to shout over the engine noise to Chad, who might or might not know the answers. He wasn't a Bundoloo, after all.

It was already late afternoon. She would be lucky to prepare the taping equipment in time, let alone her mind. The whole exercise was insane, futile, rendered even less real by her fatigue. How stupid she was to try to cram an experience like this into a day or so, one that needed weeks or months of preparation. But there wasn't any choice. She thought of Margaret Mead. She must not give in to her feelings, her depression, her desire to sleep. She would just go along, make the tapes and ask questions later.

They drove into sunshine again, climbing up above the tangled foliage, up the flanks of Kilburra, higher and higher on the rough rock terrain, the green island spreading out below, the sun falling flaming-red toward the sea beyond. It was glorious, the most beautiful sunset, perhaps the greatest spectacle she had ever seen. But she did not stop driving to watch, only snatched glimpses of the pulsing vermilion sky as the tires bit and spun on the loose rock and the track wound up steeply over black lava.

At last, the vehicle could go no farther. Claudia turned off the ignition on a high silence, the eerie whisper of wind over rock.

"We walk."

"Is it far?"

Chad shrugged. Neither knew what "far" meant to the other. Time for another quick decision. Claudia unpacked the hand-held video camera. No way to take the larger machine or most of the lights. She loaded the small tape recorder, extra batteries and portable light board into one rucksack for Chad. She carried the camera, the tripod, a flashlight, a sweater and a jacket on her own back. Before she clipped the canteen to her belt, Claudia swallowed two tablets of benzedrine. It was shaping up to be one of the longer nights of her life.

Even in tennis shoes, Claudia had trouble keeping up with Chad, who leapt nimbly barefoot among the jagged confusion of black lava. The sun had set. Heat still rose off the rock, but she knew it would soon be cold up here. They picked their way up the steep slope for an hour or more in the deepening twilight. He let her catch up to him. She was winded, breathing hard. For a few moments, she failed to see that they stood on the lip of an abyss, a void immense and indefinite as deep space, but within the earth itself, a place where you could drop a stone and never hear it hit.

Claudia shivered. Reading about the ceremony, she had pictured the setting as a sort of Tom Sawyer cave, with stalactites and maybe an underground river. How idiotic, especially in the face of this vast and terrible pit. She let out the breath she'd been holding and turned to Chad.

He was gone. Had he slipped? Fallen silently (still falling) to his death within the mountain? Her heart beat wildly. She almost screamed when he touched her arm, almost jumped over the edge herself.

"Jukka say come."

Come? What did that mean? What was she doing here? Claudia felt the panic inside her. Control, keep control. Why had she come alone? She shivered again. With fear? The cold? It's the drug, that damned speed. She stared hard at the huge full moon, rising up yellow from the eastern sea. The terror eased. She resumed regular breathing again, thinking wistfully of a carpeted room at the Hilton in Kuala Lumpur. 'Just remember why you're here. Focus your mind on that and forget about your own little problems. Concentrate. You're a pro; don't blow it.'

She took out the flashlight.

"Okay. Let's go."

Abruptly, Chad turned and disappeared into the dark crater. Beaming her light after him, Claudia saw the narrow, scuffed path in the rock. She followed carefully, pressing her body against the crater wall, aware that to her right was absolutely nothing. Even if it fell a thousand feet, the drop would have been less threatening if only she were able to see it. She needed several minutes to realize reference points did exist in the blackness. Torches were burning at intervals along the ledge path, though hardly close enough together to light the way. Chad and the others must proceed by touch. To keep her imagination in check, Claudia counted steps between torches, working out distances between them.

Descending, Claudia approached the noisy roar she thought at first must be an underground river or waterfall. The sound swallowed her up as completely as the darkness and, finally, she understood it was not water falling but drums beating, a steady rhythm echoed and magnified in the solid rock cavern. Chad took her arm, leading her off the path. She flashed the light here and there, but could not see if they had reached the floor of the crater or only a large ledge. Half a dozen drummers, men and women, were pounding on huge wood and skin drums. Claudia considered the technical problems, how best to arrange the light board. Would so much light spoil the ceremony? Chad put his mouth to her ear.

"Jukka..."

Claudia turned to face the shaman, directing the flashlight beam past him. She looked at his startling features, the intense, intelligent eyes, the hard set of his mouth. His fierceness froze the half-formed smile on her face. They stared at each other a few moments, then Claudia began to babble.

"Tell him I'm... honored to come to Kilburra..."

"Kilburra!" Jukka pounded his staff on the rock.

"...and... and I don't want to disturb anything, but I would like to ask him a few questions about what's going on and whether he'd mind if I used some lights I brought in order to..."

In the midst of this nervous torrent, Jukka shouted something at Chad and walked away. Claudia was shaking again, frightened, embarrassed, glad for the darkness which hid her humiliation. Chad leaned close.

"Jukka say talk later. You watch."

She nodded her understanding . Conversation was barely possible anyway with all the noise. She decided to risk the light board. If Jukka didn't like it, she was sure he would let her know.

Chad had apparently been instructed to remain with her at all times. Fine. She pressed him into service, having him hold this and move that while she wired the portable light board to the battery pack. As she fussed around, holding the flashlight, Claudia caught sight of something moving, off in the shadows. She aimed the light. What she saw made her gasp and grab at Chad's arm. An ape, tethered to the wall by its ankles.

"No be afraid, madam. Come."

He led her closer. She went, reluctant, but fascinated, shining her light at the creature she now saw was skinny and hairless, of the same large size and bent, simian carriage as the rock-apes she had seen in the hills of northern India. Then she knew it was not an ape, but a man. Or had been. Its eyes were large, empty, fixed on nothing. Then she noticed the others, men and women, all tethered to the rock, all in the same wasted, condition with the same vacuous expressions. Forty of them, fifty, or more.

"Who are they? What happened to them?"

"They be married gone, madam. Married gone."

Married gone? Oh yes. The Worth-Peters monograph: "The union takes place within the body of one or the other... Only one of the two will emerge physically from the Lodge of Kilburra...." These creatures were the bodies left behind by spirits gone to the bodies of dominant spouses, discarded shells deserted by their inhabitants. According to Worth-Peters' informants, they are kept alive, but confined forever inside the volcano, until Kilburra claimed them. She had heard of possession by spirits, but never of dispossession. Here it was—living, breathing physical evidence. My god. Incredible. Appalling. She had to get it on tape.

"Here, hold these. Hold them up like this, all right?"

Chad lifted the lights as directed while Claudia shot footage of the chained animals whose human souls had fled.

When she finished taping, Claudia saw that the moon had passed over the crater opening, flooding the volcano with a ghostly silver light. Reflections on facets of the rock walls gave the cavern a luminescence. Now she could plainly see the men and women in their separate groups (newly arrived or there all along?), huddling nervously together as the drums grew louder, faster. To her surprise, the light meter registered sufficient light for shooting. Perfect. Natural light would be far more effective. And she wouldn't have to disturb the ceremony.

Jukka stood,arms upraised, between the groups of men and women. He was chanting, shouting at the moon. Claudia set her camera on the tripod and began to tape again. The shaman chanted something and both groups responded. Damn, the tape recorder. Quickly she got it going, gesturing to Chad to point the microphone toward the chanters. Jukka was pairing off the couples now, holding their arms in the air, rubbing something on their bellies and foreheads, then dancing away, leaving them together as he joined the next couple. He kept chanting all the while and everyone present continued to sing their responses, while the drums grew stronger, more insistent, and the whole cacophony echoed back on itself from the lava walls, building to a deafening roar.

Then, Jukka was beside her, shouting something, gesturing. Claudia recoiled from him, afraid. Was he angry at her for taping?

"He say you put!"

She looked at Chad with incomprehension.

"You put. Everyone put."

Chad nodded. Jukka rubbed his forehead and his belly, then turned again to her. Worth-Peters did say participants and observers must be ritually anointed for the ceremony. She had to stay kosher. She nodded her assent, lifting her shirt to let the priest dab his sweet-smelling paste on her belly. He grazed her forehead with it and left without a word.

Her skin felt cool where Jukka touched it, like the eucalyptus oil-base medicine you rubbed on your chest for a cold. Worth-Peters' informants told him the Bundoloo believe the spirit leaves the body at the solar plexus and enters the body of another at the forehead. So far his information seemed to be valid.

The mountain itself throbbed and shuddered with the terrible racket. Claudia was a little dizzy, her hands cold and damp, her heart pounding. Did they all feel this way, these brides and grooms, half of whom were destined to become zombies before the night was over?

Suddenly the drumming stopped dead, leaving a silence as stunning as the din before it, echoes dying away in the dark. Jukka raised his voice in a chant, a strange haunting lament, similar in Claudia's mind to recordings she had heard of whales singing deep beneath the sea. Where the shaman's voice led, the chorus followed, filling the great cavern more intensely than the now-silent drums. He was reaching, higher, higher, as if to the moon, the other voices joining, gaining a certain pitch, then falling away to build again, still higher. The tape recorder ran on, preserving the sounds if not the feeling. Engrossed in the compelling crescendo, Claudia had forgotten her camera.

With obvious effort, Jukka reached a high scream she would have thought beyond the human range to produce, a shrill vibration which caused Claudia nearly to fall as she covered her eyes, shuddering, dying, looking up to see - one after another - couples becoming engulfed in a kind of bluish glow, then falling away from each other, reeling, spent. The transfer! Here it was, visibly happening.

Claudia fumbled with the camera. Where to aim?

"This is it, isn't it?" But she didn't need Chad's answer to know it was. "Look. They're married now. Married, my god... Get the lights on this. Chad? Pick up the..."

She broke off at the sight of Chad's face, his awful empty eyes. She turned accusingly to Jukka, who hovered nearby. The shaman spoke.

"Now you see. I did not know if it was possible with others. I wanted to know...."

Claudia tried to think what he meant, then realized she had understood his dialect.

She stared at Jukka's proud face, then into Chad's empty one.

She screamed.

"Very impressive."

"You liked it?"

"Very much."

"I'm glad."

"Drink?"

"All right."

Bob Weidemeyer rose and crossed his sunporch. He set the United Nations Global Village report on a shelf above the bar.

"You argue forcefully and logically. There's nothing sentimental about it. You must have a great sense of satisfaction, Claudia."

"Well, I was just trying to express the obvious humane position, that every cultural and ethnic group has the same right to survival..."

"Water?"

"Please."

"Well, it might seem obvious to you and to me. But I see that a lot of your fellow anthropologists would just as soon the majority of subcultures on this planet sank out of sight, the sooner the better. Most of them start from that assumption. All they want to discuss is how best to ease these people into oblivion..."

"Yes..."

"One of your colleagues has the incredible nerve to point to the Chinese seizure of Tibet as a model of efficiency..."

"I know..."

"Here you go."

"Thanks."

"Most of them come off as apologists for imperialism. The Russians are especially transparent. But I must admit, some of your opposition expresses itself eloquently. It's frightening, the way they have of twisting reason until it seems to make sense. One report I remember in particular..."

"Fong."

"What?"

"Arthur Fong. He's..."

"Is that who I mean? Let's see..." Bob retrieved the thick volume from the shelf and began leafing through it.

Yes, Arthur Fong. She could see him, sitting near the podium in that austere ballroom of the old Dutch hotel in Kuala Lumpur, smiling his polite, superior smile, waiting for her to finish speaking. Born and raised in Singapore, only a few years out of Cambridge, Fong already enjoyed a reputation as a brilliant social scientist, diamond-hard. He had published several important studies of post-colonial societies, including Singapore. Besides English, French and Chinese, he was fluent in Hindi, Urdu and Swahili. He smiled as she sweated at the podium, reading her paper to the damp, impassive faces. When she had finished, to polite applause, Fong took the floor. Smile in place, in precise Oxbridge English he made Claudia's humanitarian pleas seem childish.

"Mr. Chairman, we sympathize with our young colleague from the United States..." (Claudia bristled. He could not be much older than she. He might be younger.) "We admire anyone who, at this late date, can still believe in the equality of man. Each of us has had this dream at some point in our lives. But we are scientists, Mr. Chairman, not dreamers. We can ill afford to indulge in naiveté." (Claudia was shaking with anger.)

"The fact is, men are not equal. Neither are their cultures. In technical, philosophical, or any other terms, some are far superior to others. The so-called subcultures or minority cultures our colleague wishes to protect—out of semantic deference we no longer call them primitive, though that is what they are—these groups are evolutionary throwbacks, Darwinian freaks, doomed by their own lack of adaptation to extinction. And rightly so. Our American colleague argues for kindness. But is it kinder to perpetuate those who are hopelessly ill-equipped for life in this century, or to help them into history where they belong?"

Claudia could not restrain herself.

"I'm glad Professor Fong is not my physician, Mr. Chairman. Death is rather a drastic remedy..."

"But Miss Hardwick, if your condition were already diagnosed as terminal and certain to be painful, would you wish your life artificially prolonged, whatever the cost? Wouldn't you prefer to die with dignity?"

"You're stretching the metaphor, Mr. Fong. Peoples with different values than the mainstream cultures are not terminally ill..."

"It amounts to the same thing, does it not? Anyway, Miss Hardwick, the metaphor was yours."

The Chairman gaveled for order as laughter rippled through the conference, slightly delayed for those who required translations. Claudia was furious.

"Yes, you're right, Claudia. It was Fong I was thinking of..." Bob looked up at her from the report. "He certainly knows how to make his points, doesn't he?"

Claudia nodded, trembling with remembered rage at the conference which had ended nearly eight months earlier. Adding to her nervousness then had been the strain of carrying Twanda Chad around with her. At times she wondered if this psychological tumor weren't visible to Beth or to others. But Chad remained docile, present only when summoned, a servant within her as in his previous existence. As the months, passed she grew less uncomfortable with him, only lamenting the weak moral character and incredible ignorance of her marriage partner, whose meager dowry consisted of a few obscure island dialects and a bundle of silly superstitions, hardly anything worth having.

"Claudia, are you still on planet Earth?"

"Mmm? Oh, sorry, Bob. I'm just remembering Fong. We had a running battle at the conference, as you can imagine. I asked him why he, the child of a colonized people, sided so vehemently with the colonials."

"What did he say?"

"He said for two reasons. One was gratitude. Because the British had taken him out of the dirty, crowded streets of Singapore, educated him, let him in Cambridge. The other reason was revenge, because in spite of his brilliance, the British condescended to him. The meanest tradespeople considered him inferior because of his race..."

"So he's out to prove he's better than they are at their own game?"

"Something like that."

"That sounds just a little bit crazy, don't you think?"

"Who isn't a little bit crazy, Bob?"

"Well, now, wait a second..."

"I mean, sure, Fong's insecure, but he has his reasons..."

"Okay, okay. I agree. All I meant was it's a shame his personal insecurity has to surface as a defense of cultural annihilation..."

"Yes, that's true..."

"It's too bad he can't speak for more humane..."

"Well, I think Fong realizes he's been trying to fill his irrational emotional needs with a kind of amoral logic..."

"Really? You sound like you got to know him pretty well, Claudia."

"Yes, I... doubt he'll ever again argue for immediate acculturation of minorities by the mainstream."

"You persuaded him it was wrong? How? That's amazing."

"Well, I didn't exactly persuade him. But... well, I made him a proposition—that if I could prove to him so-called primitive societies still had things to teach modern man, he'd reconsider his position."

"You never told me that, Claudia."

"You don't know everything about me, you know."

"What did you show Fong to..."

"Oh, you know, just some things I'd been working on. But I understand he didn't go back to work. You know he was advising the Brazilian government about how best to acculturate tribes of Amazon Indians..."

"Why are the Brazilians trying to..."

"Because tribal cultures aren't functional, Bob. Brazil needs workers to help exploit its natural resources, especially minerals. So the government strips these people of their hunting culture and gets them into the consumer society."

"And a way of life is sacrificed to economic expediency. But Fong walked out on them? Well, he's a bright fellow, Maybe he realized..."

"Maybe. But Fong seems to have disappeared entirely since the conference. Nobody's seen him."

"Really? That's odd. Maybe he went into the wilderness to meditate on these matters."

"Could be..."

"...went up on a mountaintop to look about him and..."

"What do you mean, he went up on a mountaintop?"

"It's just a figure of speech, Claudia. Why the sudden intensity?"

"Oh, nothing."

"It's guilt, isn't it?"

"Guilt?" Color drained from Claudia's face.

"Yes. Here you were, fighting with this man Fong, probably hoping the earth would swallow him up. And then the earth *does* swallow him up. Naturally you're disturbed. See? Let me get you another drink."

"I don't really..."

"Come on, Claudia. Loosen up a little. My God, I thought you were a workaholic before. But since your Pacific trip last summer, I swear you're moving twice as fast."

"I'm keeping busy, that's for sure. Imagine if I'd taken the department chairmanship?"

"I'm still not sure turning it down was your wisest career decision, Claudia. The prestige..."

"The prestige isn't as important as my time. I just don't want all that administrative work on top of my own projects."

"What I don't understand is why Beth Chambers should suddenly take a job halfway across the country. She worshipped you, Claudia. She did all sorts of things for you out of loyalty you'd never get an ordinary assistant to do. Her leaving like that really surprised me."

"I guess she decided it was time to go out on her own, leave my shadow..."

"Well she certainly picked an inconvenient time. Did you want water? Oh, never mind, I remember..."

Beth had not wanted to leave. Claudia arranged an instructorship for her at a southern college, then stood firm through Beth's tears, insisting she accept. It was the only way, after what had happened. Several weeks after returning from her Pacific trip, Claudia had brazenly seduced Beth Chambers. The affair, impossible from the start, was mercifully brief. Claudia had never experimented with homosexuality before (though given her new psycho-sexual components, homosexuality was not precisely the word. There was no word.) and instantly regretted giving way to the impulse. She resolved to keep strict control of herself, amazed by what she considered her masculine rashness. Meanwhile, for both their sakes, Beth had to go.

"Here you are."

"Thanks, Bob. I guess I do need to relax."

"Glad to hear you say that, my dear. You should take more of my advice. Old Doc Weidemeyer knows his stuff."

"Oh? What else does the old sage prescribe?"

"I can think of two very important priorities."

"Such as?"

"Such as working up your U.N. report for general consumption. A larger audience needs to hear what you're saying. It's too important to be buried in a big fat tome nobody's going to read."

"I don't know, Bob..."

"Listen, right now you're a voice crying out in the wilderness for the conservation of ethnic minorities. If people knew what was happening, they'd support you. Right now, they don't. They don't have your statistics, your data. Don't you think it's a worthwhile project?"

"Of course I do, but..."

"But nothing, Claudia. These are days of ecological concern. And minority subcultures are definitely irreplaceable resources, as endangered as any species of bird or antelope. Animals are being protected, why not people?"

"That's true."

"Of course it is. You could lay the whole thing out historically. Show how the process is accelerating, a war no longer fought with guns, but with money. It would make a compelling book. Done right, it could sell like crazy and wake a lot of people up..."

"It would take a lot of work..."

"I'll help you. With pleasure. I've helped with proofreading and editing before. I can get involved in the research too, if you let me. Together we could do a great book, an important book..."

"God, I don't know, Bob..."

"Why not? You can have full author's credit."

"Oh, darling, it's not the credit..."

"Then what is it? Can you think of any other project more important?"

"No. Honestly, I can't."

"What are you working on now, anyway?"

"Oh, just some translations from the Hindi, religious..."

"Hindi? When the hell did you learn Hindi?"

"Oh, I... picked it up along the way."

"You amaze me, dear. Sometimes it's almost scary..."

"Thank you."

"Don't you think our book is more timely than your translations? Don't you think your idol, Margaret Mead, would have jumped in with both feet?"

"Probably. Maybe you're right. It should be done."

"Sure it should."

"I'd definitely need your help though..."

"I meant it when I said I wanted to be part of it. Which leads me to my other piece of advice, even more important. Marry me, Claudia. Soon. Please?"

"Now, Bob, we've been..."

"I know, I know, we've been over it and over it. But can't you understand yet that marriage to me poses no threat to your precious independence? I respect your career. Hell, I'm even offering to drop my own for awhile to help with one of your projects."

"True, true..."

"I believe in what you're doing. You know, philosophically we have a lot in common. And as a collaborator, I can offer you a lot. Besides my... incredible command of the English language..."

"Hear, hear..."

"I know German and French philosophy, European history and the literatures of several countries thoroughly..."

Claudia nodded thoughtfully.

"And, more important, I love you and I want to... share my life with you. We'd both benefit in so many ways, don't you think so, darling?"

She stared at him, drumming two fingers on her chin.

"Okay."

"What?"

"But I can only marry you on one... no, two, conditions. That I name the time and place, and that it's kept absolutely secret until after the ceremony."

She watched Bob's surprised face, his eyes looking for the joke, probing her sincerity. He was intelligent and strong. Stronger than she was? She felt a twinge. But as she continued to gaze at him, she realized it made no difference. She trusted his ideas, his instincts, his heart. The project they envisioned—and others also beyond the scope of a single human mind—must manifest. How many apparently insoluble problems now facing humankind might yield themselves to the combined wisdom of several thoughtful lifetimes focused with singular tenacity? More than she or Bob or any other individual needed their separate identities, the human species needed to go forward, to rise above itself. She believed in evolution. So did Arthur. It was the only way.

"All right, Claudia. I'm calling your bluff. I accept your terms. Now what do you have in mind?"

"Well, there's a little island I know, out in the South Pacific...".

Kathleen Thoma

And Still We Wait

Andrea Winkler

It's very easy to miss us. Perhaps people would notice us more if we lived in the Catskills, or at the edge of a somber New England village. We are expected to be in such places. Who would think to find us in a small, outworn town in Blanco County, Texas?

That is, of course, why we live there.

We're well situated for our work. Come summertime, when the afternoons stretch long and drowsy, the tourists flock over to Fredericksburg to see the German Sunday houses, Admiral Nimitz's birthplace, and the Garden of Peace. And then, since they're so close, they travel on to Luckenbach, and then the Johnson Ranch, home of the former President. And then they head toward Austin, with bushels of fresh-grown peaches, quaint German dolls, and perhaps a leaf or two taken unobtrusively from the Japanese garden. From the ranch and campgrounds, the only main road leading to Austin is Highway 290 which runs—quite literally—through what was once our front lawn.

They never stop, of course—the tourists, I mean. Only once or twice. There's nothing much that's visible in Skey. Just the post office, the feed store, and two houses. And the Motley house isn't all that much to look at. You'd see it duplicated in any small town suburb. They're really ordinary folks, for all that Addie Motley prides herself on being part of a family that's got a county named for it. It's our house that draws people.

I remember four, maybe five, summers ago when our last visitor stopped to ask for directions. "What a quaint old house," she said, smiling the way people do when they mean the opposite of what they're saying. "All Victorian and gingerbread-y." She cocked her head, glancing up at the house, and riffled her fingers through her sandy blonde hair. "Three stories, too. Has it always been that interesting color?"

The house is painted a dull lime green. My sister, always the most interested in our visitors, smiled faintly. "We like it," she said, and asked the girl if she would like a lemonade.

"I'd love one," the girl said, "but then I have to be on my way. Now that I know I'm going in the right direction, that is."

I had been sitting on the evening-shadowed porch, but now I walked over to the girl and smiled. The smile was not for her, but, not knowing that, she smiled back. "Lovely sunset, isn't it?" she asked, looking over the neat fields bordered by scraggly, unkempt scrub land. She glanced back at the house. The sun's rays shining on it made the house glow brightly against the gathering blue-black darkness on the horizon. "You and your sister are lucky," she said softly. "Do you live here all alone or do you have help to work your land?"

I smiled again. She noticed things. "Friends stay with us from time to time," I said, "and we have no land to work."

"Oh." She frowned slightly.

My sister came from the kitchen carrying a tall lemonade glass. The girl took it, and stood sipping in silence until the sun was completely hidden by the hills. In the warm Texas dusk our surroundings blurred into one another: house and road and trees were all indistinct appendages of one single creature. This was the time I liked best. This was the time that people sometimes perceived us.

And as I said, she noticed things.

It came quickly. After she finished her lemonade and thanked us, she started for her car, but then impulsively half-turned to look at the house again. In the fading light she saw us for what we are.

It lasted for a second only. Then other, rational, daylight habits took over, and she rubbed her eyes and settled into her small car. My sister rushed over to the window. "Are you feeling all right?" she asked. "Do you want to stay here for the night?"

A shadow—perhaps memory?—crossed the girl's face. "That's kind of you," she said, "but really, Johnson City's only twelve miles or so from here, you said, and from there it'll only be an hour's drive to Austin. And I've already made my motel reservation—the Holiday Inn on the river. But thank you anyway."

My sister nodded. The girl rolled up her window, started her car, and bumped back out the driveway toward the highway.

We watched her bright taillights until they faded in the distance. Then my sister said, "I'm going to fix a room for her."

"How long did she see us?"

"Long enough." My sister nodded slowly. "Long enough."

She did return, three weeks later, long past the time that I had stopped looking for her. She came just before dawn, in that time that is neither day nor night. Without saying a word she carried her suitcase and her shoulder bag into the room that she had been given. She knew the way without my telling her.

It wasn't until evening that she joined us on the porch. It was the world's evening and we sat in silence, I, my sister, the old man from Uvalde, and the maiden lady from Stonewall. The girl, who sat on the porch steps, began to fidget. At last she burst out, "Is this all you do? Sit in the twilight and look at the highway?"

I frowned. "What is your name?" I asked severely.

"I ... I don't remember." She pursed her lips and looked down at her feet. "Nobody else does, either," she said more quietly. "First they didn't remember me, and then they couldn't see or hear me." She reached down, picked up some loose stones lying at the base of the steps, and idly began tossing them toward the highway. The last one, the heaviest, she held in her hand for a moment, feeling its firm weight. Then she shrugged her shoulders and sent the stone after the others. "What does it matter, anyway? I'm stuck here."

"It does matter."

She laughed shortly. "You believe all that guck about names being powerful?"

"Are you powerful?" I countered.

"How can I be powerful when nobody can see me?" she flared. "Nobody except you."

"What is my name?"

She said nothing. After a moment, I nodded. "I don't have one. None of us do. All we have are the remnants of who we once were."

Still she said nothing. Instead, she reached down and felt about for more stones. The others remained silent, and for some moments the only sounds were the cicadas trilling their chik-chilli-chik calls, and the wind rustling the cottonwood leaves. Moodily, she began throwing her stones. When she had exhausted her small rockpile, she stretched and looked up. "It's still not dark, but I'm going to bed anyway."

My sister said placidly, "It never gets dark. It's always evening here."

"Here, here, here! Where *is* this place?"

"Neither one place nor the other: neither dark nor light, a mingling of the two where, meeting, they cancel each other out."

She sat down again on the steps. At length she said, not so much to me but to all of us, "Then why do you stay here? Why was I brought out of that bright life into this?"

It was my sister who answered. "You saw us as we truly are. We can't make anyone see. It's accidental. The quality of light has to be just right."

"But there has to be some reason!" She was crying, the first tears I had seen since the old man from Uvalde arrived. We do not cry. "What do you get out of it?"

"Power," I said. "Energy. There's none here save what people bring in from other places; it can't be generated here, and we can't move without it."

Her brows lifted. "Move?" Then she shook her head morosely. "Why? Nobody could see me anyway."

"There's always the chance." It was the lady from Stonewall, her voice rough with disuse. "Maybe there's a place where we can see into their world."

The girl jumped up, with an excess of energy which amazed me. "Then I'll go!" she cried. "I have my car; I can go forever."

"Oh, no," my sister said. "You go in order."

The girl stood absolutely still, then leaned against the porch support. "In order?" she asked..

"Of course."

"When ... when can I leave here?"

My sister stood. "When someone else sees us."

Nothing more was said that evening. When we woke, in the grey blurring that passes for bright morning here, my sister and the lady from Stonewall were gone, taking the girl's car with them.

Time of day or night means nothing here, where neither day nor night exist. We sit on our porch in the world's evening, the three of us, watching the cars passing on the highway and the endless twilight expanse, waiting for someone to notice us. It only takes a second of strangeness, a passing glance if the light is right, and then some of us will be free to move. So we sit, and listen, and rock: and still we wait.

Cover Photo: (clockwise from top) Isabella Russell-Ides, Brian Yansky, Tamara Stanfield Fish, Andrea Winkler, Kathleen Thoma, James McEnteer, Nan Cuba, Jenny Lou Peña, Diane Castleberry, Susan Rogers Cooper, Claudio Segré, Ray Reece. Not shown: Steven Phenix, Michael Reynolds, Russell Smith, Pat Ellis Taylor, John Campion.